THE FIRES OF WAR AND PASSION ENFLAME THE EMOTIONS OF A YOUNG AMERICA.

RENNO—Born a white man, raised a Seneca, the revered Sachem of the invincible Iroquois must face a devastating choice: to fight for his nation —but against his own blood.

JA-GONH—Mighty son of the great Renno, he has passed the Seneca's skill and stealth on to his only child. Now he faces deadly combat with the very son he bore.

GHONKABA—Renno's warrior grandson. In him is reborn the impetuous spirit of the White Indian's youth. His rebellious nature can make him a dangerous traitor or perhaps the greatest Seneca of them all.

ELIZABETH STRONG—Lovely blond daughter of a Colonial general, her love can make Ghonkaba a loyal friend of the colonists; her betrayal can make him a bitter foe.

GEORGE WASHINGTON—As a valiant colonel in the Virginia militia, his prowess and daring win him Ghonkaba's brotherhood. But other powerful colonists reveal a .... world.

D0816066

The White Indian Series
Ask your bookseller for the books you have missed

The White Indian Series
Book VII

WAR CRY

Donald Clayton Porter

 Created by the producers of
Wagons West, Children of the Lion,
Saga of the Southwest, and
The Kent Family Chronicles Series.

Executive Producer: Lyle Kenyon Engel

BANTAM BOOKS
TORONTO • NEW YORK • LONDON • SYDNEY • AUCKLAND

WAR CRY

*A Bantam Book / published by arrangement with
Book Creations, Inc.*

*Bantam edition / February 1983
2nd printing ... September 1983*

*Produced by Book Creations, Inc.
Chairman of the Board: Lyle Kenyon Engel*

ISBN 0-553-25589-4

Published simultaneously in the United States and Canada

*Bantam Books are published by Bantam Books, Inc. Its trade-
mark, consisting of the words "Bantam Books" and the por-
trayal of a rooster, is Registered in U.S. Patent and Trademark
Office and in other countries. Marca Registrada. Bantam
Books, Inc., 666 Fifth Avenue, New York, New York 10103.*

PRINTED IN THE UNITED STATES OF AMERICA

H   11 10 9 8 7 6 5 4 3 2

WAR CRY

Chapter I

It was no ordinary hunting party of Indian warriors that made its way slowly, cautiously through the deep forests of the Ohio Valley, west of the land that the English settlers called Pennsylvania, and north of the Ohio River. Rarely did as many as fifty braves take part simultaneously in a hunt.

That their green and yellow war paint identified them as Seneca warriors was highly unusual because these Seneca were far from their own land in the northern portion of New York. And a closer scrutiny revealed other unusual aspects of the party.

The leader was white-haired with a wrinkled face,

1

but his still-slender body and erect carriage belied his more than eighty summers. Renno, the white Indian and Great Sachem of the Iroquois League, the most powerful of all Indian alliances in North America, was a legend in his own time. Renowned and respected by the English colonists, he was feared by the French and their Indian allies. His own Seneca believed him to have almost godlike qualities, and he was seen as a larger-than-life leader by most other Indian nations.

Seldom did the Seneca venture so far from home. But it was Renno's wish to make such a journey, and as usual, his orders were obeyed to the letter.

"I dreamed a strange dream," he had told his son, Ja-gonh, sachem of the Seneca, several days earlier. "I went to the lands where the Miami nation roams, to the forests that lie north of the preserves of the Erie. Why I was in this strange territory I do not know, but I have given much thought to my dream, and I have decided that it is the will of the manitous that I go where they have directed me."

Ja-gonh, a powerful and wise leader in his own right, knew better than to dispute the will of his father. As he had said to Ah-wen-ga, his wife, in the privacy of their own dwelling that night, "As my father grows older, his resemblance to Ghonka, my grandfather, becomes more and more pronounced. He is so accustomed to having his word obeyed in all things that he tolerates no argument and no discussion. When he told me that it was his wish to hunt in the distant land of the Ohio, I assigned fifty senior warriors as his bodyguard, and I gave command of the party to Ghonkaba, our son."

"I can't imagine why Renno would wish to hunt so far from his home," Ah-wen-ga had replied in some

2

wonder. "Surely the deer are no larger and fatter than the deer that live here in our own forests. Why does Renno insist on going into an alien land?"

"He has traveled to Quebec and other places in Canada to the north," Ja-gonh had pointed out. "He has often visited Virginia, the home of my mother, and in his travels, he has gone far beyond the land of the Seminole, in the land the Spaniards call Florida, to the islands of the West Indian Ocean. He has visited at length in England as well. As his life draws nearer to its close on this earth, I suspect he is filled with a desire to visit a new region that he has not previously known."

Ah-wen-ga, who was still as pretty as the day some twenty-five years earlier when she had been abducted to France by enemies of the Seneca, nodded in accord. "It well may be that Ja-gonh is right."

"It is the privilege of my father," Ja-gonh had said solemnly, "to go where he wishes and to do there what pleases him. I have fulfilled my obligations to him by sending our most courageous and talented warriors with him, under the command of my own son, and may his exploits someday be as great as those of the famous ancestor whose name he bears."

As it happened, Ja-gonh's son was bored by his assignment. He recognized the honor of being placed in charge of the warriors responsible for the safety of his famous grandfather, but that fact in no way compensated for the annoyances of day-to-day travel. The pace of the hunt, due to Renno's advanced age, was almost infuriatingly leisurely for a hot-blooded young brave who still was eager to make his mark in the world.

But what was really bothering Ghonkaba was some-

3

thing he would admit to no one. He had lived his entire life in the shadow of renowned warriors, first his namesake, Ghonka the Elder, sachem of the Seneca, then Great Sachem of the Iroquois League—a warrior beyond compare. After Ghonka had come his adopted son, Renno, whose accomplishments almost miraculously had equaled—and sometimes even surpassed—those of Ghonka himself. Now it was Ja-gonh who wore the feathered headdress and cape of sachem of the Seneca.

Ghonkaba knew that the entire nation was expecting him to perform in both war and in peace with valor and sagacity at least equal to any of them. All his life, Ghonkaba had stood apart from his contemporaries, and was considered "different." Unlike his grandfather and his father, who were both white skinned, he was a half-breed. Thanks to the Indian blood of his mother, Ah-wen-ga, he was the first in the family since Ghonka who could truly call himself a Seneca. Yet the nation, its Iroquois allies, the white settlers in Massachusetts Bay, Connecticut, and New York—and even the tribes that were enemies of the Seneca—looked to him for great deeds, not only because of his distinguished heritage, but particularly because of his name: Ghonka the Younger.

How often Renno and Ja-gonh had lectured him: "Mighty deeds are required of a Seneca warrior simply because he is a Seneca. Your standards are still higher because you are of the family of Ghonka and of Renno."

Even his grandfather on his mother's side, Sun-ai-yee, a renowned war chief, had achieved great distinction as sachem of the nation. Ghonkaba more than once found himself wishing that he could escape the magnificent aura that surrounded him.

With difficulty, Ghonkaba was forcing himself to keep his mind on his task as he crept through the thick forest several paces to the left of Renno. The rest of the escort were strung out over several hundred feet to the right and to the left—all of them invisible from a distance of only a few paces. As a Seneca, Ghonkaba took such accomplishments for granted. The warriors of no other nation could have traveled so silently through the deep underbrush, nor could they have maintained as high a degree of invisibility thanks to the disciplined, rigorous training that the Seneca received from earliest boyhood.

Suddenly Renno halted and, leaning forward silently, peered intently through the thick foliage.

Ghonkaba stopped abruptly and signaled for the entire column to come to a halt. He could see nothing, but he assumed that Renno had perhaps caught a glimpse of a deer or some other animal that he, with his now sometimes unreliable eyesight, imagined to be a deer.

Renno reached over his shoulder for an arrow that he inserted with practiced ease to his bow, then fired; Ghonkaba followed its flight almost indolently, but suddenly he snapped to full attention. No more than thirty paces ahead of them was a brave wearing the purple and white war paint of the Erie, a nation long an enemy of the Seneca.

Before the young warrior could intervene, Renno fired a second arrow, then a third. It seemed to Ghonkaba at first that Renno was missing his target, but he quickly realized that his grandfather's aim was as accurate as it had ever been. One arrow buried itself in a tree trunk scant inches ahead of the Erie, a second pierced another tree directly behind him, and a third dropped to the ground at his feet. He was surrounded by Seneca fire, yet was unharmed and untouched.

A ring of authority entered Renno's voice as he declared softly, "Ghonkaba! Take some of the escort with you and make the Erie brave your prisoner. Do not harm him in any way; just bring him to me."

Hastening to obey the order, Ghonkaba told himself that he was on a fool's errand. Had he been fortunate enough to see the Erie first, he would have put a tomahawk into him and added a scalp to those he carried in his belt. His grandfather, he decided, must be growing soft.

Signaling to several of his comrades, Ghonkaba advanced stealthily but rapidly through the forest. The other Seneca did the same, spreading out as they moved, and in a classic maneuver, they succeeded in surrounding the Erie. The warrior, apparently having realized that he was being warned to halt, did not move as he tried to determine his best course of action, when four Seneca appeared, seemingly out of nowhere, only a few feet away.

The Erie, a man of courage, was not foolhardy, and recognizing that a fight against such odds would be futile and probably fatal, he surrendered without a struggle.

Ghonkaba, his thoughts hidden behind his impassive face, led the captive back to his grandfather.

As always in dealing with fellow Indians, regardless of their tribes, Renno was courteous. "I am Renno of the Seneca," he said, "and if you answer my questions truthfully, you will not suffer. But hear me well, O Erie—evade the truth, and you will not live!"

The Erie stared in undisguised astonishment at the white-haired man who stood before him with his arms folded across his chest. Quick to recognize the war paint of the dreaded Seneca, the brave knew the identity of his captor, the renowned Renno, by his piercing blue eyes and suntanned pale skin. What could he be doing so far from his own land?

"Why are you in the land of the Miami?" Renno demanded, his voice soft, even gentle, though he carried himself with such authority that the Erie cringed.

"I was sent as a messenger to the sachem of the Miami," he replied.

"How does it happen," Renno continued, "that the French, who live far to the north in Canada, have chosen to employ a brave of the Erie as their messenger?"

Staring in surprise, Ghonkaba wondered—not for the first time—whether his grandfather was clairvoyant. How could he have known that the Erie was in the employ of France?

The prisoner, taking seriously the warning of the Great Sachem of the Iroquois, decided to be truthful. "The Erie," he said, "have now become the allies of France."

This was news—startling and totally unexpected— and Ghonkaba and the other warriors nearby were stunned.

But Renno, showing neither surprise nor emotion, directed an order to the captive. "Give me the pouch that contains messages sent by the French to the sachem of the Miami," he commanded.

The Erie silently unwound the thong of a leather pouch at his waist and handed it over.

At least one mystery was solved, Ghonkaba thought,

7

as he recognized that burned into the rawhide pouch was the faint but unmistakable symbol of the fleur-de-lis, the emblem of France. To his grandfather, it had been a telltale indication that the brave was a French messenger, and Ghonkaba now felt slightly abashed for having doubted Renno's eyesight. Extraordinary all his long life, it was still superior to almost anyone else's.

Renno opened the pouch and unrolled a parchment scroll containing a message written in French and, below it, a translation into the language of the Algonquian, a large tribe that was a traditional ally of France.

Dated no more than two months earlier, in April 1755, the document was signed by the Marquis Louis Joseph de Montcalm de Veran. Renno knew of General Montcalm as the military commander in chief of the armies of King Louis XV of France in the New World.

The message itself was a simple one: France was engaged in a great crusade to drive the English colonists out of North America for all time. With him in this grand design were several large and powerful Indian nations, among them the Algonquian and Huron, the Ottawa and the Erie. The Miami were being invited to join in the alliance. In return for their fealty to France, they would be supplied with the most modern French firearms and ample ammunition. French military instructors would be sent to teach them how to use these remarkable weapons.

And even greater benefits could await the Miami in an alliance with France. The nations of the Iroquois League, as allies of the British colonists, would be a principal object of the campaign. Once the Iroquois were defeated, their lands would be confiscated and would be shared by the victorious Indian nations. Though the message said nothing about the fate of the people of the Iroquois, tradition dictated that any who were not killed in combat would be enslaved.

Renno felt a deep dismay as he read the invitation to the Miami. Almost all his adult life had involved warfare against the French; he had taken part in several major campaigns. In a significant way, his reputation rested on his achievements in those campaigns. Now France, still ambitious and greedy, was planning on a new attempt to drive the British out of their seaboard colonies and to annihilate their Iroquois comrades.

Renno was discouraged and weary. But suddenly blood started coursing rapidly through his veins again. The cause for which he had fought so long and honorably was coming to life again, and now his people were threatened by danger. The Seneca and the other nations of the Iroquois needed him, and he would have to respond to the challenge without delay.

Impatient throughout the exchange, Ghonkaba was relieved to see that it seemed to be nearing an end. Now, he thought, the Erie would be turned over to him, and he could dispose of the brave promptly and add a scalp to his belt.

But his grandfather surprised and dismayed him again. "If I were to follow the custom of the wilderness," Renno told the captive, "I would hand you over to these warriors and allow them to deal with you as they please."

The Erie warrior's face fell in horror. "On this occasion, however," Renno went on, "I shall spare your life."

Ghonkaba was disgusted. His grandfather was becoming soft and senile, he felt, but he could do nothing.

"You will return to the land of the Erie without delay," Renno instructed the warrior. "I assume you are not the only messenger who was sent by your sachem to the Miami."

The Erie swallowed hard. This aged Seneca had an uncanny ability to read his mind. "I was but one of several couriers sent to the Miami," he acknowledged. "Three others were given the same assignment."

"You will relate to the sachem of the Erie and to the elders of his council what has befallen you in the wilderness," Renno now instructed. "Then you will give them a special message from Renno of the Seneca, Great Sachem of all the Iroquois. You will remind your listeners that they have been enemies of the Seneca from the time when my father's father was very young. Many times through the long years the Erie have broken the peace with the Seneca. Each time they have resorted to arms, they have lost. Their warriors, the cream of their nation, have been killed in battle, their squaws and their children enslaved and forced to work for the Seneca until the end of their days.

"Unfortunately, the Erie seem to have learned nothing from their tragic experiences," he went on. "You will tell the sachem and the council of the Erie to listen to the words of Renno of the Seneca and to heed his advice. The Seneca and the Erie are now at peace. The Erie are free to hunt and fish where they please, their women grow bountiful crops, and their children grow strong and sturdy. But if the Erie once again break the peace, all that will change. This time, the Seneca will grind them into the dust as kernels of corn are ground at the bottom of a bowl to create the dust from which bread is made. If the Erie persist in their intention to join the French, long the enemies of the Iroquois nation and of the English settlers, they will receive no mercy from the Seneca and the other nations of the Iroquois. Their towns will be put to the torch. Their warriors will be scalped; their women will be taken captive and used for the pleasure of Seneca warriors. Even their youngest children will not escape the curse of the Seneca and will be made to suffer all their lives because of the foolish mistakes made by their fathers."

The Erie warrior listened intently, committing to memory Renno's words, which were not the idle boastings of a vain and pompous elder. These were solemn words of warning from the greatest of living Seneca, a warrior whose very name struck fear into the hearts of his foes.

"Go!" Renno commanded. "And may the manitous guide you safely to the land of your people."

The Erie needed no further urging as he darted off into the wilderness.

Though Ghonkaba averted his face, Renno seemed to understand instinctively how he felt. In a gesture of affection, he clasped the younger man by the shoulder. "Ghonkaba is sad," he said, "because he feels he has been cheated out of the scalp of an enemy. But it is better, far better, that the Erie live and deliver the warning of Renno to the leaders of his people. I do not expect the vain and stubborn Erie to heed my warning. But my mind is at rest, and if we are forced to do battle with them, I will know that I did all in my power to prevent their extinction."

Not daring to dispute his grandfather, Ghonkaba nonetheless could see no sense in his words. If the Erie would not listen to the warning but would persist in

11

waging a new war, the messenger's life was needlessly spared.

Renno saw the situation from a far different perspective: though the chance of preserving the peace might be slim, he considered the risk was well worth taking. As one who had seen countless wars and had become all too familiar with death on the battlefield, he wanted to avert a new catastrophe if at all possible. His conscience was clear, and he would still be able to hold his head high when he faced the final reckoning of the manitous. That was increasingly important to him: the time was fast approaching when he would cross the great river to the land of his ancestors and there be reunited with his wife, his parents, and so many others he had loved in this world.

Ja-gonh, sachem of the Seneca, was an Indian, yet the civilization of his white ancestors, Renno and Betsy, had marked him, too, just as his father was marked.

Ja-gonh sat cross-legged before the cooking fire still burning in the open pit outside his house and ate stolidly, occasionally smacking his lips in appreciation of the dish of squash, beans, and corn that Ah-wen-ga had prepared according to an old family recipe. His brother-in-law, No-da-vo, senior war chief of the nation, sat opposite him, and he, too, ate steadily. Their wives, Ah-wen-ga and Goo-ga-ro-no, had absented themselves to prepare the dessert—mashed inner bark of birch trees, sweetened with the natural syrup of maples.

"In the house of No-da-vo," the senior war chief declared with typical self-depreciation, "this dish is often served, but its taste is inferior to that prepared by Ah-wen-ga. She must use different herbs from those Goo-ga-ro-no puts into her cooking pot."

By custom, the Seneca did not talk during a meal, but No-da-vo felt free to do so now because the main dish had been eaten, and dessert was not yet ready for them.

Ja-gonh smiled politely. He considered his wife to be a far superior cook than his sister, but he was sensitive, as always, to the feelings of others.

"Have you learned," No-da-vo was asking, "why Renno sent a courier racing back from his hunting grounds in the land of the Miami with the urgent request that the leaders of all the Iroquois be summoned to a conference without delay?"

Ja-gonh replied carefully. "Before I sent the summons to our brothers in the Iroquois League, I questioned the courier at length," he said. "All he told me is that Renno captured a messenger of the Erie and talked with him before releasing him. Then the hunting trip was canceled, and the courier was sent here with that request."

Further words between them were unnecessary. The High Council of the Iroquois League was called into formal session only on occasions of great importance. It was apparent to both of them that Renno had acquired urgent information that demanded the combined efforts of the other Iroquois nations, as well as the Seneca.

"If my father felt it was proper for us to be told in advance of the significance of the meeting, he would have given word to the courier," Ja-gonh said. "All we can do is to be patient until Renno arrives."

Ah-wen-ga, slender and strikingly handsome, arrived

on the scene with her plump sister-in-law, both of them carrying the dessert gourds. "How often through the years," she observed, "we have waited for word from Renno before taking action on either peace or war."

"Ever since my mother passed on to the land of our ancestors on the far side of the great river," Goo-ga-ro-no added, "I have tried so often to persuade my father to yield the place of leadership to a younger man. El-i-chi, my uncle, and Deborah, my aunt, have added their voices to mine, but Renno does not heed our advice. Our voices are like the wind that whistles and sighs through the treetops."

Ja-gonh declined to discuss Renno's devotion to his duty. He was sure that no man could be more conscientious, more dedicated to the cause of his people than Renno, and Ja-gonh believed that Renno's children and their mates should not be carping about one of his greatest qualities. Like Renno and like Ghonka before him, Ja-gonh used words sparingly, and he turned quickly to another topic.

"What disturbs me," he said, "is that Ghonkaba heard the talk that passed between Renno and the Erie brave. The courier was very certain on that point. But he was equally certain that Ghonkaba was distressed and that he did everything that he could to try to show his disapproval of what was said."

As No-da-vo replied, his features remained placid, masking his feelings, but the disapproval in his voice was evident. "It well may be," he said, "that Ghonkaba does not agree with whatever it is that his grandfather has decided."

Ja-gonh sighed. "It would not be the first time," he conceded.

Ah-wen-ga sought to change the subject promptly,

for if Ja-gonh began to dwell on their son's attitudes he would become so upset that he would ruin his digestion and lose his appetite for the dessert, which was a rare delicacy he relished. She began to speak quickly about how to boil certain plants in order to provide the green stain for Seneca war paint.

But her husband refused to be distracted. "I really don't understand my son," he said vehemently. "When I was his age, I always obeyed my father, in all matters. As for my grandfather, Ghonka, I revered him above all other human beings. I still think he was the greatest person it has been my privilege to know. Perhaps my father is equally great; I find it hard now to distinguish between them. But Ghonkaba! He must go his own way, always. He disagrees with his grandfather, and I'm sure that I have yet to win his approval for anything that I say or do."

Goo-ga-ro-no tried to defend her nephew. "I am sure all of you recall the trouble I caused when I was young, by being rebellious and restless," she interjected with a smile. "Ghonkaba will change his views as he matures."

Her brother did not agree. "I would mention this to no one outside the family," he said, "but sometimes it almost appears that Ghonkaba rejects the values that we Seneca have held near to our hearts for many generations. Do these things have no meaning for him? I cannot really believe that to be true. His mother and I have tried speaking to him about these matters many times, and though he is always polite and listens to us, he says nothing. I have no evidence one way or the other, but I cannot understand why he turns his back on what the Seneca value most."

15

Now it was Ah-wen-ga's turn to defend her son. "He is young and lacks experience," she countered.

Ja-gonh's lower jaw jutted forward, his blue eyes blazed, and he bore a striking resemblance to Renno as he exclaimed, "Ghonkaba is not as young as you seek to imply. He is old enough, after all, to hold the rank of a senior warrior, and it is time that he makes it clear to me and to all the Seneca that he truly accepts the standards of our people!"

"I think there's a simple explanation for his apparent attitude," Goo-ga-ro-no suggested. "Remembering my own rebellion, I was confused because my father was the natural son of white-skinned parents, and my mother had white skin. I was a Seneca and was accepted by the entire nation, and yet I felt different. I stood apart from all whom I had known since earliest childhood."

"My father and mother were of Indian stock," Ah-wen-ga remarked, "and through me, Ghonkaba has inherited Indian blood. So I don't see why he would feel alien."

"Try to understand," Goo-ga-ro-no said, appealing both to her brother and her sister-in-law. "Of all the many hundreds of senior warriors who live in the Seneca nation, how many are there who are not completely of Indian ancestry? I know of none except Ghonkaba. He is alone in this respect."

Ja-gonh was losing patience. "No leader of our people has done more for our nation than Renno, the son of Ghonka!" he declared hotly. "As for me, my record of fidelity speaks for itself. It is nonsense to even suggest that my son is shamed by his white blood!"

"I do not say that he is shamed," Goo-ga-ro-no replied, ignoring the subtle efforts of No-da-vo to silence her. "Based on my own experience, I only suggest that perhaps he feels different because of his white-skinned ancestry."

Ja-gonh decided that the discussion had gone far enough, perhaps too far. "What my son feels is strictly his own affair," he said with a tone of finality. "All that really matters is that he remembers now, and always, that he is a Seneca. As such, he will respect his elders, obey his superiors, and do nothing that will bring discredit to the nation!"

The return of the hunting party to the main town of the Seneca was expected in about ten days, but no one, not even Ja-gonh, counted on the stamina and strength that Renno displayed. Six days after he and his party set out from the land of the Miami, the drums of Seneca sentries echoed through the forests, bringing word that the Great Sachem of the Iroquois was en route to his home.

El-i-chi and Deborah both tried to persuade him to rest before meeting with the Seneca council. But he was adamant.

"There will be time for me to sleep later," he said. "It is urgent that I meet with the Seneca council at once."

Renno, in spite of his grueling journey through the wilderness, showed no signs of fatigue as he related the latest conspiracy against the Iroquois and the English colonies that he had so fortuitously uncovered.

"On more occasions than I can recall," he told the assembled elders, war chiefs, and medicine men of the nation, "the Seneca have responded to the call of duty

17

when our land was endangered by the French, who have coveted it. We have again and again marched off to save our land and the land of our neighbors and good friends, the English colonists, from devastation. Now we are being called, once more, to protect our people and to preserve the freedoms that are precious to us. I have heard it said that General Montcalm, of the French, is a great and noble man, but I do not think this is so. He serves King Louis of France, so he must be greedy and treacherous and full of hate for the liberties that we and the English cherish."

Ja-gonh was not surprised that Louis XV of France now wished to expand his realm in the New World. It was true that he had once been kind and generous to Ja-gonh and Ah-wen-ga—but like all Frenchmen, Ja-gonh reflected, his lust for land had gotten the better of him, and the result would be a new war.

When Renno was finished with his address, the assemblage stood and cheered.

Then Ja-gonh, always practical, rose and asked, "What are the plans of Renno to counter the moves of the French and their Indian allies?"

"The French," Renno replied, "have perpetrated their new perfidy silently, in secret, as we might expect they would do. They have formed their customary alliance with the Algonquian, the Huron, and the Ottawa. Now they have reached out their hands and have formed friendships with the Erie, and perhaps by now with the Miami also. So far, only the Seneca know of this vast conspiracy. We have been chosen by the manitous as the instrument for bringing together those who love freedom and are willing to fight the French. The elders of the other Iroquois nations will arrive soon in this town and we shall inform them of the plot

against us. I have no doubt that they will join us in de-
claring war on France and the Indian nations that
serve her.

"In the meantime, our brothers, the English colonists, must be told of the grave danger that threatens
them," Renno reminded the council. "I propose that
we send a courier to each of the English colonies. I will
write a letter to them in their own tongue and explain
what we have learned. Then a trusted messenger will
deliver it to the militia chiefs of each colony. Then
they, too, will become aware of the danger and will
join forces with us."

His plan seemed so logical that the Seneca council
approved it without a dissenting voice, and a call was
promptly issued summoning all warriors of the nation
to mobilize without delay. Renno, keeping his promise,
composed a letter to the militia chiefs of various key
colonies.

The warrior assigned to carry the message was
Ghonkaba, who was to proceed immediately to Boston.
There he was to deliver the letter to Major General
Kenneth Strong, commander in chief of the volun-
teer forces of Massachusetts Bay. He would then
proceed on to other major colonies—particularly New
York, Pennsylvania, and Virginia—and other braves
would carry the message to certain other colonies.

The hunting party from which he had just returned
had in no way dissipated Ghonkaba's energy, and he
was still restless as well as irritated. After eating his
evening meal with his mother while the council meeting
was still in session, he wandered to the southeast
quadrant of the town, where the female captives who
were forced to serve Seneca warriors had their dwellings. He went straight to the hut of Toshabe, a girl

of the Erie nation whom he had visited on several occasions in the past. Toshabe, her face streaked with juices of red and black berries, her doeskin shirt carelessly unfastened to reveal her charms, was pleased to see Ghonkaba, who always treated her considerately and paid her considerably more than the fee to which, under Seneca law, she was entitled.

He made love to her in earnest, and quickly, then began to relax somewhat. He unburdened himself, telling Toshabe in detail about the experience in Ohio with the messenger—who was, like her, an Erie—and explaining his sense of unrest and dissatisfaction with his grandfather's decisions.

Experience had taught Toshabe that listening to her clients was an important role for her. So as she sat on a bed of corn husks covered with a blanket, and with her head to one side, she did not interrupt while Ghonkaba spoke at length.

He did his best to describe his confused feelings about his responsibility to his family. "I am especially concerned about the continuing alliance of our Seneca nation with the English colonists," he said. "I am afraid that this arrangement is strongly supported by my grandfather because of his own personal background. After all, he was the white child of white colonists in the Fort Springfield area—his parents had lost their lives in a Seneca raid, and this resulted in his capture and adoption by Ghonka when he was only an infant. He grew up knowing only Seneca ways, but nevertheless, he had the heritage of the white man. And then, when he was a young man he met and married a Virginia woman, Betsy Ridley, and the ties of sentiment that had already bound him to the English colonists were strengthened.

"I can't forget that he and Betsy were even presented at the royal court of the King and Queen of England, and obtained their favor.

"So it is only natural, it always seems to me, that Ja-gonh, my father, has felt as sympathetic to the cause of the English colonists as his own mother and father did.

"All this, I believe, is the cause of much trouble for the Seneca and for all the Iroquois. It is the presence of white men in our leadership that distresses me, and I wish to do all I can to counteract this unfortunate influence. No matter how much I respect my father and my grandfather, I think they are wrong in their attitudes and in their policies."

When his account was finished, he glanced at Toshabe sharply and saw that she continued to have a half smile on her face, her expression unchanged.

"What does Toshabe think?" he demanded.

Her expression remained steady. "If Ghonkaba is satisfied that his inner feelings are right, it does not matter what a captive of the Erie may think," she replied evasively.

"We have known each other for a long time," he remonstrated, "and I have told you many secrets. It is only fair that you tell me what passes through your mind when you hear me speak."

She hesitated for an instant, then brushed a long, thick strand of her blue-black hair across her shoulder. "It is the opinion of Toshabe," she said, "that Ghonkaba is wrong in all that he thinks."

He reacted as though she had slapped him. "Why do you say such a thing?" he asked in an aggrieved voice.

"In some things," she said, speaking softly but firmly, "the ways of the Seneca and the ways of the

21

Erie are different. But in other matters—in those that are the most important—the ways of our two peoples are the same. In both lands, the old warriors who have won great glory in battle are revered by the young for their courage and for their wisdom. In the land of the Seneca, no man is honored as Renno is honored. Only once did he deign to speak to me, and I clearly recall every word he said. In your veins flows the blood of Renno. You should rejoice because you are related to him—you should be proud and happy beyond measure. Instead, you are ashamed. This is not right."

"But you don't understand," Ghonkaba told her. "I certainly am not ashamed of his great deeds or of his renown. I have great love and respect for him; he is the finest of men. I am shamed only by the fact of his pale skin, and the pale skin of my father."

Toshabe shook her head in wonder, her eyes round and enormous in her painted face as she stared at him. "Did the pale skins of Renno and of Ja-gonh make them less valorous in battle?" she wanted to know. "Did it rob them of courage or deprive them of cunning? I think not! I am a mere woman, who knows nothing of war and of battles. But even I heard much about Ja-gonh and about Renno before I was captured and brought to this place. The names of Renno and his son must be known to every Indian nation in this vast land. Ghonkaba should rejoice because he is descended from such great warriors."

Because she was not telling him what he wanted to hear, much less sympathizing with him, Ghonkaba shortly took his leave. The council meeting had come to an end. Only in the longhouses occupied by bachelor warriors and by eligible maidens were candles still burning. But Ghonkaba had no desire to discuss with an excited group of his colleagues the possible developments in the coming campaign against the French and their Indian allies. Instead, he wandered through the silent town to his parents' home.

There, to his surprise, he found his mother was awake and apparently waiting for his return. Though realizing that she was spoiling him, Ah-wen-ga went to the larder and brought him a joint of venison and a gourd of cold beans and corn left over from the evening meal. As he devoured the food ravenously, Ah-wen-ga saw that no matter what might be troubling him, his appetite remained unaffected.

"You need your sleep," she told him. "You'll be leaving for Boston in the morning, carrying an important message from your grandfather, and then you must continue your journey to other distant cities."

Ghonkaba made a slight face and continued to eat.

His mother still watched him. "You're not surprised, I gather."

"Indeed I'm not," he replied. "It appears that we're going to follow the same routine as so many times in the past. The Iroquois nations will be alerted and will march to a rendezvous somewhere in the wilderness. The only difference between this march and those in the past is that my grandfather is now too old to lead the warriors in person. So I assume that they'll be led by my father or my uncle."

Aware of the disrespect in his voice, his mother peered at him still more closely. "Are you being critical of the military arrangements planned by Renno?" she demanded.

Her son, smiling sourly, shook his head. "Not at all," he said. "I know in advance every step that will be taken, that's all. The English colonies will be notified and they'll mobilize their militia. They'll meet the Iroquois at some predesignated spot in the wilderness, and the two armies will march together against the French and their allies. Their forces will maneuver, our forces will maneuver, and ultimately, we will meet in battle. We will be the winners, of course, because no Indians in all of America can stand up and survive against the combined power of the the the Iroquois. Similarly, the armies of the French fight in the European style, and those of the English colonists, having learned from the Iroquois, use the Indian methods of fighting. So the English will triumph, also. We will claim that we've won a great victory and bonfires will be lighted in all the towns of the Iroquois and in the cities of the English colonists. Then there will be peace again for a few years—until the whole business must once again be repeated."

Ah-wen-ga was appalled as she listened. Remembering her own long visit to France a quarter-century earlier, when she had been abducted, and rescued by Ja-gonh, she vividly recalled, despite the passage of the years, the court of Louis XV and the grasping, greedy nobles who dreamed of expanding their empire in North America at the expense of the English and their Indian allies. "You don't think that the cause for which we fight is worth a major battle?" she inquired.

"I see no difference between the English colonists and the French," Ghonkaba replied firmly. "All are white-skinned men, all come from the far side of the Atlantic Ocean, and all steal the land of the Indian nations."

"There is one major difference between them," his mother said, her manner gently reproving. "The French insist that all who live in the lands they conquer must abide by their rules. They insist that their God be worshiped as they choose to worship him. The chiefs of the Indian nations and of the colonies are not allowed to raise their voices in criticism of the king of the French or of the governors who represent him in the New World. They are required to give their animal skins and furs to the French so the French may enrich themselves."

Ghonkaba seemed unimpressed.

"If we had our way," Ah-wen-ga told him earnestly, "we would live side by side in peace with New France. But we are faced with a choice. Either we must surrender and give up the freedoms we cherish, or fight. Your father has fought long and hard in defense of those liberties. Both your grandfathers have devoted their lives to protecting the freedoms that we cherish. You are their inheritor, Ghonkaba, and you have no choice, either. It is up to you to finish the task that they started."

The young warrior sighed. It was odd, he thought, that he had been given similar advice by his mother and by Toshabe.

Aware of his boredom and indifference, Ah-wen-ga lost her ability to remain calm, "Hear my words carefully, my son," she warned him. "The day is at hand when you must choose. Either you will fight in the tradition of your grandfathers and of your father, or you will be disowned as a disgrace to the Seneca. The choice is yours, Ghonkaba—yours alone!"

Chapter II

Ghonkaba trotted at the same, unvarying pace
through the wilderness for mile after mile, despite
any obstacles that he encountered. He was conscious of
the wild animals and of the sentries of various tribes
through whose territory he passed. His war paint identified him as a Seneca, so he had nothing to fear. No
Indian nation would needlessly endanger relations with
the most powerful and warlike of tribes by molesting or
halting a Seneca runner. The ability to travel without
rest was a special knack of the Seneca, one that other
nations tried in vain to emulate. Actually, the "secret"
that they sought so eagerly did not exist. The Seneca

began training at a very young age to become tireless runners. Small boys practiced trotting through the forest, and as they grew older, the exercise became increasingly rigorous. So by the time a Seneca reached manhood and achieved the status of senior warrior, he was capable of what other nations regarded as incredible feats. When necessary, he could even run without tiring while carrying a deer carcass or a wounded comrade on his back.

Ghonkaba took his talent for granted, seeing nothing out of the ordinary in such accomplishments. As with many other aspects of Seneca living which would be considered remarkable elsewhere, he regarded them as only ordinary.

Scarcely pausing in Fort Springfield, where his father and his grandfather had many lifetime friends—and where Renno had, in fact, been born—he continued on his eastward journey. His journey took him on dirt roads past cultivated farms as he approached the civilization of the English colonists. Still, he did not slow his pace, and when colonists who saw him recognized his distinctive yellow and green war paint, they realized that something of importance was in the wind.

At last Ghonkaba reached Boston, which he was well acquainted with. He had accompanied his father on journeys to the white man's settlements, and one of these had brought him to Boston. Though on that occasion, he recalled, General Strong had been absent from the city on an official visit to London, he quickly was able to find his way to the spacious, white clapboard Beacon Hill home of the general. The militia commander's residence faced the Common directly below the mansion built by two prominent shippers, Thomas Hancock and his nephew, John.

Ghonkaba did not slow his pace until he reached the stoop and raised the polished brass knocker to announce his arrival.

The door was opened by a young woman whose features and expression seemed to him to belie the modesty of her high-necked, long-sleeved gown of dark brown linsey-woolsey. Blond hair, the color of ripe wheat, tumbled down her shoulders. Her features were set in a classical mold, and her eyes, a deep, almost startling shade of green, suggested a mischievous personality. She showed no surprise at the sight of an Indian warrior in war paint, and her full, scarlet lips parted in a smile that hinted at a greater interest than mere politeness demanded. "May I help you?" she asked pertly.

Ghonkaba replied in his perfect, unaccented English. "I am Ghonkaba of the Seneca, and I bring a private message to General Strong."

Hardly prepared to find a savage so familiar with her language, Beth inspected him candidly. She saw a tall, rangy Indian, whose skin was far lighter than that of any of the savages she had ever encountered. His hair was black, to be sure, but with strong hints of brown in it. His eyes, which were hazel rather than the deepest brown, revealed that he was a half-breed, rather than a full-blooded Indian. She immediately wondered if he was related to the renowned white Seneca of whom she had heard much.

"I am Elizabeth Strong," she said cordially. "Won't you come in? My father is out at the moment, but I am expecting him to return shortly."

With due deference to the custom of the colonists, Ghonkaba carefully wiped his moccasins on the doormat before he entered. As Beth led him down a corridor toward the parlor, Ghonkaba could not help noting her superb figure; she was broad shouldered, with a tiny waist, and exceptionally long limbs that her floor-length skirt somehow could not completely conceal.

"Do I gather you've come a considerable distance?" she asked politely.

"I have traveled here from the land of the Seneca," he replied.

She waved him to a chair, and realized with some surprise that he appeared very much at home as he seated himself in it; he was hardly a stranger to the homes of settlers, so she offered him a glass of sack or a mug of ale.

He surprised her once more by replying, "If it's no trouble, ma'am, I would prefer a cup of tea. I have tasted alcoholic beverages so infrequently that I've no liking for them."

She tugged the bell rope, and when a serving maid appeared, she ordered a tray of tea. As they awaited General Strong's return, Beth satisfied her curiosity about this unusual Indian and learned that, as she had suspected, he was the son of Ja-gonh. "Are you by any chance connected with the family of Renno and Ja-gonh?" she asked.

Ghonkaba frowned and looked down. "They are my father and grandfather," he said at last, and then went on to change the subject as quickly as possible. "I am sure you think of your own father simply as your father, not as commander in chief of the Massachusetts Bay militia."

Beth graciously conceded the point, and sensed that he had no desire to talk about his family. She began to search for topics that would interest him. She quickly realized that Ghonkaba was able to hold his own in almost any conversation. He knew a great deal about life in Boston, as well as the political situation in the closing years of the reign of King George II in England. Here was truly an extraordinary brave!

Their conversation was interrupted by the arrival of General Strong, a lean, gray-haired man whose chiseled, rugged features carried an air of authority that spoke more forcefully than the epaulets of his blue and gold militia uniform. With him was a young man, who was introduced to him as Samuel Adams, a newspaper editor and writer for several Boston publications.

Ghonkaba assumed that Adams might be a suitor for Beth Strong's very attractive hand, but quickly learned that his guess was wrong. Adams's interest was in writing a series of articles on the state of preparedness of the Massachusetts Bay militia. Adams and Beth treated each other with a formality that soon suggested to Ghonkaba that they were merely cordial acquaintances.

Samuel Adams gave scant evidence of the qualities that would make him known as the Father of the American Revolution. Mild mannered, he enjoyed the mug of ale that he was served, and with it, he devoured handfuls of roasted kernels of corn that Beth offered. Inclined toward plumpness, Adams had a liking for food, which was further proven by the numerous spots on his tailcoat, waistcoat, and cravat. The spots, ranging from new to those that had begun to fade with time, suggested that he was an enthusiastic, if not careful, trencherman.

Ghonkaba, having paid his own respects to General Strong, handed him the letter that Renno had sent, and then rose to his feet, intending to take his leave.

But the general would not hear of his departing so soon. "You have traveled a very great distance without rest, and knowing the ways of the Seneca, I'm confident that you have eaten nothing but parched corn and jerked meat on your journey."

"That is so," Ghonkaba admitted, seeing nothing unusual in his feat.

The general insisted that he dine with them that evening, and that he remain as their guest before continuing on his mission. When Ghonkaba tried to protest, the general used a simple stratagem to overrule him. "It's very possible that I will want to answer the letter sent to me by Renno," he said, "and you will be needed to deliver it."

Ghonkaba realized he was being outsmarted, but he subsided, and for once, he did not actually object strenuously. He couldn't remember meeting a more attractive young woman than Beth Strong, and despite his traditional belief that a warrior should marry a woman of his own nation, he hardly had an objection to getting to know Beth much better.

General Strong studied Renno's letter at length, then read it aloud for the benefit of Sam Adams and his daughter.

Both were deeply disturbed by it, though neither showed surprise.

"We have been fortunate," Beth murmured, "more than we realize. We've been at peace with France for many years now, but apparently that era is coming to an end."

Sam Adams remained remarkably cheerful. "This French threat to our security," he said, "may well be a blessing in disguise."

"How so?" General Strong demanded.

"Each of the colonies stands alone," Adams replied forcefully. "There is no cooperation between any of us, and each is totally isolated. We in Massachusetts are far more interested in events that take place three thousand miles away in England than in what happens in the lands of our neighbors, Connecticut and Rhode Island. The same is true of every other colony. So this threat can prove to have a fine therapeutic effect. The danger can bring the colonies together and enable them to start working for the common good. There's no telling what could happen if the colonies were to act in concert for some important aim. They might well prove to be invincible."

Ghonkaba had to concede, silently, that Sam Adams had analyzed the situation sensibly and described it well. The rivalries between colonies were as senseless as those that had driven the Indian nations apart. The one achievement of his ancestors of which he was truly proud lay in the result of the efforts of Ghonka and Renno in uniting the nations of the Iroquois League and keeping them at peace with each other.

General Strong drummed on the arm of his chair, and frowned as he looked off into space. "I must admit," he said finally, "that it won't be any too easy to alert the several colonies to the danger that they face. They are inclined toward complacency, just as we are here—particularly after having enjoyed a peaceful respite for a quarter of a century."

"I gladly will do everything in my power," Adams told him, "by writing articles that will help to awaken people to the dangers. What's more, General, I have newspaper colleagues in New York, Philadelphia, and other towns who will cooperate."

"I will be eternally grateful for anything you can accomplish," General Strong assured him. "The strongest ally of the French, I find, is the lethargy of our colonists!"

Beth turned to Ghonkaba. "How do the Indian nations achieve unity?" she asked. "I don't believe the tribes of the Iroquois League encounter the difficulties in cooperating with each other that our colonies have."

Ghonkaba saw no reason to be less than candid. "My grandfather," he said, "as was his father before him, is a forceful man who knows his own mind and permits no one to disagree. When my grandfather states an opinion as a fact, the warriors of the Seneca accept it as a fact. So do the Mohawk, the Oneida and Onondaga, the Tuscarora and the Cayuga."

Sam Adams raised an eyebrow. "You sound as though you don't always approve of what your ancestors have done," he commented.

Ghonkaba made a belated attempt to be discreet. "I am a young senior warrior of the Seneca," he explained, "and my voice carries no weight in the councils of my elders. So the opinions that I may hold are of little consequence."

A serving maid announced that supper was ready, and they adjourned to the dining room. There, a further surprise awaited Beth when she observed how familiar Ghonkaba was with knives and forks, plates and glasses, and napkins. She was steadily revising her opinion of life among the savages. Later, she would learn that he had taken part in visits with his father, grandfather, and uncle to Fort Springfield, and particularly to the home in Virginia of his late uncle and his cousins, the Ridleys.

Adams remained curious. "I have no right to insist

on a reply," he said to Ghonkaba, "but you really haven't answered my question."

The young warrior promptly discarded discretion. "As you insist," he responded. "I will tell you what I truly think. Because of the firm rule of Renno, and of Ghonka before him, we warriors of the Iroquois do not think for ourselves. We do what we are told, regardless of whether it is good or bad for us."

General Strong paused while serving a fragrant soup from a large tureen. The dish, a typical Bostonian recipe, consisted of clams and mussels, shrimp and crabmeat, simmered in chicken stock with liberal quantities of herbs. Just prior to its serving, thick cream had been added.

"Speaking for myself, as well as for Massachusetts Bay," the general said, "I am delighted that the Iroquois are going to be marching and fighting beside us." To this, Ghonkaba said nothing.

Again, Adams correctly interpreted his lack of comment. "Do I gather that you disapprove of your grandfather's decision for the Iroquois to take part in the coming campaign?"

"The basic dispute," Ghonkaba said, "is between the English colonists on one hand, and the French on the other. Each claims that it is pure and honorable, and that the other is a nation of villains. The French have attracted several Indian nations who have become their allies, just as the English colonists have won the loyalties of the Iroquois. But it is my opinion that all the Indians who are going to take part in this war are simply playing the white man's game."

Kenneth Strong exchanged a startled glance with his daughter. Neither had heard a supposed ally express such a blunt rejection of the English colonies.

"Those who came to these shores from England and Scotland, from Ireland and Wales," Ghonkaba continued, "settled on land that for centuries had been the hunting grounds of Indian nations. The Indians were expelled from these lands, and when they tried to recapture them by force, they were driven off by the firesticks of the settlers. The English have taken the furs and the skins of animals and have sent them across the Atlantic, earning great profits. The French have done precisely the same thing. They have taken lands that have belonged to one nation or another for hundreds of years. They have paid the Indians nothing, and in order to pacify them, have sold them some old-fashioned firesticks, and have made gifts to them of inexpensive blankets and cooking utensils of metal. These objects the Indians accepted gratefully because they didn't know any better. The French, too, covet the furs and the skins of animals, have bought them for virtually nothing, and have earned great fortunes for themselves in Europe with these goods.

"If I had my way," he went on, looking at each of the surprised trio in turn, "I would urge the Seneca and the other nations of the Iroquois League to shun both the English and the French colonists. Let them destroy each other, and then let the land be returned to the Indian nations that made their homes here for so long!"

A stunned silence followed as he devoted himself to his soup. General Strong felt constrained from becoming involved in an argument with a young warrior who was the grandson of Renno and was, therefore, too potentially influential to be needlessly antagonized. Adams followed his host's lead.

But Beth Strong felt under no compunction to keep her views to herself. She was so angered by Ghonkaba's statement that no power on earth could have prevented her from replying.

"Your arguments are specious and shortsighted," she cried. "I won't argue with you that the colonists who first came to these shores were wrong when they appropriated lands that belonged to various Indian nations. Since that time, however, in colony after colony, people have paid the Indians for their hunting grounds, and the towns and farms of the colonists have been built on ground that they have purchased legitimately. But your biggest mistake is in equating the English and the French. Surely, as one who is descended from whites, as well as from Indians, you cannot claim that all white men are alike. That would be like saying that all Indians are alike. Would you claim that no differences exist, for example, between the Seneca and the Algonquian?"

"The record of the Seneca speaks for itself," Ghonkaba replied stiffly.

"So do the records of the English and the French," she declared with spirit. "In England men are free to worship God as they choose, free to write and say what they think, free to meet with those of like mind, regardless of whether King George or his government agrees with their beliefs. In France that is not true. Only one religion is permitted, and all others are banned. Those who speak or write ideas that are opposed by King Louis and his ministers are sent to prison and are held there without a trial for many years. The same is true on this side of the Atlantic. In the English colonies there's freedom; in the French colonies there's repression. And how can you possibly say that there's no difference in the way that we and the French treat the Indian nations? That is utterly absurd, and shows your abysmal ignorance! We go out of our way to be fair at all times. Don't take my word for it! Ask your father and your grandfather why they have made treaties with us. Then ask them whether the French have ever offered to treat them as fairly. The only reason the French have any allies is because they provide certain Indian nations with liquor, which is bad for them, and with firearms, which they're encouraged to use."

Silence fell again as the maid, having cleared away the soup plates, returned with roast beef and a platter piled high with potatoes and other vegetables.

General Strong smiled as he observed mildly, "My daughter feels rather passionately on this subject, and as you can see, she doesn't hesitate to speak her mind—a trait I fear she shares with her late mother." The general sighed. "I've tried to caution her about this but to no avail. But in this one instance I happen to believe she's right."

"No question about it," Sam Adams added, though without heat. "The difference between the English and French ways of life is as great as freedom is from prison chains!"

General Strong responded to the threat from the north by applying to the governor and legislature of Massachusetts Bay for a declaration of a state of emergency. His request was promptly granted, and he immediately informed the entire militia force of the colony to be prepared for a call to active military duty if the circumstances did not improve.

In the meantime, he made arrangements with John Hancock to borrow a fast-moving sloop to carry the word of the crisis to the other seaboard colonies. "I'm not for a moment doubting your ability to make splendid time through the forests," he told Ghonkaba, "but you'll manage the feat in far less time if you travel by sea."

A sloop was readied for the voyage, and in the interim General Strong asked a favor of Ghonkaba. "You made it clear," he said, "that you really don't see the point of our taking a stand against the French because you do not see the difference between the various Europeans who have come to America. But inasmuch as we're intending to bend every effort in that direction, I hope you can be persuaded to lend your own efforts toward convincing the tribes of this area that it will be in their best interests to join us."

Ghonkaba could not refuse such a request, since he would not openly oppose the principle espoused by his father and grandfather. Therefore, when the general summoned leaders of the two largest Indian nations of the Boston area, the Massachusetts and the Wampanoag, he went to the Boston Common to meet and speak with them.

The leaders of the Wampanoag, short, dark men who were inordinately shy, refrained from coming forward, and showed considerable reserve when they saw Ghonkaba. The Massachusetts, more outgoing and self-assured, greeted him cordially, but also with a measure of reserve. He realized that they looked up to him simply because he was a Seneca. Every member of his nation was accorded such treatment, and actually considered it only proper. Under the circumstances, though, Ghonkaba felt that he was making an appearance under false colors.

Speaking in the language of the Massachusetts, General Strong introduced the young Seneca, stressing his parentage. Ghonkaba sounded and looked self-assured as he addressed the assemblage in the Algonquian language. He explained what was at stake in the coming military campaign, and he found himself relying heavily on the arguments that Beth had used. He could see that he was making an impression, and by the time he had finished, the reaction of the Wampanoag and the Massachusetts was evident. Leaders of both tribes had been persuaded that it was wise for them to join with the Iroquois and the colonists in fighting the French.

As Ghonkaba made his way back to the Strong house, he could see Beth standing at a second-floor open window, presumably having stationed herself there to hear his speech. As she caught his eye, smiled, and withdrew into the house, he felt color rise to his cheeks, and was suffused with shame. The arguments he had presented were her views rather than his own.

What surprised him was that Beth appeared to have understood him, even though he had been speaking in the language of the Algonquian, a language all nations of the Northeast were familiar with. Beth opened the door for him, and Ghonkaba, somewhat flustered, spoke the first words that came to his mind. "You are familiar with the tongue of the Algonquian," he exclaimed.

She seemed to find nothing particularly praiseworthy about her accomplishment. "Yes," she said. "I learned a number of Indian languages over the years. I've always felt that it's only fair to speak to them in their own languages rather than expecting them to know ours. But we're digressing, aren't we? Your address was very stirring, and very effective."

"If it was," he replied, forcing a smile, "it is due to

you and your ideas. I simply repeated what you said to me the other evening."

"I was impressed," Beth assured him, and it was evident that she meant what she said. "You showed loyalty to the Seneca, even though you don't happen to believe in their cause. That took a great deal of courage, to stand up for a position that isn't really yours."

Rather than saying that he had actually felt foolish, particularly after he discovered that she had heard him, he reflected that if an attractive young woman chose to think highly of him for such a peculiar reason, he would not seek to dissuade her.

Later that day, when General Strong escorted him to the sloop that would carry him south, he was pleased that Beth accompanied her father. She wished him well on his journey, and when they parted, she held out her hand to him, English-style. She would be a very difficult person to forget.

The sloop, manned by expert seamen, put in to Providence, the capital of Rhode Island, and then, entering Long Island Sound, stopped at New Haven and again in New York. At each place Ghonkaba delivered his warning to the appropriate militia authorities.

When the sloop put in to port in Delaware, the colonel commanding the colony's militia agreed to send a messenger to Philadelphia, thus shortening Ghonkaba's travel. Instead, he was able to continue to his last major call, Williamsburg, the capital of Virginia. After Massachusetts, that was perhaps the most important of all the English-speaking colonies.

Ghonkaba was assured a warm welcome there because the militia commander was his own first cousin, once removed. He was Brigadier General Thomas Ridley, who also bore the Indian name of Linnick. Because of the pressures of colleagues in the military, he had long gone by the name of Thomas; on the contrary, Ja-gonh, whose English name was James, had chosen to use his Indian name because it was appropriate in the land of the Seneca.

Tom Ridley, who had returned many years ago from South Carolina Colony, where he had for a time been a cotton grower, was delighted to see Ghonkaba. He promptly introduced him to Governor Robert Dinwiddie, who assured him of Virginia's complete cooperation.

General Ridley then insisted that Ghonkaba accompany him to his house, and there they were joined by Colonel George Washington, an aide-de-camp, in whom, Tom said, the governor had great confidence. After the general, a rather stocky man of medium height, hospitably made his guests at home, Colonel Washington, a lean, tall surveyor and gentleman-farmer who looked and acted considerably older than his early twenties, peppered Ghonkaba with questions.

"How many men are the French assembling, do you know?" he asked. "Are they colonial militia, or are they regular troops imported from France? Are the Indian allies of the French committed to service beyond their own borders, or are they intending to fight a defensive war?"

"I'm afraid I can't answer any of your questions, Colonel," Ghonkaba replied, smiling at his earnest intensity. "All I know is what I've related in my message. The details aren't yet available."

"I have great respect for the knowledge that the French seem to have of the topography of the New World and for their ability to maneuver in the wilderness," Washington said. "So I expect that they'll move down through the lakes and rivers—particularly the Ohio River—and try to cut us off from the west. Then with their fleet blockading our coast and their own armies to the north of us in Canada, they would have us totally isolated."

"Fortunately," Tom Ridley said with a faint smile, "we have you functioning on our side, rather than on the side of the enemy, Colonel. I trust that the French will prove to lack your perspicacity."

"Well, sir," the younger officer replied seriously, "I've never had the privilege of meeting General Montcalm, but I have read several of his treatises on the subject of how to conduct a military campaign. I would be surprised if he didn't employ such a strategy as I have described."

Ghonkaba, who had little use for the colonial officers he had met, considered even General Ridley inferior to most Seneca warriors. But Colonel Washington seemed different; perhaps because he exuded an air of self-confidence, or possibly because he knew his subject so well. In any event, the young Seneca found himself regarding him with quiet admiration. Here, he thought, was a militia officer he wouldn't object to fighting beside. His own knowledge of warfare and his confidence in his own abilities were solidly based, and in young Colonel Washington he recognized a similar spirit.

"I'm afraid," Tom Ridley said, "that we'll have to allow the campaign to take shape as the French elect to shape it. They are prepared for war, and we are not. I realize that this may not be a popular judgment, or in a strategic sense, even the correct one. But from a strictly practical point of view, what else are we to do? We here in Virginia, and General Strong in Massachusetts, have the only militia forces of consequence. The other colonies have been lulled by too many years of peace, and their regiments are woefully inadequate."

Washington reluctantly agreed with that estimate.

"It strikes me," the general went on, "that our only hope is to persuade the War Office in London to send us adequate troops for our defense."

Washington, who seemed about to reply, remained silent. Ridley was aware of his reticence. "Don't be bashful, young man," he urged. "Speak your mind freely here!"

"All right, General," Washington replied, "I will. It might be better to use our own militia and deploy such regiments as we have ourselves, along with those of our Indian allies that we can feel confident are reliable—such as the Iroquois nation," he added with a slight tilt of his head in Ghonkaba's direction. "I've seen any number of regular troops from Great Britain, and they don't impress me. I am not deploring their ability as fighting men. They're surely as brave and as resourceful as the most intrepid of our colonists. But they haven't been trained for wilderness warfare, and it's a far different matter to fight a battle according to European-style combat than to maneuver in the forests of the New World."

Here, Ghonkaba thought in amazement, was a militia officer who made great sense! Colonel Washington was one of the few senior officers he had encountered who recognized the need to employ the wilderness to its greatest advantage rather than to regard it as a handicap that had to be overcome.

Ghonkaba reflected that it would be interesting to ascertain whether this young Virginia militiaman felt as he had slowly come to feel—that the threat posed by

France might be somewhat exaggerated. The idea had been taking root in his mind for some days past. "Do you think, Colonel Washington," he asked, wording his question with great care, "that we'll be able to triumph over the French and their allies in this campaign?"

The Virginian showed amazement that anyone would even ask such a question. "There's no doubt in my own mind that we'll win!" he said briskly. "We've beaten the French in every campaign that we've fought, because our manpower has been superior to theirs. I have no doubt that we'll demonstrate, once again, that our forces are superior and that we'll win the day."

His self-assurance was so great that, as the conversation drew to a close, Ghonkaba misinterpreted his remarks. Already persuaded that the danger facing the English colonies was slight, he took Colonel Washington's statement as a corroboration of his own views.

His immediate mission having been fulfilled, Ghonkaba left the following morning for his return journey overland to his home. He enjoyed himself thoroughly, as he always did in the wilderness, shooting game and catching fish for food, and relishing the mastery of his environment that was such an important part of his Seneca heritage. Only when he passed through the land of the Erie did he observe more than normal cautions. Only because they were now the foes of the Seneca, and not because of their alliance with the French, was he careful to avoid them.

He felt he had done his duty and could not be criticized by either his father or grandfather. But all that he had seen and heard—particularly his conversation with Colonel Washington—had convinced him that the threat posed by France to the English colonies was an exaggeration, and that the danger to the Seneca and their neighbors was actually very slight.

Traditionally, the secretary of state for foreign affairs claimed the largest office in the massive stone building in Whitehall occupied by the British Foreign Office. But the Duke of Newcastle was no ordinary foreign secretary. Recognizing that he was forced to function with a recalcitrant House of Commons that often changed its mind, and that his task was further complicated by the Hanoverian obstinacy of George II, he preferred to operate modestly and quietly. Hence, the chamber that ordinarily would have been his office was now a conference room used for receiving dignitaries from abroad. The duke himself, balding but not deigning to hide his scalp beneath a fashionable wig, worked in a small, cramped chamber adjacent to the large office. The room was barely large enough for his desk and several leather-covered chairs for visitors.

Two of those chairs were currently occupied. In one sat Henry Pelham, the duke's younger brother, who actually had attained even greater political success. For several years, he had been prime minister, and held onto that office despite his precarious health. The family resemblance was marred by his full head of hair, which he wore long and carefully powdered. His attire, as usual, was dazzling: a swallow-tailed coat, waistcoat, breeches, and stockings, all of pure silk. The buckles on his shoes were of solid gold. But if Pelham gave the impression of being overly concerned with the superficial, that was only because the role suited his pleasure. Actually, one of the shrewdest men in England, he had risen on merit to his high post.

The third man was in the room because the brothers had no choice: if they expected to accomplish anything in Commons, they needed his support. William Pitt, the leader of the Whig party, bore scant resemblance to the superb politician he had become. Tall and broad shouldered, he had developed an increasingly ample girth, bearing testimony to his considerable enjoyment of good food and drink. His habitually bland, seemingly innocent expression had fooled many men in the king's service, but by now everyone recognized that no one could be more shrewd, more clever, or more ruthless. Pitt was already recognized as a powerful orator; his ambition, it was reputed, was to become prime minister himself. He did not bother to deny these conjectures.

"Occasionally, gentlemen," the Duke of Newcastle was saying in the singsong voice that his opponents in the House of Lords found so annoying, "one finds a delightful strip of bacon sizzling and bubbling in a frying pan. Delectable though it may appear at first sight, it is so hot that anyone who attempts to remove it will burn his fingers on bacon grease. Consequently, it is deemed best to let the piece of bacon simply burn itself out."

Pleased with his analogy, he folded his hands over his paunch and, beaming, leaned back in his comfortably padded chair.

"Quite so," the prime minister declared, "and well put, if you don't mind my saying so. The letters from the governors of the New World colonies appear to be just such a piece of bacon."

The duke beamed. "You catch my meaning entirely, Henry. How clever of you!"

Pitt, slouching indolently, remained silent. His pale

eyes were hooded like those of a hawk, and any man who had dealings with him in the past could have told the brothers that he was at his most dangerous.

"The colonial secretary," the duke declared, "didn't know what to do with the communications, and the secretary of war was so horrified that when I offered to take charge of the matter, he practically threw the letters at me!"

Pitt seemed to uncoil as he reached out and picked up one of the documents from the desk. "May I?" he asked mildly and proceeded to study it, though he already knew the contents. Signed by eight royal governors—Massachusetts Bay, Rhode Island, Connecticut, New York, New Jersey, Pennsylvania, Delaware, and Virginia—the letters were as plain as they were urgently worded. France, the governors declared in their various communications, was in the process of preparing to make war on the English colonies after two decades of peace. The very able French commander, General Montcalm, had enlisted many powerful Indian nations in the struggle. Therefore, the governors said, massive military aid was needed in the immediate future. Specifically, they wanted no fewer than ten thousand troops to be dispatched from the Mother Country, in addition to an equal number of muskets, bayonets, and ample supplies of ammunition for their own men.

Pitt seemed to be weighing the matter. "I'm inclined to take this threat seriously," he said, "because men of the caliber of Robert Dinwiddie, for example, don't panic easily. I regard a threat to the colonies to be very serious."

"What I find of even greater significance," the Duke of Newcastle said forcefully, "is that the ambitions of

Louis XV appear to have been reawakened. You'd think he'd learned a lesson, having lost several wars to us in his attempt to gain possession of our colonies, but it's typical of the French that he's learned nothing. When the French activities in the New World become public knowledge, Henry, I anticipate a great clamor throughout the British Isles—and consequently in Commons as well—for a declaration of war against France."

"I suspect," Pitt said dryly, "that you can count on precisely such a clamor, Your Grace."

Newcastle never knew when Pitt was serious; it was impossible to determine from his expressionless face. "I'm glad we're in agreement, Pitt," he said, and glanced at his brother.

Having already discussed the subject in private with the duke, Pelham knew precisely what role was expected of him now. "It seems to me," he put in, "that the colonial governors aren't very practical. A declaration of war against France—which is inevitable—is going to mean an equally inevitable strengthening of the British army and navy here at home. After all, we're separated from France by only twenty-one miles of a common waterway."

"Are you intimating that we can't afford to meet the needs of the colonies and to expand the armed forces at home as well?" the duke asked.

Pelham shook his head. "The question isn't whether we can or cannot afford such expenditures," he explained. "Rather, it's a matter of our willingness to do so. The English people will pay the new taxes on goods that will be required by the war, provided those funds are spent close to home on items that will assure us victory. But the public—and consequently Commons—

will protest rather strongly in the event that large sums are expended for the protection of colonies that don't bring us enough revenue in the first place."

The brothers' arguments were smooth, having been well rehearsed, but William Pitt remained unconvinced. "I know of nothing," he said, "of greater importance to Great Britain than our colonies in North America. Their potential, both financial and political, is enormous. Properly developed, they can add immeasurably to our power as a nation. I would truly hesitate to abandon them in their time of need."

Pelham forced a laugh. "Really, my dear Pitt. That's too much!" he exclaimed. "Apparently I haven't expressed myself well. Under no circumstances do I propose that we abandon the colonies or leave them to their fate against a French general of high caliber. Any Englishman in a position of authority who took such a stand would be guilty of criminal negligence."

Pitt's frown was erased from his face, and he seemed more at ease. "Apparently I did misunderstand you," he said quietly.

"I believe my brother has worked out a scheme," the wily Pelham said, "that will meet your complete approval, Mr. Pitt, and I'm sure you'll deem it worthy of giving it the unqualified support of the entire Whig party."

The duke smiled blandly. "Since the problem has been given to the Foreign Office for a solution—the army and the Colonial Office having abdicated the responsibility—I've made it my business to look into the matter in some depth. I have learned that the most eligible officer in the army is a brigadier named Edward Braddock. His superiors think very highly of him, and are in general agreement that he is by far the most promising officer currently wearing the king's uniform."

"What experience has he had?" Pitt wanted to know.

"I asked the same question, but that doesn't appear to be important," the duke said casually. "He's an avid student of military strategy and tactics, and is said to know more than any of our other generals on those subjects. Furthermore, he's a strict disciplinarian who nevertheless wins the unqualified support of the troops he commands. I propose, therefore, that he be promoted to the rank of major general, and receive the command of the military forces in North America."

Pelham took up the discourse. "We can't spare ten thousand troops," he said, "for a conflict with the French. But I am willing to do the next best thing, and send two thousand of our most seasoned veterans under Braddock."

Shrewd William Pitt ordinarily would have seen that Pelham and Newcastle were merely throwing a sop to the colonies. The strategy was to send a token force under an officer who reputedly was exceptionally able, in order to convince them and the public at home that the colonies were not being neglected. So sincere were the duke and the prime minister in their declarations, however, that Pitt reacted exactly as the brothers had hoped.

"We live in an imperfect world," he said, "a world in which it's necessary, more often than not, to compromise. I'll grant you that it would be helpful if we could raise a large enough military force to protect the British Isles, and at the same time, send a major expedition to the colonies. Under the circumstances, however, the colonial administrators will have to take steps on their own initiative for their self-protection."

"It isn't as though they're totally helpless," Prime Minister Pelham pointed out. "After all, they do have competent regiments of militia, and they've worked out treaties with their major Indian allies, particularly the Iroquois League."

Pitt sighed. "Are you intending to propose to Commons the scheme you've outlined to me?" he demanded.

"I am, sir!" The time for decision had arrived.

"Then I shall give you my unqualified support," Pitt assured him.

The prime minister breathed more easily. It was true that the colonies had been shortchanged, but the protection of the British Isles, his primary consideration, must take precedence over all else.

Out of the seemingly impenetrable Canadian wilderness lining both sides of the great St. Lawrence River, a city suddenly rose that offered testimony to the skill, stamina, and spirit of the Frenchmen who had carved a major metropolis out of the forest.

On a high plateau that soared above the river were the homes and shops, the schools and churches, and the counting rooms of the French who engaged in the fur and lumber trades, and in shipping.

And at the plateau's high crest stood a great stone fort, the Citadel, a complex of buildings that included stout defensive structures where powerful cannon guarded the commerce in the river below and kept would-be attackers at bay. Barracks housed thousands of troops behind the parade grounds, and farther on stood private dwellings for ranking officers.

Of these structures, one that resembled a miniature

fort was the traditional headquarters and home of the commander in chief of the military forces of New France. It was currently occupied by the Marquis Louis Joseph de Montcalm de Veran, whose youthful, handsome appearance seemed at odds with his rank of major general.

With him in his comfortable office-drawing room were two of his principal subordinates, the gray-haired Comte de Beaufort and the lean, ascetic Marquis de Lavelle, both generals in their own right. They could have outranked their superior, but they accepted his higher position with good grace. The entire French high command was united in the firm conviction that General Montcalm was a military genius. In their view, the fact that he was stationed in North America gave them a decided advantage in the forthcoming hostilities with the British colonies.

Not the least of Montcalm's assets was his ingratiating charm. At no time did he make himself obnoxious or try to assert authority capriciously over his subordinates. Leaning back comfortably, in a chair that was a gift from Mme. DuBarry, the latest mistress of King Louis, he inhaled the pungent odor of the brandy that swirled in the bell-shaped glass he held in his delicate hands. "It strikes me, gentlemen," he said, "that we shall have a natural advantage over the English."

"I'm glad to hear it," General Lavelle replied, "but I'm afraid I don't follow you."

"Nor do I," General Beaufort said as he took a sip of his brandy.

General Montcalm looked like a youth in his early twenties as he grinned. "We're fortunate," he said. "We have a king and a cabinet in France who understand our situation thoroughly here and are prepared to cooperate with us in every way. The English are shortsighted, according to my informants in London, and I pray that they'll stay that way. Specifically, they're offering very little concrete assistance to their colonies. They've just passed bills through the House of Commons under which they're sending a meager two thousand troops, and they're placing great reliance on their new commander, Braddock."

Lavelle sniffed his brandy. "I've never heard of him," he said.

"I know a few things of interest concerning him," Montcalm mentioned. "What's important is that it's very likely that he's totally unfamiliar with the principles of warfare as it's fought on this continent."

General Beaufort raised an eyebrow. "You mean he has no experience in wilderness fighting?"

"None," Montcalm said flatly.

"Astonishing," Beaufort said, and chuckled.

General Lavelle looked contemplative. "The English," he said, "are not a stupid people, and their military leaders are men of considerable stature. Why should they be so nearsighted about the importance of their colonies?"

"Perhaps they have an island mentality," Montcalm said. "We have recognized the importance of the New World for a great many years. Even during the reign of Louis XIV, our general staff knew that the nation that established control here would become a great power, probably the greatest in all of Europe. The English have yet to awaken to that fact."

"By the time they wake up," Lavelle said, a cutting edge in his voice, "it will be too late for them to respond effectively."

"I sincerely hope so," Montcalm replied, and rising

from his desk, he crossed the room to a heavy iron safe, which he unlocked with keys that he produced from a chain in his pocket. From the safe he took a map and spread it on a large, oblong table. Then, with his subordinates flanking him, he studied it at length. "This," he pointed out, "is the region to our west and the lands lying south of that region. It shows the course of the Ohio River, the greatest stream in the eastern part of the continent—not including the St. Lawrence, of course.

"The history of French military ventures in America is an unhappy tale, gentlemen," he continued. "The English have defeated us in the past in war after war because we have ignored certain basic principles. We have built great fortresses in Canada, like the Citadel, where we now sit, and Fort Louisburg on Cape Breton Island. This approach has been inadequate. We should instead take the initiative by carrying our rivalry with the British down closer to the territory they claim. We have a strong base here in Canada, and we must establish another, equally strong, west of the English colonies. That will enable us to engage in a pincer movement. If we attack them simultaneously from the north and the west, their resistance will crumble. This is especially predictable when you consider that they have inadequate forces at their disposal. Therefore, the key to winning this campaign—and with it establishing our absolute control over all the continent—depends on just one factor." He took a razor-sharp dagger from its place in his belt and tapped a point on the map. "Here is where we win or lose North America!"

His colleagues saw at a glance that he was referring to the place where two rivers, the Allegheny, from the north, and the Monongahela, from the south, join to form the Ohio. The spot was in territory claimed by both England and France—but the French, as all three of her generals knew, had achieved a natural advantage. Where the rivers converged, a wooden fort that the French called Duquesne had been built, and there they unobtrusively maintained a small but secure garrison.

"I propose," General Montcalm said, tapping his dagger on the map for emphasis, "to strengthen Fort Duquesne. I intend to send at least one thousand troops familiar with wilderness warfare there in the immediate future, and to bolster that garrison with as large a number of braves selected from our Indian allies as proves practical."

"Very clever," General Beaufort said, immediately grasping his intent. "You plan to make Fort Duquesne the pivot of our position in the west!"

"Exactly," Montcalm replied. "With an impregnable Duquesne firmly under our control, the English will have no way to wrest control of the region from us. We shall keep adding to the personnel of the fort, which will become a perfect springboard for our pincer movement from the west, just as Quebec is an ideal base for a movement from the north."

His colleagues were silent for some moments as they digested his plan. Then, General Lavelle exhaled slowly. "I can find no fault with your plan," he said.

"Nor can I," General Beaufort added. "It seems to me that if we're successful in strengthening Fort Duquesne, we're going to reverse the tide of history that's run against us for more than a half century."

"I assure you, we cannot, and shall not, lose," General Montcalm said firmly. "And I fully anticipate that what we have done will come to the attention of the

English. The Mother Country may be stupid and short-sighted in its dealings with them, but the colonies are sharp witted, and they're certain to recognize its significance. So they'll see no choice but to attempt to take Duquesne from us by force."

Beaufort chuckled. "And thus," he exclaimed with delight, "they'll be playing right into our hands."

"That," General Montcalm told him, "is the ultimate aim of my plan. Let them send a force through the wilderness that will expend its energies in the mountainous terrain to which they are unaccustomed. They'll be tired, and will be running short of necessary supplies by the time they reach Duquesne. There our men, well rested, will await them—and will defeat them in the battle that I predict confidently will prove to be the key to the control of North America for centuries to come!"

Chapter III

Having received the stunning news that the military assistance being sent from England would be only a fraction of what they anticipated, the militia leaders of five colonies—Massachusetts Bay, Connecticut, New York, Pennsylvania, and Virginia—convened in Boston in an atmosphere of disbelief, anger, and frustration. They could do little save try to cope with the gloomy situation. Nor did they have any confidence in General Braddock, an unknown quantity to them. As Governor Dinwiddie had written, they were being forced to rely on their own resources.

Facing a potential threat to their existence, they

recognized that their actions in the months immediately ahead would determine whether they would remain a free people or surrender to the French.

The officers' meeting was brief; they had no choice but to promise every effort to win the war against overwhelming odds.

As soon as they adjourned, General Strong set out for the land of the Seneca. A meeting with Renno was imperative, he felt. General Ridley, who would normally have been a natural choice to represent the colonies, declined because of his family connection to the great Seneca leader. In the long run, he explained, the other tribes of the Iroquois could be expected to be more amenable to the colonies' proposal if they were approached by someone other than a relative of Renno's, who might be influenced by family ties.

Accompanying General Strong was his daughter. Beth's presence raised the eyebrows of officers from other colonies, but those from Massachusetts were agreed that the general had made an appropriate choice for an interpreter. Renno and Ja-gonh spoke and understood English perfectly, but most of the Iroquois did not. And the general thought it would have been most impolite for him to have asked either of the sachems to take on the mundane role of interpreting for him. That would have been easily construed by the Seneca as a degrading assignment. No militia officer was Beth's equal in the tongues of the Indians. And so she gladly accepted the assignment.

For the journey, she dressed in trousers, boots, and an open-throated shirt—garb that made her resemble a boy.

The officers and men of the militia escort, well aware of her femininity, kept their distance. Not only was she the general's daughter, but she was known for her high, unwavering standard of morality, and anyone who sought to violate it would have ample cause for regret.

General Strong and Beth heard the throbbing of Indian drums in the distance as they crossed the land of the Mohawk, largest of the Iroquois nations. They assumed that the sentinels of the Iroquois were announcing their moves.

Consequently, they expected to be intercepted by a Seneca at some point, but nevertheless there was still an element of surprise early one morning when a tawny warrior, clad only in a breechclout and moccasins, his face and torso smeared with Seneca green and yellow war paint, appeared out of nowhere and stood directly in front of them.

"Welcome to the land of the Seneca!" Ghonkaba called.

Astonished at his ability to elude the advance scouts of the escort so successfully, they recognized him instantly. Beth was surprised, too, by her pleasure at seeing him again.

Their amazement multiplied when twenty other warriors materialized out of the wilderness. The young officers of the escort understandably were chagrined and apprehensive.

Ghonkaba knew that it was unbecoming to boast, but he could not resist remarking, as he did, that "The Seneca always know when strangers are abroad in their land. We have been expecting you for three days, ever since you came to the land of the Mohawk. I bid you welcome, and I welcome you, too, in the names of Renno and of Ja-gonh."

General Strong promptly placed himself and Beth in

Ghonkaba's custody for the last stage of the journey. As they continued on, they noted an absence of contact between the Seneca braves and the young militiamen, though they nominally were allies. The warriors soon revised their low opinions of these white men, whom they had assumed were neophytes in the forest. The troops, demonstrating that they, too, were no strangers to the wilderness, walked quietly, leaving a minimum of tracks. Although they could not move with the speed and agility of the braves, they nevertheless gave a reasonably good account of themselves and encountered no problems. For their meals, they shot game, bringing down deer and smaller animals skillfully, and they prepared their food on open fires. Never had the warriors seen white men so at home in the forest, and while the two units talked but little, the tensions of their initial encounter appreciably lessened.

On the afternoon of their second day in the land of the Seneca, the drums again throbbed furiously. Suddenly a tall, older warrior, wearing an elaborate feathered bonnet, appeared on fhe trail. Ja-gonh had come to welcome the honored guests. He conducted them past the fields where the women grew corn, squash, beans, and other vegetables, and they came to the high palisade surrounding the town.

Everyone in the town turned out to greet the newcomers. Senior warriors by the hundreds appeared, as did their juniors, who were distinguished by a lack of war paint. Squaws and younger women stood silently, while most of them scrutinized Beth with great care. Children, most of them boys, joined in the procession, accompanied by dogs that barked furiously but amicably wagged their tails. The militiamen, directed to a longhouse where they would be quartered, were reluctant to go until assured by General Strong that he and Beth were safe.

Assured that Beth, as well as her father, wanted to proceed forthwith to the business that had brought them, Ja-gonh conducted them to the council chamber, a long, low building where a fire burned day and night beneath a hole cut in the roof.

Here Beth had her first glimpse of the fabled Renno. An elaborate bonnet of hawk feathers sat squarely on his head. Over his shoulders was thrown the badge of his high office, an intricately feathered buffalo robe, which only the Great Sachem of the Iroquois was entitled to wear. Sitting in a body behind him were his principal counselors, war chiefs, medicine men, and, above all, El-i-chi, his brother, who, like Renno, did not show his great age.

Speaking easily in unaccented English, Renno greeted General Strong, then transferred his attention to Beth, who was stunned by the impact of his words of welcome. The pale eyes, which seemed to strip away her inner defenses, were infinitely wise and equally shrewd. She discerned that here was no freak, a white-skinned savage. On the contrary, she had never encountered anyone who instantly conveyed so great an aura of dignity.

In a deep, resonant voice, Renno's greetings were remarkable principally for their brevity, as he reminded them all of the many ties binding the Seneca and the citizens of Massachusetts Bay. General Strong, well aware that Indian ceremonies were interminable, knew that Renno was being thoughtfully terse, and he, too, spoke only briefly. Beth translated for the warriors.

For the sake of his own people, Renno soon switched to the language of the Seneca. Translating for her father's benefit, Beth was uncomfortably conscious of the atmosphere in the council chamber. The interior of the lodge was smoky because the fumes from the fire did not rise rapidly enough toward the ceiling. Her eyes smarted, and she suspected that the Indians must have felt equal discomfort, but they gave no sign if that were true. They were accustomed to it in their stoic manner.

Among ranking members of the Seneca nation permitted to sit behind Renno, was Ja-gonh, whom she had already met. She reflected on his strong resemblance to Ghonkaba. One other Seneca obviously was a key figure. He wore only a breechclout, and he was heavily smeared with war paint. As his dark eyes glittered challengingly, he appeared to overlook no nuance in General Strong's expression or in Beth's. Later, she learned that this high-ranking warrior was No-da-vo, Ghonkaba's uncle. Another high-ranking warrior was, she assumed, Renno's brother, El-i-chi, about whom she had heard. He had married the widow of a Fort Springfield clergyman many years earlier.

When her eyes became accustomed to the chamber's gloom, Beth glanced about until she found Ghonkaba, who was present only as a senior warrior, and not as a participant. He was one of three braves armed with tomahawks who were stationed immediately inside the entrance. His two colleagues, paying no attention to the proceedings, kept their eyes fixed on a skin draped over the doorway. Presumably they were ready to attack anyone who had the temerity to enter.

Ghonkaba, however, was devoting his attention exclusively to Beth. She felt an almost physical jolt when she realized that he was staring, seeming to drink in every detail of her appearance. The difference between him and other young men of her acquaintance soon became apparent. Any young Bostonian, regardless of whether he was a suitor, would have quickly transferred his gaze elsewhere when she became aware of his scrutiny. But Ghonkaba, in true Seneca fashion, resorted to no subterfuge. As he continued to study Beth, a twitching at a corner of his mouth, resembling the beginning of a smile, was the only sign that he knew she had found him watching her.

Uncertain at first whether to be flattered or annoyed, Beth decided that she liked the attention of a man who made no secret of his interest. She found it difficult to force her mind back to business.

For the first time, Ghonkaba began to understand how it had happened that his grandfather had elected to marry his grandmother, a white woman. He had a glimmering, too, of why El-i-chi had chosen to marry Deborah, and why his great uncle, Walter, was included in the family circle. He had been overly hasty, perhaps, in deciding that he should marry only a Seneca. Perhaps he would be wise to widen the scope of his interests.

General Strong minced no words in describing the reasons for his journey. Having expected substantial help from London in the struggle that was taking shape, he told the Seneca, the colonies instead were receiving only token assistance—two thousand regular troops and a commanding general of distinction. Even more disappointing, he pointed out, was the news that no additional muskets or cannon, ammunition or even gunpowder, would be forthcoming.

The colonies now intended to fight alone if need be, the general said candidly. Factories for the manufacture of muskets and pistols were being constructed in

Connecticut; larger foundries in Massachusetts and in New York could produce cannon; and a company was being formed in Delaware for manufacture of gunpowder on a substantial scale.

The Iroquois, General Strong told them, had the right to know the truth. If they elected now to withdraw from their alliance with the colonies, that was their privilege. He, for one, could not blame them for such a stand, but he hoped that their posture would remain unaltered. The colonies needed their allies now, as never before. But it was only fair for the Iroquois to know that in adhering to the alliance they would face a very difficult role.

Renno, having listened carefully to the general, first when he spoke and again when Beth translated his words for the Indians, arose, and to Beth it seemed that the effort tired him.

In a voice husky with emotion, Renno recalled that for nearly ten times seven years, the Seneca and other Iroquois nations had been the allies of the English colonies. Together they had suffered adversities, and together they had won great victories. He recalled the suffering of militiamen and of warriors alike in the fields where they were raked by the great cannon of Fort Louisburg. He remembered the long march to meet the combined forces of the French and the Spaniards on the lower reaches of the Mississippi River. Now—undoubtedly for the last occasion in his own lifetime—the Iroquois were being called, once again, to stand shoulder to shoulder with their brothers.

Renno made it plain that he could not speak for the other Iroquois nations, who would have to determine their stand for themselves, but he would immediately summon a meeting of the Supreme Iroquois Council.

Though assured of their continued loyalty in the Great Council held several weeks earlier, he did not feel he could commit their forces to battle—now that the English were sending only a limited force—without first summoning their leaders again to a Great Council and explaining to them the most recent facts as he now understood them.

In the meantime, he could assure General Strong of two things: first, he would use all his influence to persuade the other nations to honor their commitment. Second—and equally important—he believed he could speak for his own nation, in expressing confidence that the Seneca would keep their sacred word and march into battle beside the colonists.

His words galvanized all the Seneca, who leaped to their feet, shouting their ferocious, high-pitched war cry. No one shouted more loudly than did Ja-gonh. Even the crafty No-da-vo seemed to accept Renno's words without reservation, and El-i-chi shouted until he became hoarse.

Though greatly relieved by the loyalty of the Seneca, Beth was shocked to realize that Ghonkaba was not taking part in the demonstration—perhaps, she hoped, because he was present only as a sentinel. Whatever his reason, he was staring down at the dirt floor of the lodge, his wooden face concealing his feelings. Beth noted that the other two sentries were cheering Renno's declaration.

The meeting came to an end when Renno invited the guests to remain in the town until representatives of the other Iroquois nations arrived. It would be well, he emphasized, for General Strong to address the Iroquois Council.

Renno led the general to a small house being made

available to him as his quarters. Ja-gonh escorted Beth to another small house made of logs with mud between the chinks and skins over the doorway and windows. There an elderly white woman greeted her. Even before being told her identity, Beth correctly guessed that she was Deborah, the wife of El-i-chi. She had cast her lot with the Seneca more than a quarter of a century earlier.

The hut was bare, except for her bed—a low, shelflike protrusion from one wall, on which corn husks had been placed—and crude pegs on which to hang clothes.

"This evening," Deborah told her, "you will dine with Ja-gonh and Ah-wen-ga." She paused, and then smiled. "Ghonkaba's parents," she added. Beth was horrified to feel color rising to her face, but Deborah appeared not to notice. "Ah-wen-ga is eager to learn more about you," she said, "and she felt that you might be equally interested in her and Ja-gonh."

Beth was at a loss for a reply to such an unexpected statement.

"I understand how you must feel," Deborah said, patting her lightly on the shoulder. "The ways of the Seneca are rather shocking to those who have been reared as you and I were. There's no lack of subtlety in their relationships, to be sure, but there's a candor that we—coming from a supposedly more advanced civilization—are likely to find unsettling."

"To say the least," Beth replied with a nervous laugh.

"The situation is quite simple, really," Deborah explained. "Ghonkaba has always been a trifle strange. That is, he's far more inclined than most warriors to keep his thoughts to himself. He's something of a lone wolf, you see, and he has very few close friends, male or especially female. But when word came from the Mohawk sentries that you were en route with your father, Ghonkaba seemed to almost explode with happiness. So his mother is eager to see the young woman who can arouse such a reaction."

Not knowing what to say, Beth remained silent. Deborah studied her for a moment. "It must be wonderful," she said, "to be young and to have your whole life stretching ahead of you. I'm not for a moment prying into your possible feelings for Ghonkaba, but it's evident that you're interested in him. Well, that's as it should be."

"I—I assure you, ma'am, that Ghonkaba and I have never exchanged a serious personal word!"

"I'm sure you haven't," Deborah replied serenely, "but that doesn't in any way alter his mother's curiosity. Perhaps I shouldn't have said anything, but I felt it was better if you knew. Enjoy your supper tonight, as I'm sure you will. Ah-wen-ga is a splendid cook, and uses a great many of the oldest of Seneca recipes. And tomorrow you'll come to my house for a New England meal." She slipped away, and Beth thought she showed considerable agility for her advanced years.

The idea that Ghonkaba's parents intended to meet her as a potential daughter-in-law was unsettling in the extreme, but Beth was reconciled to facing the situation to the best of her ability. She wandered outside. Finding a bucket of cold water near the door, she washed her hands and face, combed her hair, and felt considerably refreshed. But before she could attain a state of mental calm, Ghonkaba appeared unexpectedly.

"My great-aunt has told you that you will come with

me to the house of my parents to eat," he began. Though Beth knew she should confine her words to a minimum, she found herself jabbering nervously. "Yes, and I certainly hope that your mother isn't going to any trouble on my account."

He made no reply as he started off across the town. Beth increased her own pace in an attempt to keep up, then realized that was not expected of her. A Seneca woman did not walk beside a man, but followed him by several paces. Walking behind Ghonkaba, she thought that she would find it difficult, if not impossible, to adjust to the life of a Seneca wife.

The hut of Ja-gonh and Ah-wen-ga was large, as befitted the sachem of the Seneca nation, and although Beth was very much on edge, she quickly was put at ease, and felt very much at home. Her father, she learned, was at the dwelling of Deborah and El-i-chi, where he and Renno could confer in private.

Beth fell into a contented but rather faraway attitude, and Ja-gonh apparently thought that she might desire a cup of sack before the meal, for he observed without any previous introduction of the subject, "Liquor does not mix well with the simple life that we lead."

"That's not to mention," Ah-wen-ga added, "that most Indians have an aversion to alcoholic beverages. We and liquor just don't seem to mix. My husband doesn't suffer from such an effect because his heritage is white. My son, of Seneca blood through my side of the family, suffers frightful headaches if he indulges."

Ghonkaba frowned, clearly thinking that his mother was speaking too freely.

Ah-wen-ga, accustomed to saying whatever came to mind, went on. "Oddly," she said, "it's only the men who can't drink. I don't care for the taste of alcohol, but I could tolerate a glass without ill effect."

Beth, fascinated by such disclosures, found herself feeling even more at home. Their meal was as delicious as it was unusual. They started with an extraordinary soup, as thick as porridge, that seemed to blend several different distinct tastes. Beth was informed that it consisted of fish boiled for a long time in a stock that included duck bones, which was then coarsely strained to reduce it to a smooth consistency. A variety of wild herbs had been added as a finishing touch.

The main course was roasted wild turkey, which had been first smoked in order to preserve it. Stuffed with corn meal and small wild onions, it was served with squash and a reddish pastelike substance. This, Ahwen-ga explained, was a concoction of boiled cranberries sweetened with maple syrup.

The personalities of Ja-gonh and Ah-wen-ga were not at all as Beth had imagined. The sachem's head was shaved except for his scalp lock, and he wore only Indian attire, but he spoke a colloquial English so easily that Beth was reminded of certain friends in Boston. As for Ah-wen-ga, who was as vivacious as she was attractive, she astonished Beth by her sophistication. She and Ja-gonh had spent many months in France years earlier, where they had won the friendship of Louis XV after foiling a plot against him. Ja-gonh was familiar, too, with London, and because he was related to the Ridleys of Virginia through his mother, they knew some of the most distinguished residents of that colony.

Both exerted themselves to put Beth at her ease, and she found that her visit was no strain; on the contrary, she enjoyed herself enormously.

Ghonkaba, on the other hand, seemed to shrink

within himself in his parents' presence. Beth couldn't be sure whether her imagination was playing tricks, but it seemed that he was tense, and certainly withdrawn. He volunteered almost nothing, and replied in monosyllables when addressed. His parents appeared to take his conduct for granted, and if he seemed surly, they gave no sign of being upset.

Ja-gonh was called away when the delegation from the Onondaga nation, closest of the neighboring Iroquois, arrived for the forthcoming Council session. It was Ghonkaba's role to attend his father on such an occasion, so the two women were left alone at the supper fire.

Ah-wen-ga filled two gourds with a pungent herb tea that tasted slightly bitter when first sipped, but afterward developed a far more mellow, pleasant taste. "I'm glad," she said, "that we have a natural opportunity for a talk."

For the first time, Beth was overwhelmed by self-consciousness.

"I had to meet you," Ah-wen-ga went on, "because of the great impression that you've made on Ghonkaba."

Beth felt her face growing hot. Ah-wen-ga smiled at her and patted her hand. "I don't mean to embarrass you in any way," she said, "and if I'm causing you distress, I sincerely beg your pardon. But for years we've wondered about Ghonkaba's future. He has never showed the slightest interest in any girls of the Seneca nation, nor has he responded to any of the young ladies in Virginia who seemed to have set their caps for him. I believe that he has attended to his physical needs with our captives, after the manner of young bachelors, and otherwise he paid no attention to women. Then, suddenly, after he met you, he could talk of nothing else. Now that I've met you, I can certainly understand his enthusiasm. You're all that he claims, and a great deal more."

Beth lowered her head and tried not to show how flustered she felt. "You're very kind," she murmured.

"Not at all," Ah-wen-ga assured her. "I'm speaking only the truth."

"You've been candid with me," Beth said, "and I must be honest with you in return. I've realized from Ghonkaba's attitude that he likes me, but he hasn't revealed his feelings by a single word."

"That doesn't surprise me in the least," his mother said. "He will hold his own counsel until such time as it suits his purpose to speak more freely."

"I see," Beth replied.

"I'm not sure you do," Ah-wen-ga told her. "Ja-gonh and I have discussed you at some length, and have wondered how to deal with the problem. Now that I've come to know you slightly, I feel I must be completely honest with you."

Beth didn't understand what she meant.

"My son," Ah-wen-ga said, "is no ordinary warrior. As one who is descended from Renno and Ja-gonh, he could not be like other men, particularly when his blood is mingled with that of a war chief as illustrious as Sun-ai-yee. The extraordinary mixture of ancestry in Ghonkaba is almost explosive."

"In what ways is he different?"

"It is possible to predict how most young warriors will react to any situation," Ah-wen-ga said seriously. "You know in advance what they will think and what they will do when faced with questions of war and of peace, of family and of personal problems. But you never know what Ghonkaba will think or what he will do. It is said that his great-grandfather, Ghonka, for whom he was named, was such a man, also. But Ghonka became a great leader of his people, and it is thanks to him that the Iroquois League was formed and has flourished. But sometimes it seems that my son actually is ashamed of his ancestors—in fact, that the presence of white blood in his heritage is a blot on our history. He bewilders us."

Beth looked at her searchingly. "Why are you telling me all this?"

"Because I could tell from the way you looked at Ghonkaba, from the way you replied when you heard his voice, that his interest is at least somewhat reciprocated. It is not difficult to guess where this might lead."

Beth took refuge in sipping her tea and looking down at the coals of the cooking fire, which were still glowing.

"You appear very worldly, very sure of yourself," Ah-wen-ga said, "but I expect that this is a convenient attitude only, and that you really are not at all what you appear to be. I have been candid with you for your good, for the sake of your future. I don't want you to be hurt by Ghonkaba."

"But how or why on earth would he hurt me?" Beth asked, her confusion growing.

"I do not say that he would ever do or say anything deliberately that would cause you harm or pain," Ah-wen-ga replied. "That is not his way. He is not mean or vindictive or cruel. But he has, I am afraid, recently been a source of pain and chagrin to his grandfather, whom he loves. For reasons that I cannot fathom, he is mercurial, and I hope you will not allow yourself to become involved with him in a way that will open you to possible hurt."

Chapter IV

Beth found it virtually impossible to remember Ahwen-ga's advice during the days that followed. While her father waited for the leaders of the Iroquois League to assemble, Ghonkaba became her constant companion. He made it his business to be beside her at all times. She accompanied him on hunting trips into the wilderness and marveled at his skill, and at his seeming sixth sense whenever game came within reach of his bow and arrow. To her surprise, he shunned the use of firearms.

"I was taught to use a rifle and a pistol when I was very young," he said. "I believe that I am correct in stating that I qualify as an expert shot with them. But I can take no pride in my marksmanship with weapons that fire bullets. In my visits to the colonies, I have seen many dolts and buffoons who have become expert shots also. I prefer the bow and arrow and the tomahawk of my ancestors, because effective use of these weapons requires long training, intelligence, and great skill."

Beth marveled at Ghonkaba's knowledge of the wilderness. As they walked through the forest, he pointed out numerous plants, some of them delicious and edible, others that would be used primarily as seasoning, and still others that were utilized by the Indians for many purposes—one was a dye, another would cure fevers, and a third added a protective, waterproof coating to clothing. Nothing in the forest seemed to escape Ghonkaba's attention.

Just when Beth became convinced that he was always serious, his mood suddenly changed. One morning, as the sun beat down through the leaves of the tall trees, they came to a small lake whose waters were green, cool, and inviting. Ghonkaba promptly stripped, plunged in, and after swimming with powerful strokes from shore to shore, invited Beth to join him.

Had he been a fellow colonist, she would have refused, in part because of modesty, in part because of the complications that would follow, and partly, too, because her reputation would be at stake.

But this situation was different. She was certain from Ghonkaba's guileless expression that his invitation was innocent.

Making up her mind swiftly, Beth removed her clothes and plunged into the lake's cool waters. Because she could accept Ghonkaba without subterfuge or reservations, she found herself greatly enjoying the experience. As they raced, she was pleased to discover that, though he was a more powerful swimmer, he could not greatly outdistance her.

They swam until exhausted, and then, panting for breath, climbed out of the water onto a mossy bank to dry in the sun. Again, Ghonkaba's attitude seemed completely natural, and Beth's initial discomfort soon passed. But she knew a man and woman strongly attracted to each other could not indefinitely sit in the nude, sunning themselves in such an isolated area. Gradually, as Beth became more and more aware of Ghonkaba's lean, hard-muscled body, she knew that he was becoming aware of her too, and she felt a growing discomfort at the unusual situation. Her common sense warned her to extricate herself from a potentially delicate problem while she had the opportunity, so she reached for her clothes and, continuing her conversation, quickly dressed. To her infinite relief, Ghonkaba did the same. If he had been aware of mounting sexual tensions, he gave no sign.

In the evenings, the young couple ate supper either with Ghonkaba's parents or with his grandfather. As Beth came to know Renno, she regarded him with increasing awe.

"I've never encountered any human being quite like him," she said one day to her father. "He's so wise, and he knows so much about so many things! It's hard to believe that he was personally responsible for beating the French in battle after battle, but Ghonkaba assures me that the stories about him are no exaggeration."

"Those stories are true," General Strong said, "just as the stories about the exploits of Ghonka and Jagonh are also true. They're three generations of a remarkable family, one that has left its mark not only on the Iroquois but on every colonist who has come in touch with them."

"I can begin to understand how Ghonkaba feels," Beth said thoughtfully. "He must live under terrible pressure knowing that he's expected to perform great deeds and to always take a stand in favor of principles that are right and just."

Her father looked at her curiously. They had not discussed Ghonkaba, and he had no idea what she meant. Beth saw no reason to explain. Ghonkaba had appeared to be at peace within himself in recent days, and she told herself that perhaps his antagonism to white settlers was a passing mood that he was overcoming. Still uncertain whether her relationship with the young warrior would develop into a full-fledged romance, she would not prejudice her father against him unnecessarily.

When the representatives of all the Iroquois nations had arrived, Renno summoned the Council into formal session. At his invitation, General Strong was to address the assemblage, so Beth prepared to attend as his translator. From Ah-wen-ga, she had learned that no woman had ever attended a meeting of the Iroquois Council, so she readied herself with great care. Her face scrubbed clean of all cosmetics, she tied her long blond hair at the nape of her neck. Wearing her man's shirt, breeches, and boots, she also buckled on a sword and carried a pistol in her belt in order to heighten the appearance of a man. Even so, the Indian leaders ogled her when she followed her father, in his blue and gold dress uniform, into the lodge. They were not the only ones who gaped, however. She was particularly conscious that Ghonkaba, again acting as a sentry, scrutinized her with infinite care. She had no idea what he found particularly fascinating about her looks, and she tried in vain to shut him out of her consciousness.

Renno, who could be succinct when the occasion called for brevity, was an accomplished orator in the Indian tradition. He opened the conference with an address that seemed interminable to Beth, who translated for her father in a low tone. After sketching the long history of the alliance between the nations of the Iroquois League and the English colonists, he launched into an equally long description of the military history of the alliance. His memory was extraordinary, as he detailed every battle of every campaign fought against the French and their Indian adherents.

Beth assumed that the other Iroquois leaders were familiar with these battles, but they appeared fascinated by his words, and sat motionless throughout his address.

Occasionally, Beth glanced in Ghonkaba's direction and noted that he was stifling yawns from time to time. She couldn't blame him; in fact, she felt much as he did.

At last, Renno finished speaking and it was General Strong's turn. Beth, trying to remain inconspicuous, remained seated and translated his words into the language of the Seneca, sentence by sentence.

The general described the uneasy peace that had prevailed in both the New World and the Old World for many years. France, he declared, had appeared to have reawakened her hope of gaining control of the English colonies and of their allies—the Indian nations.

But those hopes were doomed to certain disappointment. Louis XV was old and vain, and men close to the throne had persuaded him that glory awaited him in a campaign against his hereditary enemies.

Therefore, France had secretly sent strong reinforcements to the New World and had also strengthened her already powerful fleet. In addition, arms were offered to any Indian nation that would ally itself with her, as well as gifts of blankets, metal cooking utensils, mirrors, scissors, and other objects prized by the Indians.

Then France had set about the task of winning converts to her cause. The Huron and the Ottawa, her unwavering, faithful allies had joined her again. So had the large Algonquian nation, their leaders apparently having forgotten the thorough drubbing that Renno had administered to them years earlier.

In addition, the Erie and the Miami had been recruited, and their mere presence in the camp of New France constituted a grave danger. Although no one knew the strategy that the French generals and the sachems of their allies would employ, it seemed reasonable to assume that they would try to establish a stronghold in the west and would use it, as well as Quebec, as a launching site for attacks.

The English colonies and their own allies, including the nations of the Iroquois League, faced a severe crisis. To survive and preserve their heritages, they had to win.

General Strong carefully refrained from mentioning the appointment of General Braddock as the British commander in chief for North America, about which he and his colleagues were skeptical. Nor did he refer to the two thousand troops that were to be sent to the New World. The number was so inadequate that he knew he would find it virtually impossible to explain to these savages—who nevertheless had shrewd military minds—why London was refusing to take the French threat seriously.

The Oneida were the least cooperative, the most independent minded of the Iroquois nations, and consequently their sachem was the one who stood up first after the general's remarks were concluded. He demanded to be told why it was necessary for the nations of the League to honor their alliance with the colonies. Peace had reigned for many years, he said, and he was not even certain that the treaty of alliance was still in effect.

General Strong stood aside while Renno replied in detail. The Iroquois League, Renno declared, was a solid, indissoluble alliance of nations that stood together in good times and in bad. They had conquered with the able assistance of the English, and would conquer again. Did the Oneida think that the nations allied to the French would leave them unmolested if they stood aside and remained at peace? Did they think that the Erie and the Miami, the Huron and Ottawa and Algonquian, all of whom wanted hunting grounds that belonged to the Iroquois, would remain at peace with them?

The sachem of the Oneida finally was persuaded, and agreed that his people would join their Iroquois brothers in their war effort.

Deeply moved by the debate, Renno declared fervently that the Iroquois nations, united with each other and with their old and faithful friends, would once again triumph. He concluded with the customary ringing Seneca declaration, "If anyone doubts my words, let him step forward!"

The entire assemblage was stunned when a young Seneca sentry stationed at the entrance came into the lodge and moved down to the base where the speakers customarily stood.

"It is not the place of Ghonkaba to doubt or deny the words of his grandfather," the young warrior said. "He intends no lack of respect to his revered grandfather by questioning the position he has taken. But he cannot help but observe that the Seneca and the other nations of the League have been mistaken for many years. They have viewed the colonists from England and the colonists from France as being different breeds. That is like saying that the Ottawa, the Huron, and the Algonquian are different because they are different tribes. But they are all Indian nations, and they are all opposed in all things to the Iroquois. Similarly, the French and the British, both being white, must be alike in many respects."

Translating for her father in a low tone, Beth was shocked. The opposition of Ghonkaba to his grandfather and his father seemed incredible.

Ja-gonh, in fury, gripped the handle of his tomahawk so hard that his knuckles whitened as he forced himself to remain silent until his son had finished. No-da-vo was even angrier and seemed ready to throw himself at Ghonkaba in order to silence him.

Only Renno remained calm, and as Beth looked at him, she recognized that his serenity was little short of remarkable. His attitude was genuine and unfeigned; he was not putting on a front for the leaders of his fellow nations, but she found compassion in his eyes—and something more. Beth interpreted the look as reluctant admiration for his grandson, who had the courage to speak out and express his own views.

"The grandson of Renno," Ghonkaba said, speaking quietly, "believes that the colonists of England and those of France are alike. Their dress is similar, they live in houses that are like the houses of the others, and they like food that looks and tastes much the same as their own food. Most important of all, they fight in similar ways. They use firesticks, large and small, and they also carry long knives which they handle with great dexterity."

At last the Great Sachem intervened. "The grandson of Renno is mistaken. Renno has lived in England and his son, Ja-gonh, has lived in France and has visited England, and will certify that the words Renno speaks are true. The men of England and the men of France are *not* alike."

Ja-gonh now had regained sufficient self-control to speak. Jumping to his feet, he cried out, "That is so! The men of England are free, and fear no one. It is my experience that the men of France are craven and fear their own shadows. The men of England worship their God as they wish, and they do not interfere with their allies who are free to worship as they please. I defy any man present to say now that any Englishman has ever dared to tell him that he must abandon his gods and accept the God of the English."

In the long moment of silence that followed, no one spoke up.

"The English colonists," Renno went on, "have presented the nations of the Iroquois with many gifts as a sign of their friendship. They have given the Iroquois blankets and knives, cooking utensils and mirrors, beads, and even firesticks and ammunition. I cannot recall when they asked for a favor in return. The French, on the other hand, always demand their due in return for the gifts that they give to the tribes who are allied with them. These Indian nations realized too late that they are no longer free to choose their own destiny. They are servants of the French, and deserve to be treated as the slaves they have become, rather than as free men."

His listeners rose spontaneously to their feet and cheered raucously.

Beth, who had difficulty in finishing the translation for her father above the hubbub, stole a glance at Ghonkaba and was aghast. He glared at his father and his grandfather, unrepentant.

Beth felt extremely sorry for him. She saw his defiance as only the rebellion of youth.

No-da-vo leaped to his feet, and in a choked voice demanded a vote by all leaders of the Iroquois who were entitled to have a voice in the proceedings.

Without a single dissenting vote, the sachems and elders, medicine men and war chiefs voted to support Renno in his position that the English colonies deserved their help without qualification in their pending war with France.

Ghonkaba, lacking a vote, could only stand at attention at the door with his fists clenched. The vote of his elders was a sharp, direct rebuke, a denial of all that he had said, but instead of being humiliated, he seemed defiant.

The conference was at an end, and Renno, though shaken by the direction the proceedings had so unexpectedly taken, was nevertheless highly pleased with the results. He promptly invited General Strong and Beth to his house for supper in order to discuss a coordination of the military plans of the Iroquois and the colonies.

Beth had been hoping that she would have an opportunity to see Ghonkaba and talk with him. At the very least, she hoped he could shed some light on his reasons for taking such a strange, harsh stand so diametrically opposed to the views of the colonists and of his elders.

He had disappeared, however, and she could find no sign of him anywhere. At the house of Renno, Deborah, his sister-in-law, was preparing supper. For want of anything better to occupy her, and wishing to make a gracious gesture, Beth pitched in to help. This was the first meal that she had taken a hand in preparing, and she enjoyed the experience.

While Ja-gonh conversed further with the leaders of the other nations, No-da-vo went directly to his brother-in-law's house. As he had anticipated, he found that Ghonkaba had preceded him there.

"I cannot recall a time," No-da-vo said, speaking with great severity, "when I have heard a warrior of the Seneca contradict the beliefs of his elders, especially his father and his grandfather, who is noted among all nations for his great wisdom."

"Would you have had me bite my tongue rather than express my true feelings?" Ghonkaba demanded.

His uncle looked him up and down. "I respect the opinions of my father and my grandfather so much," he said, "that I would tear my tongue out by its roots rather than dare to contradict them."

Ah-wen-ga was so upset that she could not bring herself to listen to their conversation, and instead busied herself with preparing the evening meal. Never in the long and honorable history of her family or her husband's family had any young person shown such disrespect for his elders. The unprecedented scene in the Council Lodge, as it had been described to her, was shocking beyond measure, and she was so upset that she felt incapable of facing the son whom she loved.

When Ja-gonh returned, his expression was grim, his mouth set in uncompromising lines. After one look, Ah-wen-ga knew he had reached a decision regarding Ghonkaba. As sachem of the nation, he was entitled to make his own decision without discussing the problem with anyone, and it appeared that he had done just that. Although she was closer to him than most Seneca wives were to their husbands, Ah-wen-ga did not dare inquire about his judgment. He would make his position clear when he chose to announce it, and until then, she was expected to keep silent. And as a Seneca who had spent her life obeying the customs of her people, she did as expected.

No-da-vo also was too discreet to question his brother-in-law. When Goo-ga-ro-no arrived ahead of her daughters, she immediately busied herself at the fire, helping Ah-wen-ga. Of all the members of the family, she had the greatest sympathy for Ghonkaba and could understand his rebellion because of her own escapade so many years earlier when she had run off with a Frenchman. But she knew from her brother's face that he had made up his mind, and under no circumstances would she raise the subject herself.

When the time came to serve the meal, a stiffness prevailed in the air, and Seneca protocol was strictly observed. Tonight the head of the household was served first, and no one ate until he had tasted his portion.

Ghonkaba himself was thoroughly confused by the day's climactic events. Certainly he had not planned to defy his grandfather and his father, and he had been almost as unprepared as anyone else when his defiant speech had suddenly emerged from his mouth, virtually unbidden.

As he had told No-da-vo, he was not sorry that he had spoken up, because he sincerely believed every word. On the other hand, he was abashed because he had defied the tradition of his people, a tradition that he cherished. Most of all, he felt remorse because his defiance had been directed at his grandfather and his father, whom he loved and respected. He really didn't want to say or do anything that would injure them and cause them pain. On the other hand, he believed it wrong to keep his own counsel if he believed they were mistaken.

Ghonkaba knew that he would not escape unscathed from the scandalous event, but he was not afraid of what might happen to him. His convictions remained firm, and to him that was all that mattered.

Ja-gonh's silence set an example for the others, as always. The Seneca custom that forbade conversation during the meal was ordinarily honored without fail. When he was finished eating, he left the cooking fire and returned in a few moments wearing his feathered headdress, and carrying in his belt an ancient stone knife that resembled a long arrowhead. These were symbols of his rank and power; it was apparent that he was about to pronounce sentence on his son.

He drew the stone knife from his belt and pointed the chipped blade directly at his son. Then, folding his arms, he said ponderously, "Hear the words of Ja-gonh, sachem of the Seneca!"

A deathly quiet enveloped the little group. Ah-wenga realized she had been holding her breath and exhaled silently, then drew in fresh air. Ghonkaba braced himself, his face devoid of all expression.

"He who decries the thoughts and the words of the Great Sachem of the Iroquois does not deserve to live in the same place where the Great Sachem dwells," Ja-gonh intoned. "Therefore, I have decided that Ghonkaba, my son, will travel to the land of Virginia and will apply there to his blood cousin, General Thomas Ridley, for the right to make his home there. While in Virginia, he will observe the English colonists there and will learn why his grandfather and his father favor their cause so completely. Only when he has absorbed this lesson, and has learned it well, will he be permitted to return to the land of the Seneca and resume his place here with his own people."

The verdict was as fair as it was mild and merciful, and Ah-wen-ga was greatly relieved. It was within Ja-gonh's province to have condemned his son to make his way alone into the wilderness, and to live there in repentance for as long as a year.

Ghonkaba, though dismayed by the verdict, only bowed his head in acceptance of his father's will. He knew it would be easy enough to spend a short time in Virginia, and then to pretend to have a new admiration for the English, but he had no intention of indulging in any such deception. Honest to the core, he planned to remain that way.

His honesty made strange demands on him, however, and when at last he raised his head, his eyes met those of Ja-gonh. "Will the sachem of the Seneca grant me one boon before I leave for the land of Virginia?" he asked.

Ja-gonh sat motionless, neither agreeing with the request nor denying it.

"I would like to pay a visit to the Great Sachem," Ghonkaba said, "and explain to him that I meant him no personal harm when I disagreed with him."

"You may visit him," Ja-gonh replied gruffly, pleased that his son at least had the basic decency to ease Renno's hurt.

Afraid his father might change his mind, Ghonkaba rose swiftly and walked the short distance to Renno's dwelling. As he approached it, he stopped short; it hadn't occurred to him that they might be entertaining guests at dinner, and he was nonplussed when he saw Beth with Deborah, washing gourds, wooden planks, and skewers in a large wooden tub outside the house.

Beth saw the young warrior's haggard expression, and conscious of the anxiety in his eyes, she felt desperately sorry for him. His situation was far more complex than the simple rebellion that met the eye.

As always, Deborah handled the situation smoothly. "If you're looking for your grandfather, Ghonkaba," she said quietly, "you'll find him inside the house."

He continued on his way, afraid he might lose his nerve if he stopped. Within, he saw Renno and El-i-chi bending over a large map, which General Strong had unfolded and was discussing. All three were absorbed as they studied the map in the light of two large, sputtering candles.

Ghonkaba halted, and as he cleared his throat more forcefully than was necessary, they all looked up. When Renno saw his grandson, he smiled. That smile spoke volumes, and in it Ghonkaba saw genuine love and a warmth and pride that would not be denied.

"I am being sent into exile," the young warrior said,

speaking more loudly than he realized, "but before I go, I had to see my grandfather in order to assure him that the words I spoke at the meeting of the Iroquois Council were not directed personally at him. I have great love and great respect for my grandfather. If some of my thoughts are not in agreement with those of my grandfather, that in no way takes away the depth of my feelings for him. He is the finest of living men, and I am privileged beyond belief to be descended from him."

Renno beckoned; his grandson moved slowly toward him.

Reaching out, Renno placed a hand on Ghonkaba's scalp lock. "It grieves me," he said, "that my own flesh and blood should be sent into exile. But I am proud that my son had the strength and the courage to pass such a sentence on you, and I am proud, too, that you have the courage to accept this punishment in the spirit in which it is meted out to you. May the manitous who watch over the destinies of the Seneca continue to protect you from all harm. And may the hawks who, as their representatives, have guided the warriors in our family for so many years, hover over you and lead you to safety and to glory."

Ghonkaba came within a hair's breadth of disgracing himself. A Seneca warrior was expected to contain his emotions at all times, never revealing his feelings. But he felt a lump rising in his throat, and to his horror, his eyes felt moist. He blinked rapidly and the tears disappeared as his vision cleared. He wanted to hug his grandfather, and longed to tell him that he wished with all his heart that they could agree on the worth of the colonists. But that, too, was forbidden in a land where warriors' attitudes were taken for granted and candid discussion was unsuitable.

Squaring his shoulders, Ghonkaba turned and ran out of the house, in his haste blindly brushing past Beth, who was aware of his emotional upheaval. But it was not her place to volunteer comment about him to his relatives, so she kept her views to herself.

Deborah knew what the younger woman was feeling, and her expression disclosed that she, too, did not disapprove of Ghonkaba.

Whether Ghonkaba had made an actual impression on his grandfather was far more difficult to judge. Beth heard Renno's voice picking up the military discussion where it had been interrupted.

The following day, General Strong and his daughter left for home, accompanied by their militia escort. Renno and Ja-gonh saw them off, as did a number of other Seneca, but Ghonkaba was nowhere in sight. No mention was made of him, and Beth assumed that he had already departed for his life of exile in Virginia.

For several days as they made their way with their escort through the wilderness, the general refrained from making comments about Ghonkaba's scandalous behavior.

One night on the trail they feasted on roast venison, a militiaman having shot a deer. With their meat, they enjoyed a variety of wild vegetables. Beth had been busy in the land of the Seneca and had gathered the plants, basing her search for them on knowledge she acquired from Ah-wen-ga and from Deborah as well as from Ghonkaba. She brewed strong coffee, and after she and her father had finished a satisfying meal, they sat in the open, beside the banked fire, sipping the strong brew.

Kenneth Strong appeared to feel that the time was at hand for an intimate personal discussion. "Unless I'm very much mistaken," he said, "you've found Ghonkaba to be especially attractive."

Though not fully expecting his comment, Beth answered it as best she could. "He interested me as few men ever have," she confessed.

"That was very evident," her father said bluntly. "It was also plain to me that he returned your interest."

"Oh, do you think so?" she inquired, and laughed.

General Strong frowned. "I hope you've tempered your liking for him with a strong dose of common sense," he said.

"I've never given you cause for undue concern," she replied a trifle stiffly.

He sipped his coffee, then reached out and patted her hand. "I'm not interfering in your private business, Beth," he said. "As your father, I'm interested in your welfare, and above all, I don't want to see you hurt."

"Thank you for your concern, Papa," she said, "but your worry is unnecessary. I've certainly made no commitment to Ghonkaba. I don't deny that it seemed at times that we struck sparks together, but nothing came of it, and I think it unlikely that anything will in the future."

"I thank God for that," General Strong said emphatically.

"I gather that you disapprove of him, Papa?"

He frowned again and chose his words with care. "He's the inheritor of a great tradition. No one in North America can boast a family line as notable and as distinguished. But I'm afraid that Ghonkaba is a renegade."

She couldn't help coming to his defense. "I believe you don't understand him, Papa," she said. "His heritage is a terrible burden for him."

"I'm in no position to judge such matters," her father replied. "All I know is that Ghonkaba has made it very plain that he dislikes colonists, and I'm just human enough to respond that if he doesn't like me— then I say to hell with him, too."

Beth knew her father sufficiently well to realize that he would scoff if she told him that, in her opinion at least, Ghonkaba was really rebelling against his own white ancestry, which he was ashamed of, while at the same time feeling pride in the achievements of those white ancestors.

Besides, it was a waste of time and effort to stand up for Ghonkaba. She was sure he had forgotten her, and with so much on his mind she certainly couldn't blame him for forgetting a woman, no matter how much he was attracted to her.

Her father studied her in silence as he filled a pipe and lighted it with a coal from the supper fire. "If you are sure that you aren't going to be hurt," he said, "I am willing to dismiss the matter from my mind."

"I'm quite sure," Beth said, but she was by no means certain.

Her father puffed on his pipe, then looked down at the tobacco burning in the bowl. "I'll grant you," he said, "that Ghonkaba is no run-of-the-mill suitor. In fact, he bears scant resemblance to any of the young men whom you have ever known. And for that reason—combined with his extraordinary family background—I can understand why you were drawn to him. But I ask you to keep one thing in mind. It often happens that there's one rotten apple in a basket of prize apples. That may be true in this case."

Beth made no reply. Her father had made a surface judgment of Ghonkaba based on the young warrior's regrettable conduct, and nothing she could say would change his mind.

What Beth thought she did know—beyond all doubt—was that Ghonkaba possessed qualities that would make him the equal of any of his distinguished forebears. It was useless for her to express such ideas, however. She wished she could put Ghonkaba out of her mind, because it was unlikely, after all, that she would ever see him again.

Chapter V

Governor Dinwiddie glanced at the fire burning in the hearth opposite his desk, lighted to rid his office of the autumn's early-morning chill, and then returned to the document that he had been reading.

Brigadier Thomas Ridley waited patiently for the governor to absorb its information. It had been gathered by a lieutenant who had just returned from a scouting expedition to the western frontier.

At last, the governor broke the silence. "This is the fourth report in as many weeks, General," he said, "stating that the French are making strenuous efforts to strengthen their garrison at Fort Duquesne. What do you make of it?"

"There's no doubt in my mind, Your Excellency, that the French *are* strengthening their Duquesne garrison," Tom Ridley asserted flatly. "As to the significance of their effort, I'm afraid it's all too clear. The nation that dominates the Ohio River controls the west, and the nation with a firm grip on Fort Duquesne undoubtedly can control the Ohio."

Dinwiddie dropped the report onto his desk and frowned. Though he had consented to send a letter to London requesting military aid, actually—like most Englishmen who came to the New World as holders of high office—he found it difficult to grasp the significance of various moves readily understood by the colonials who had spent their entire lives on the edge of the forest. "Combine that fact," he said now, "with the reports we have received, to the effect that France has formed alliances with the Erie and Miami tribes, and what do you conclude?"

They had covered the same ground in a previous discussion, but General Ridley remained patient. "The conclusion that I draw is inescapable, Your Excellency," he explained. "The strategy of France is to cut us off from the west, and encircle us with what will become a stranglehold. She's doing exactly what I'd do if I were wearing the boots of the general in command of her forces in Quebec."

Governor Dinwiddie struck his desk with an open palm. "But that's outrageous!" he declared. "France has no valid reason to try to drive our English settlers into the Atlantic, as I interpret your prediction to mean ultimately."

"Her reasons are self-evident, I'm afraid," Tom

Ridley replied dryly. "She covets territory—a great deal of territory—that happens to belong to us, and the only way that she's going to get it is by taking it from us by the most effective strategy open to her."

"I find that a prospect unworthy of a civilized country," the governor replied scathingly. Tom Ridley could say nothing in reply.

"I don't want to go down in history," Dinwiddie continued tartly, "as the man responsible for sacrificing any chance that may exist for peace between Great Britain and France. I'm prepared to take this action on my own authority, without the benefit of additional consultations with other governors. I want you to send a representative to Fort Duquesne, General. Let him be an officer of high enough rank that he can speak with authority. Let him inform the commandant that the Royal Crown Colony of Virginia will resist any further enlargement of the French garrison at Duquesne. And needless to say, I trust the officer you choose will have the good sense, while traveling through the wilderness, to keep his eyes and ears open for any further French reinforcements."

The gesture was foolhardy, in Tom Ridley's opinion, but a direct order from the governor had to be obeyed to the letter. So he gathered together his documents, packed them into his portfolio, and rising to his feet, saluted. "An expedition will be dispatched without delay, Your Excellency," he said as he took his leave.

At his home, he was surprised when his housekeeper told him that his Indian cousin had arrived unheralded and was in a guest chamber. A few minutes later, Tom was closeted with him, as Ghonkaba explained fully and candidly why he had been sent to Virginia in exile. He would be the Ridleys' guest, and could only hope that the imposition would not prove to be too onerous for them.

Tom grinned and shook his head. "You're a son of Ja-gonh, no two ways about that," he said.

Ghonkaba knew this was not the appropriate moment to inquire about whatever his father's own rebellion against authority as a young man might have been. He doubted that it could have been as outspoken as his own.

Studying him, Tom liked what he saw as much as he always had. "I assume," he said, "you're prepared to earn your keep here?"

"I have never asked for charity," the Seneca replied tersely. "I am quite ready to do whatever you may ask of me."

Tom took no offense. "Good," he said cheerfully. "I may have employment for you much sooner than you might think."

He dispatched a messenger at once to Colonel George Washington, and late that same afternoon the young surveyor sat in his office with him.

Ridley described in detail the latest development in the Fort Duquesne situation.

"It sounds ominous to me," Washington told him.

"It is ominous," Tom replied. "It's my own feeling that we're wasting our time by appealing to the commandant of Fort Duquesne for reason, but an order by Governor Dinwiddie must be obeyed. Will you carry out the mission for me, Colonel?"

Washington could have found many reasons to sidestep and avoid the assignment. But it was typical of him to reply quickly and quietly, "Yes, sir!"

"As I see this assignment shaping up," the general said, "I think you should travel with as small a party as you can manage. Take a couple of aides—if for no other reason than to impress the French—and we'll find you an Indian guide who is thoroughly familiar with the territory. Also, I have an additional member of the party to recommend to you—my own cousin, Ghonkaba, a senior warrior of the Seneca, who has just arrived here for an indefinite stay with me. You met him some time ago when he visited, having brought a message from the Great Sachem of the Iroquois to the governor."

Washington's interest was immediately aroused, for he did recall Ghonkaba, and quite favorably. The colonel accepted an invitation to stay for supper, and he and Ghonkaba had an opportunity to speak, finding their mutual pleasant impression of the first occasion had weathered well. The young Seneca had to admit to himself, again, that Washington seemed to be a colonial who did not fit his preconceptions. It was unlikely, he reflected, that any French officer would be as direct and forthright, or would know as much about the Indian nations and their relationships.

It was only a few days later when the pair set out for Fort Duquesne, accompanied by a party of three others, including a Miami warrior who had been in Virginia Territory and who was said to have remained loyal to the English in spite of his people's defection.

Ghonkaba had an opportunity to learn a great deal about Colonel Washington. His first discovery was that Washington was as much at home in the wilderness as were the braves. He was the first white man, other than Ghonkaba's own father and grandfather, whom the young warrior had ever seen display so much self-confidence in the remote outland beyond the pale of civilization.

They chose a simple route of travel, marching generally northwestward across Virginia, and crossing the rugged, wooded peaks of the Blue Ridge Mountains. Ultimately, in the territory that eventually would be known as West Virginia, they came to the more rugged Allegheny Mountains, and when they came to the headwaters of the Monongahela River, they followed it as it flowed, knowing that it would bring them to Fort Duquesne.

The Miami brave who acted as a guide for the party was a sullen, withdrawn man, who made it evident from the start that he had been hired for one purpose only, and that he intended to establish no new relationships.

Colonel Washington was not disturbed by this, but Ghonkaba had his own reservations about the man, and kept a close watch on him. The Miami were reputed to be occasionally guilty of treacherous behavior, and he suspected that the guide might betray them.

The hunting season was at its peak, game having fattened on the foliage of summer, and food supplies were plentiful. Ghonkaba, who quickly became the chief hunter for the party, as always preferred his bow and arrows rather than the rifles of the settlers. "I see no reason for us to advertise our presence in these parts, Colonel," he told Washington. "We should not take unnecessary risks, and if any war parties of Miami or other nations are abroad, I prefer to let them search for us, rather than to give them a clear notion of our whereabouts."

Washington, who already was of like mind, heartily approved.

From the outset, Ghonkaba developed a rapport with the young officer that transcended words. This ability to communicate with each other almost by instinct was fortunate, as events one afternoon on the trail proved. They were traveling in their customary formation, with the Miami guide about fifty yards in advance, and with Ghonkaba leading the other three men.

Always alert in the forest, Ghonkaba heard a faint sound deep in the foliage off to his right that might have been the movement of a wild animal. Then, a moment later, he heard a similar noise to his left, and he knew that they were being stalked by humans.

The Miami guide continued to move steadily forward, apparently unconscious of the presence of strangers in the wilderness, and Ghonkaba's misgivings increased. It appeared likely to him that they were moving into a dangerous trap.

Halting, he raised a hand and gestured.

Colonel Washington grasped his meaning instantly, and followed his example as the Seneca dropped to the ground. The two young aides, although startled, were sufficiently familiar with the forest to immediately lower themselves to the ground.

Reacting instinctively, Ghonkaba reached over his shoulder, removed an arrow from its quiver, and fitted it into his bow. Then, concealed by high grass, he waited, straining for any sound of movement.

His vigil was rewarded very soon when he heard a muffled sound on his right. Neither Washington nor the Virginia militiamen heard it, but they were not endowed with Ghonkaba's extraordinary hearing. He discerned the exact location, then his bow became taut, and a slight, singing noise could be heard as the arrow sped toward its target.

Not stopping to check the accuracy of his aim,

Ghonkaba drew another arrow, notched it into his bow, and released it.

But he could not neglect the sector to his left where he also heard movement. Again he drew an arrow, and again sent it speeding off. He followed this with a fourth arrow almost instantaneously.

At moments such as this, Ghonkaba realized that he existed primarily for the purpose of engaging in combat. Only at such times was he fully alert, fully alive, with all of his senses attuned to the fine art of survival.

Those who thought he was without fear in battle were badly mistaken. He recalled a conversation he had held with Beth Strong, in which she had gleaned the wrong impression. He had been emphatic when he had told her that if he had been taught anything by his father and his grandfather, he had learned that fear was the great common denominator in combat. Only the warrior who truly appreciated the hazards of a battle, who took them into consideration and made allowances accordingly, lived to fight again.

At moments like this, Ghonkaba fully appreciated his Seneca heritage. Drilled thoroughly in the fundamentals of combat, he fought without conscious effort. Every move, every gesture, every action, every reaction, had become instinctive.

It dawned on him that he was not alone in his feelings, that the American frontiersman who had taken up a position a short distance to his rear also was a natural-born fighting man. George Washington also knew precisely what he was doing and fulfilled his obligations seemingly without effort.

The click of a hammer behind him told him that Colonel Washington was preparing to fire his musket. Preferring to maintain the silence that gave them such a decided advantage, Ghonkaba raised a hand forbiddingly. Washington promptly halted.

The encounter was ended almost before it began. Satisfying himself that no other enemies were approaching, Ghonkaba raised himself to one elbow and found that, as he had hoped, he had disposed of four warriors.

The Miami guide, bewildered by the silence behind him, turned back, intending to investigate. Ghonkaba had seen enough to assure himself that the guide was indeed guilty of treachery. The four dead warriors, like the guide, wore the war paint of the Miami.

In theory, Ghonkaba should have waited and obtained Colonel Washington's permission before acting. But the fundamental law of the wilderness surpassed conventions of men. The Miami was demonstrably guilty of perfidy, and Ghonkaba was judge, jury, and executioner. He drew his tomahawk from his belt, and though stretched prone on the ground, he nevertheless was able to throw it with great force and accuracy—a feat, as Washington later wrote, that had to be seen to be believed.

The tomahawk's sharp blade penetrated the Miami's forehead, and he crumpled to the ground, instantly dead. The party not only had escaped intact from the trap set for them, but the enemy warriors had themselves been killed.

Colonel Washington demonstrated his understanding of Indian ways by waiting while Ghonkaba cut away the scalps of the five Miami and added them to the collection he carried proudly in his belt.

Only when the bloody ritual was completed did George Washington speak. "We're ready now to resume our march," he said, without mentioning the dramatic incident; Ghonkaba also chose to ignore it. Among those who lived on the frontier, it was the custom to take violence and death for granted. The killings now belonged to the past, and were to be forgotten.

"I'll act as your guide," Ghonkaba offered.

Colonel Washington smiled. "It won't be too difficult for us now to follow the Monongahela north," he said. "But we will need you as an advance scout to warn us of any more enemies who may be lurking. How you knew the Miami warriors were waiting for us is beyond me."

Ghonkaba refrained from explaining that he had been gifted from birth with extraordinary hearing. Why he wanted the Virginian to think well of him, he did not fully understand, but it seemed very important to him.

For several days, they followed the Monongahela as the river wound its way through the hills. At last, hearing drumbeats in the distance, Ghonkaba immediately halted and listened.

"We are approaching the great fort of the French," he said. "Their Indian sentries who send the signals of the Miami are warning of our approach, and are inquiring as to our identity."

"In that case," Colonel Washington said, "we must let them know who is calling on them."

He and his aides removed their blue militia uniforms from their bedrolls and put them on, becoming easily identifiable. Although a hint of frost was in the air, Ghonkaba removed his buckskin shirt and painted his torso, as well as his face, with the yellow and green colors of the Seneca. It was important to him that the French recognize at once that the Virginians were accompanied by a representative of the mighty Seneca nation, proof that they were maintaining their alliance. It never occurred to him that, in spite of his views that had caused him to be exiled from the land of his own people, he already was making a choice between the English and the French. The perfidious attempt of the Miami on his life and the lives of his companions was responsible for influencing his judgment.

As the little party approached a triangle of land where the Monongahela and Allegheny rivers met, and caught a glimpse of a large log fort, a group of defenders came out to meet them.

Both Ghonkaba and Washington were impressed by the apparent caliber of these men.

Bearded and rugged, the defenders cared more about the practical aspects of survival in the wilderness than about their appearance. All were in faded buckskins that had seen long wear in the forests, as had their soft moccasins. They wore ammunition belts and carried French infantry rifles; most also carried pistols or throwing knives in their belts.

Ghonkaba realized that these Frenchmen had lived for years on the frontier and were accustomed to its hardships. They seemed to be aware of his identity as a Seneca, and as they stared, he took a fierce pride in his heritage.

The leader of the detail approached Colonel Washington, saluted, and identified himself. His manner made it plain that he expected the strangers to state their business.

Washington gladly obliged him. "I'm the representative of His Excellency, Governor Dinwiddie of the Royal Crown Colony of Virginia," he said, "and I have been sent by him on a special mission to meet with the commandant of Fort Duquesne."

A member of the French unit promptly raised a white flag, and the combined groups proceeded toward the fort.

Ghonkaba had visited a number of forts and was rather familiar with them, principal among them being Fort Springfield in Massachusetts Bay, the Battery that guarded New York Town, and Fort Charles, the citadel that protected Richmond. Never had he seen a structure as imposing as Fort Duquesne. Standing behind high, stout palisade walls, the bastion was made of heavy logs and was the equivalent of a building of about four stories in height. Catwalks were everywhere, each protected by a miniature palisade, and numerous platforms were capable of housing entire platoons of infantry. Even more impressive were the open gun ports, behind which the muzzles of cannon could be seen. It was apparent that Fort Duquesne would not be taken without a long, hard fight by an enemy willing to sustain very heavy losses.

When they reached a guardroom just inside the entrance, the French captain announced, "Your Seneca guide will meet you here." He plainly had no intention of taking Ghonkaba on a visit to the commandant.

Colonel Washington instantly repeated the order in the universal language of the Algonquian. Nodding affirmatively, Ghonkaba understood at once what Washington had in mind: he was to pretend ignorance of English and of French as well; thus, he perhaps could glean useful information that otherwise might not be available. He adopted the role immediately.

Washington and his aides were taken by a circuitous route inside the palisade to a closely guarded area where sentries armed with muskets and bayonets stood guard. There they waited no more than a few moments before being conducted into a chamber that astonished them. Although constructed of simple logs, it was handsomely furnished, as only the French could decorate. A thick rug covered the bare floor. Paintings stood on two walls, and a handsome tapestry covered a third. The furniture, fashioned in the style of Louis XIV, was substantial yet delicate, obviously the work of skilled craftsmen. Behind a large desk sat a bearded officer in buckskins, who, like Washington, was only in his early twenties. He introduced himself as Lieutenant Colonel Proche, the fort's commandant.

After Washington introduced himself and his aides, Colonel Proche summoned an orderly, who poured glasses of wine. Colonel Washington offered a toast to His Christian Majesty, Louis XV.

At last, after the amenities had been exhausted, both sides got down to business. "I've been authorized by Governor Dinwiddie to inform you," Colonel Washington said, "that Virginia is aware of the fact that France is sending heavy reinforcements to this fort. The augmenting of your garrison could have only one purpose—the launching of aggression against Virginia and her sister colonies that fly the flag of England. Therefore, I am authorized to inform you, with all due respect, that unless your garrison here is reduced to its former size without delay, steps will be taken to insure its permanent reduction."

Colonel Proche, in no way taken aback, smiled—or at least bared his teeth—in response to the threat. "I trust you'll be good enough, Colonel, to inform your governor that we, who represent Louis XV, do not regard as serious any threats to our safety and welfare. Any nation foolish enough to attempt to reduce Fort

Duquesne would suffer thoroughly unpleasant consequences."

Washington understood completely: the French colonies were informing the English to mind their own business and were, in fact, daring them to attack. He bowed solemnly, and Proche returned the gesture. Then they raised and drained their glasses simultaneously. Both understood that a challenge had been made and accepted, and that hereafter the issue would be settled on the battlefield. The next time they met, they would be enemies.

When Colonel Washington and his aides were led out of the sentry guardroom, Ghonkaba remained behind with the two warriors assigned to guard him. Within only a few moments, an authoritative figure in buckskins—part Indian and part white like Ghonkaba himself—came into the guardroom. "What have we here?" he demanded, speaking in French. One of the sentries explained in halting French.

Ghonkaba pretended to have no knowledge of the language, although he understood every word.

The half-breed glared at the two guards. "Are you stricken dumb because this man is a Seneca?" he demanded. "Can't you see that we've been given an opportunity and that we'd be fools not to exploit it?"

The pair looked at him blankly. The half-breed's manner changed, and his smile became ingratiating as he addressed Ghonkaba in the language of the Algonquian. "It is hoped," he said, "that the mighty warrior of the Seneca will forgive the lack of hospitality shown by these Miami dolts. As the Seneca are said to know all there is to know about the art of making war, perhaps the visitor would like to make a tour of this greatest of forts."

Although delighted by the opportunity that so unexpectedly presented itself, Ghonkaba tried to sound vaguely bored as he agreed.

The tour was thorough. The half-breed, quite evidently a man of some authority in the French high command, had one object in mind. He was determined to overwhelm the Seneca with a display of French power, hoping that the visitor would return to his own people with word that the French were invincible. It did not occur to the guide that the young warrior with the bland expression had received countless hours of instruction in military strategy and tactics from Renno and Ja-gonh, and that he had read as many as thirty books on the subject by the leading authorities of Great Britain, France, and Prussia.

Ghonkaba played his part to the hilt, showing no enthusiasm, and seeming to barely recognize equipment of significance.

His guide's timing was perfect, and he arrived back in the sentry room just as Colonel Washington and his party were being escorted there from the commandant's office.

The visitors set out without delay on their return journey to Virginia. Several hours of daylight remained, and they made excellent time as they again followed the Monongahela, this time southward.

Washington's comment was brief. "I am sure we won't be molested on our homeward journey," he said. "The French are now most desirous that we arrive safely and deliver the message that they refuse to be bluffed."

They paused at dusk beside the river, and Ghonkaba

showed his companions how to catch fish in the swiftly flowing stream. In the meantime, he built a cooking fire and eventually half a dozen fish were sizzling in a frying pan.

Only then did Ghonkaba reveal his own information. "The French," he said, "thought I was a stupid warrior and tried to impress me by taking me on a tour of the fort.

"At present," he continued, "the garrison numbers about five hundred men. But the size of the defense force is far less important than the armaments that they carry to defend themselves."

Washington leaned forward eagerly.

"I was astonished to discover," Ghonkaba said, "that they have two twelve-pounder cannon." Colonel Washington whistled under his breath. Twelve-pounders were exceptionally powerful weapons, and very few of them were anywhere to be found in the New World.

"I suspect, however," Ghonkaba went on, "that they're good principally for show, perhaps to improve the spirits of the French troops and their allies. Neither cannon looked as though it had ever been fired, and I don't believe they were forged in a foundry accustomed to such work. I could even see the seams in the barrels, and if I were commanding the battery, I'd be afraid that they'd both explode when they were discharged. So I'm inclined to believe that we can forget the twelve-pounders."

Colonel Washington chuckled. The young Seneca was truly remarkable!

"I counted five nine-pounders," Ghonkaba went on, "all of them pointed toward the east. If you launch an infantry attack on Duquesne, those cannon would lay down a very heavy barrage.

"They also had a great many small cannon. We didn't pause long enough for me to make an accurate count, but I would estimate I saw twenty-five to thirty six-pounders. That number, of course, can be somewhat deceptive. Transporting them from northern Canada all the way to Fort Duquesne must have been a difficult task, and several appeared to me to have been damaged. I have no idea how many of them can actually be used, but it might well be the case that at least half are like the twelve-pounders—only for show, bolstering the morale of troops who are expected to hold a fort a very great distance from their home base."

Colonel Washington was highly pleased by the thoroughness of Ghonkaba's report. The long journey, which had resulted in a defiant reply from the French commandant to the English demand, had not been made in vain. The information that the young Seneca had gleaned was worthy of the efforts of a master spy.

Chapter VI

Dispatches from Virginia were delivered to General Strong's home as he ate his noon dinner. Beth knew that the news they contained was not good. Her father frowned repeatedly, shaking his head, and immediately lost interest in the beefsteak on his plate.

"I'm afraid," he said at last, "that war with the French is unavoidable. At the governor's instruction, Tom Ridley sent a colonel of his out to Fort Duquesne to warn the French to refrain from fortifying it, and the commandant almost laughed. So the reports we've been hearing are proving to be true. General Montcalm is getting ready for a major struggle."

"Does that mean that you're going to send some regiments down to Virginia, Papa?"

The general shook his head. "The Virginians seem to be in no need of additional manpower," he said, "and we're going to have enough trouble strengthening our own sector. We have a long frontier with French Canada to protect, particularly as the Algonquian have joined forces with the French."

Beth was deeply concerned. "Is there no way that a major war can be avoided?"

Her father sighed. "It appears as though the French are determined, as they've been so often in the past," he said, "to try to take our lands from us. I consider it a very bad sign that the commandant of Fort Duquesne chose to rebuff the colonel from Virginia. I assume he was merely following orders. And that means that the French are going to fight, no matter how hard we might try to preserve peace."

"You're going to call your militia to active duty, no doubt?"

"Almost all, without delay!" he replied. "I've procrastinated as long as I could because I wanted to give our farmers time to harvest their crops and to let the townsmen work at their posts. But I'm afraid the time has now come when every able-bodied man is needed in uniform." He picked up the letter, glanced at it, and went on. "There is a scrap of news from General Ridley that you'll be pleased to hear," he said. "It concerns your rebellious young friend, Ghonkaba."

Beth immediately grew tense.

"He went with a Colonel Washington on the expedition to Fort Duquesne," General Strong said, "and he appears to have distinguished himself. General Ridley doesn't go into any detail, but I gather from this information that he's decided that he prefers the English cause to the French after all."

Beth smiled broadly, and her voice was buoyant. "I could have told you from the outset," she said, "that Ghonkaba would decide to fight on the side of his nation and his distinguished relatives. He's like a great many of the colonists I know. In fact, I find him very similar in temperament to Sam Adams, whom you admire."

"I'm afraid," the general demurred, "that I fail to see the similarity."

"Each in his own way, as I see it, is a rebel," Beth explained. "They have a contrary streak in their temperaments that makes them dissatisfied with blindly following the course that's expected of them. But their hearts are in the right place, and so are their loyalties. I'm confident that neither you nor anyone else ever will have to worry about whatever position Ghonkaba takes."

Her father peered intently at her. "Just how serious are you about this young man?"

Color rose to her cheeks, but she held her ground. "It's premature," she replied evenly, "to suggest that I'm in the least personally interested in him, much less serious about him, but I'm not denying that I'm interested. I find him attractive, possibly because he's as civilized as any of the many frontier dwellers whom I've met. But whether I ever could be able to think seriously about a future that included him is a question that I can't possibly answer right now."

General Strong's stern features relaxed. Beth had always been the most sensible of girls, and he was pleased to learn that she had not changed. He had no need to warn her that a romance with an Indian warrior, who lived with his people and followed their precepts, might create untold difficulties for her. He was content to leave the matter to her judgment. She had made it clear that she was aware of the problems involved, and this was all that he could ask at present.

After Colonel George Washington reported on his journey to Fort Duquesne, the leaders of the Virginia militia went into closed session to consider the problems. They debated at length, and finally Governor Dinwiddie arrived to join in the discussion. General Ridley summarized their conclusions for him.

"Your Excellency," he said, "we've been examining the various options that are open to us. I think Colonel Washington should explain his views—views held by most of us here."

The young colonel rose to his feet. "Since my visit to Fort Duquesne, Your Excellency," he said, "I have no doubt whatsoever that the French high command in Quebec is determined to strengthen the fort. Whether they were planning an aggressive campaign against Virginia and Pennsylvania, or whether they hope to entice us into attacking them, is of course another question. But for our purposes, I don't think it really matters. The reinforcement of Fort Duquesne means the weakening of our own relative position. Therefore, it seems to me that in order to protect our towns and farms, our people and their land, we must make the first move and strike as heavy a blow as we can against Duquesne."

"That's virtually our unanimous opinion," General Ridley said. "Some of us have reservations, Your Excellency, although the question is a matter of degree, rather than of disagreement in principle. We considered the possibility that we should delay, and force the French to make the first move. But that's been ruled out, and quite rightly so, I believe. I see nothing to be gained by delaying until the French are so firmly entrenched at Duquesne and elsewhere that it would be almost impossible for us to dislodge them. We'd have far higher casualties, and our chances of success would be vastly diminished."

"Does the militia have a specific course of action that it recommends?" Governor Dinwiddie asked.

"We do, sir," General Ridley replied crisply. "We believe that we'll be best served if we dispatch an expedition as rapidly as possible. At the very least, we must make the French aware that we're not going to sit by while they take over more strategic points in the wilderness, although I can't guarantee that any expedition is going to drive the French back into Canada."

Governor Dinwiddie, who, like the Duke of Newcastle, scorned the use of the wig traditional for men of high station, ran a hand through his gray hair. "Let me recapitulate what I understand. Although a clear-cut victory would be desirable, naturally, the militia would be satisfied with an engagement that inflicts sufficient casualties and does enough damage to Fort Duquesne to warn the French that further incursions into our lands would be resisted."

"That's precisely right, sir," General Ridley said, and looked at Colonel Washington for corroboration.

"The French seem to be moving rapidly, Your Excellency," the colonel said, "and consequently we must do the same. If we could, we'd wait until General Braddock and the force of regular army troops from England arrives. Although they may be inadequate in numbers, they're certainly better than nothing. But, unfortunately, he has been delayed and we can't wait; we're obliged to act rapidly, as I see it. A warning blow will lose its force if we don't act immediately and vigorously."

"From all that you say, gentlemen, combined with what I already know of the situation," Governor Dinwiddie declared, "I think the position you're taking is sound. By all means, do what you think best and move without delay!"

Colonel Washington, already familiar with the terrain, was chosen as the commander of the expeditionary force. His fellow officers approved unanimously when General Ridley proposed to appoint him to the post. Some expected that months would be required to train and equip the force, but when Washington issued a call for volunteers, five hundred men familiar with the wilderness responded promptly.

Every militiaman, Washington told them, would supply his own rifle and would be responsible for procuring his own bullets and gunpowder. In addition, each man was to carry a week's supply of emergency rations such as the parched corn and jerked venison Indian warriors usually carried on the march. Beyond those rations, the expedition would live off the land.

Another of Washington's acts was to seek out Ghonkaba. "I hope," he said, "that I can persuade you to march with us as a scout."

Ghonkaba smiled slyly. "You already know the way," he retorted. "You have no real need for a guide."

"You'll note," Colonel Washington said coolly, "that I didn't ask you to serve as a guide. We'll hardly have trouble in locating Fort Duquesne, I can assure you. But with the French already expecting trouble, some of the Indians allied with them are sure to be forming a protective network in the forest. I'll need you to keep us adequately posted on the whereabouts of our enemies in the wilderness."

Ghonkaba knew that in Colonel Washington's place he also would be eager to obtain the services of a Seneca as a scout. But he could not resist saying, "No doubt you have learned from General Ridley that I am regarded as unreliable in my own land. Are you sure that you want a warrior whom you may not be able to trust?"

Washington's expression remained bland, but his voice was coldly incisive. "You've already served with me on one mission," he said, "and you've done more than enough to justify my issuing you a formal commendation. I would place my trust in you at any time."

"Then it will give me great pleasure to serve with you again," Ghonkaba replied promptly. Here was an officer he could admire and trust.

"I admire the spirit that Colonel Proche displayed when he rebuffed the emissary from Virginia," the Marquis de Lavelle declared, "and I also like the result that his response is very likely to provoke in Virginia, as well as in other English colonies."

"So do I," the Comte de Beaufort said. "He was waving a red flag under the snout of John Bull. There's no doubt in my mind that the Virginians will now prepare themselves for an attack on Fort Duquesne."

General Montcalm's grin was almost boyish. "I am willing to wager," he said, "that they will launch an assault on Duquesne before the snow flies on the Monongahela River. If we were dealing with the English, we could expect endless procrastinations. But their colonials have learned to act swiftly and decisively, just as ours have. In any event, our tactic of luring them into an attack on a position that they cannot possibly take from us seems to be progressing very nicely. We have reason to be pleased indeed!"

"Your wise move in augmenting the bastion as you declared you expected to do, Louis, will almost certainly make it possible for us to turn them back," General Lavelle commented. "I realize that the British and their colonies still outnumber us, but fortunately they're incapable of mobilizing their manpower and using it to its maximum capacity."

General Beaufort expressed a qualm. "Under the new policy that you've initiated, Louis," he predicted, "it's going to take many months of special training to prepare any further regiments that France may send."

"Indeed it will," General Montcalm responded cheerfully. "I will insist that every French soldier has rigorous wilderness training before actually engaging in combat. That is essential."

"You seem unworried by whatever threat the Virginians may pose to Fort Duquesne," Lavelle observed.

"Well, keep in mind, if you please," Montcalm explained, "that I intend to transfer a large number of Miami Indians to Duquesne in the immediate future. If need be, we'll also bolster the garrison with some well-qualified Huron braves. That will be of great assistance in assuring a successful defense.

"The English colonies do have treaties with a great many tribes," he added, "but each operates within a limited area, and the treaties are strictly defensive in nature. Their only attack force of consequence is the Iroquois."

General Lavelle found it necessary to remind him that, as he said almost sarcastically, "the Iroquois nations have the most highly developed attack force in all of North America."

"To be sure, they have just that," Montcalm replied. "But we've had no report that any of the Iroquois nations have moved their own warriors out of their own homelands. So the Virginians presumably will be marching against us by themselves. Yes, if they were accompanied by a vast horde of Seneca or Oneida or Mohawk, it would be a far different story. But I'm sure our Miami, and perhaps a number of Huron, added to the strength of our garrison, will be adequate to contain those Virginians."

His two associates remained dubious, but offered no further objections. Montcalm was unorthodox in his strategic thinking and in his deployment of forces, but they had discovered that he had the instinct of a genius for the assignment of French troops and Indian warriors.

"Just one other observation," their commander remarked with a smile. "We have observed that the Monongahela, one of the key elements in our strategy, is a river that is quite unusual here in North America—it flows north. In my mind, I liken that fact to the direction of the river that flows just below us, the St. Lawrence, and in that coincidence I see a most fortunate omen for our success!"

The Virginians were only five hundred strong as they marched through the wilderness toward Fort Duquesne. But Ghonkaba, deeply impressed, was convinced that he had never encountered more competent troops. In fact, as he said to Colonel Washington one evening, the five hundred seemed the equal of twice as many warriors of any nation with the exception of the Seneca.

The reason for the militiamen's competence was self-evident. All carried the long rifles of the frontier, and all were remarkably accurate marksmen. Not even a band of Seneca could expect to do as well with their bows and arrows as these quiet Virginians could with their rifles.

Another positive factor lay in the militiamen's familiarity with the frontier. Colonel Washington had chosen the makeup of his force carefully, and without exception, the men were genuinely at home in the forest.

The autumn was already far advanced, and signs of approaching winter were everywhere, but that did not matter to these men. Leaves were dropping from trees and from bushes, but the veterans had acquired the knack of concealing themselves behind such vegetation. Able to move with catlike silence through the deep woods, they needed no one to tell them where to tread lightly, and to spread out to reduce the likelihood of being seen.

Though they could not hope to travel with the speed of a column of Seneca, they nevertheless made astonishingly good time. As Colonel Washington explained to Ghonkaba, experienced troops ordinarily could cover twenty miles in a day's march. These militiamen, however, were able to march thirty miles and more every day without difficulty. They kept up the unrelenting pace while crossing the rugged mountains that stood between their homeland and their goal.

Ranging through the forest far in advance of the main column, Ghonkaba covered at least twice that distance as he scoured the forest for signs of the enemy. He moved effortlessly at his familiar Seneca trot, and the militiamen, aware of what he was accomplishing, were astonished by the stealth of his movements. No matter how fast he ran, they could neither see nor hear him. In order to prevent a tragic misunderstanding, Colonel Washington established that when Ghonkaba turned back at sundown to rejoin the main body, he would identify himself to the sentries as he reentered their lines.

To the surprise of Washington and his staff, he found no sign of Indian activity anywhere. The Virginians had expected unfriendly warriors to be lying in wait for them in the forest. But the French were using a different technique. By the time the column had reached a point on the Monongahela a scant thirty miles from Duquesne, Ghonkaba had found no sign of enemy warriors.

No militia officer was more courageous than George Washington, and few were as cautious. He believed that any action taken, either offensively or defensively, should be based on a thorough knowledge of enemy strengths, potentials, and intentions. For that reason, he now sent his regiment into a bivouac. Hunting parties were instructed to use bows rather than firearms to bring down game that they needed for their meals.

That same night when Ghonkaba returned from his day's scouting, Washington asked him to eat supper with him, and they squatted side by side in front of a small campfire where meat was roasting and a potatolike root was baking in the coals. The colonel was already acquiring a reputation for the thoroughness of his preparations.

"I am sure," Washington said, "that you recall—as I

do—the conditions of our previous visit to Fort Duquesne."

"I remember them well," Ghonkaba assured him.

"Do you suppose that you would be recognized if you ventured into the fort again?"

Ghonkaba instantly understood Washington's intent. "I have no doubt," he replied, "that I could disguise myself in ways that would make it difficult for anyone there who saw me previously to recognize me."

"What might you do to avoid discovery?" Washington asked.

"The colonel realizes," Ghonkaba said, "that because of my ancestry on my father's side, my skin is lighter than that of most Indians. But at this season of the year, the walnut trees are ripe and vast numbers of walnuts are available for picking. The meat of walnuts, when boiled, produces an oil that is a marvelous stain. I will make such a stain and spread it on my skin. Then I will be darker than any Seneca—as dark, in fact, as a warrior of the Miami."

Washington responded approvingly. "Good thinking!"

"When we visited Fort Duquesne," Ghonkaba continued, "I observed the Miami warriors with great care, and I am certain I can reproduce their war paint so that none will realize that I belong to a different Indian nation."

Washington, while pleased with Ghonkaba's planning, recognized that great obstacles were still to be overcome if his disguise was to be completely effective. "What of your speech?" he asked. "Do you know the language that the Miami speak well enough to speak it yourself?"

When Ghonkaba seemed cheerfully unconcerned,

Washington went on, "I'm afraid your plan won't do. When one of the Miami braves sees you, he will address you in his own language. When you are unable to respond, he'll know at once that you are an impostor."

Ghonkaba's expression was solemn, but a twinkle in his eyes showed that he was enjoying the suspense he was creating.

"The speech of the Miami," he said, "is similar to that of the Erie, which I have long known. I anticipate no problem in understanding what might be said to me."

Washington was impatient. "I'm afraid you miss the point I'm trying to make," he said somewhat irritably. "I don't doubt your ability to understand what a Miami brave might say to you. It's what you say—or don't say—to him in return that concerns me."

Ghonkaba opened his mouth and, leaning toward the fire, pointed inside. Washington, looking at him, was astonished. The young Seneca had managed to contort his tongue in such a way that it appeared deformed.

"The braves of the Miami," Ghonkaba then said after closing his mouth, "and their French allies, as well, will look at the inside of my mouth as the colonel has done, and they will understand that I cannot speak. It will not be necessary for me to say words that would reveal my true identity."

Washington chuckled at the audacity of the young warrior, and after weighing the matter, finally approved. "If you think you can carry it off," he said, "go ahead. But just remember that we really are at war with France now, though neither side has yet declared it, and if you're found out, you'll probably be hanged as a spy. And you know that they wouldn't hesitate to torture you."

"In no way," Ghonkaba assured him, "could I be forced to reveal anything about this regiment. In any event, I do not intend to be caught in any trap, and my identity will not be revealed. Once I become a brave of the Miami, I will remain one as long as it is necessary to learn whatever the colonel wishes to know." He paused, then asked ingenuously, "What information *does* the colonel seek?"

Washington was surprised; Ghonkaba, whose courage was unquestioned, required instruction in the art of war as white men fought it. "I need to know as much about the men at Fort Duquesne as you learned previously about the cannon there," Washington said. "I want information on how many French troops are stationed there, and how many of their Indian allies, also."

"I will gain that information for you," Ghonkaba promised.

Ghonkaba promptly went about the task of gathering walnuts, cracking them, and extracting the meat. When he had enough to almost fill a small cooking utensil, he added water and put the ingredients on the cooking fire to simmer. He had also dug up a number of plant roots, and these he boiled in a second pot. The brews cooked for hours, while Ghonkaba dropped off to sleep. He awakened from time to time to check the pot of walnuts and then dozed again.

Finally, in the early morning, he was satisfied and, removing the walnuts from the fire, allowed the now oily contents to cool. Then he smeared the substance on his face and body. As he took great care to leave no gaps, his body eventually shone in the moonlight.

128

At dawn he was awake again and went down to the bank of the Monongahela to bathe. To Colonel Washington's amazement, when he returned his skin looked several shades darker. The sheen of the oil had vanished, making his face and body look more natural. Ghonkaba then daubed himself with the vermilion paint of the Miami, using the mixture created by boiling the roots. Now his transformation was complete.

Washington called the sentries' captain to his command post. "Take a good look at this Indian," he ordered, "and mark him well so that you can describe him accurately to all our sentries. He will be returning to us at some time in the days ahead. I can't tell you when he will appear or under what circumstances. What I want to impress upon you is that when you next see him, he is to be admitted swiftly and without question."

The militia captain, studying the disguised Ghonkaba at length, took notes, and satisfied himself that he and his subordinates could be sure to recognize the brave.

Colonel Washington grasped Ghonkaba's hand. "I wish you well," he said, "and may you return in safety. As much as I regret it, I can do nothing for you on this mission; I can offer no protection."

"I expect none," Ghonkaba replied, "and I need none. I will be safe, and I will come back with the information that you require."

Washington had never encountered anyone who seemed less concerned about his own welfare. He wondered if this was a Seneca pose, but decided it was only indicative of Ghonkaba's self-confidence: he felt certain of his own survival on this dangerous mission.

129

Ghonkaba overlooked no detail prior to setting out; he naturally gave primary importance to his weapons. Fortunately, his natural curiosity had asserted itself on his first visit to the fort, and he had covertly acquired a full set of Miami weapons. It was a simple matter to substitute the bow and arrow, the tomahawk, and the knife of the Miami for his own weapons, which he left in Washington's care. He believed the substitutes were inferior, but he was obliged to carry them to bolster his deception.

Leaving the bivouac area late in the day, he traveled at the Seneca trot northward along the Monongahela. When night fell, he continued to run steadily, his eyes and ears attuned for the slightest movement indicating the presence of French troops or their Indian allies.

As dawn approached, he rested in a small hollow and ate emergency rations; then he stretched out to rest, as Renno himself would have done. Ghonkaba had learned to sleep soundly for one to three hours, but even while gaining the rest that his body required, he was able to keep one corner of his mind alert for the approach of strangers.

He remained unmolested, and after sleeping for nearly three hours, he awakened, much refreshed. He daubed more Miami war paint on his face and torso and then resumed his journey, knowing that soon he would reach the fort.

He easily avoided the French and Indian sentries stationed in the woods on the approach to Fort Duquesne, and he at last reached the heavy, long gate—now open—which was the fort's main entrance. Ghonkaba quickly saw that a French lieutenant was in charge of several sentinels, including buckskin-clad French troops and several Indian braves.

The sentries' system soon became clear to Ghonk-aba. A Miami sentinel, seeing the war paint of the newcomer, challenged him. "Identify yourself," he called in the language of the Miami.

Ghonkaba halted and went through an elaborate pantomime, showing his deformed tongue to prove that he could not speak properly.

As he had hoped, his ruse satisfied the sentinels, and the Miami appealed to the French lieutenant, who waved him onto the premises.

Now he was safely inside, in itself no mean achievement, but he knew better than to wander aimlessly, for then he would be sure to be stopped and questioned. So he walked purposefully, wrapping the upper portion of his body in a small blanket. He was hopeful—and as it turned out, justifiably so—that the half-breed whom he had met on his earlier visit to the fort would not be encountered this time. He kept a sharp eye for that well-remembered figure.

Unlike the English colonial forts that Ghonkaba had visited, Duquesne was an exclusively military establishment, and no civilian enterprises flourished here—no manufacturing nor farming, and no section of the town was devoted to civilian homes, schools, and churches. The soil looked promising, particularly near the rivers, and it was plain that waterpower was available for sawmills and similar enterprises. But the French, being realists, had chosen the site for defense purposes, and the entire community was no more than an army post.

After walking for several minutes, Ghonkaba came to an area that he was seeking, where two large cooking fires were attended by Miami squaws, who were preparing food in iron vats supplied by the French. A number of Miami warriors were seated on the ground, eating, and it was apparent that this was a bivouac area.

Ghonkaba promptly sat, assuming that none of the Miami would think his attitude unusual. All Indian nations were alike to a degree, and he had gambled that the Miami would honor the custom that a brave was entitled to privacy when he ate.

He did not have long to wait for food. One of the squaws—all of them homely, scrawny women, by his standards—saw the newly arrived brave seat himself, and dipping a gourd into a pot, she filled it with a steaming stew, which she brought to him with a wooden eating device that resembled a spatula.

Had Ghonkaba been at home, he would have thanked the squaw for serving him. But in the role of the uncommunicative Miami warrior, he barely acknowledged her attention with a curt nod.

He filled his spatula, dropped food into his mouth—and almost gagged. The stew was inedible, the worst he had ever tasted—chunks of greasy, tough bear meat, and squash, beans, and corn lacking the herbs that made vegetables so delectable when prepared by Ah-wen-ga or Deborah.

Small wonder that an advanced nation like the Seneca considered the Miami to be savages—they had no idea how to prepare a meal! Ghonkaba realized he must conceal his feelings and pretend that the stew was satisfactory, eating it as the Miami braves were doing. So he forced himself to chew the unpalatable mixture, and curbing a strong desire to shudder, he resolutely swallowed a mouthful. At least, he consoled himself, he was maintaining his disguise expertly—if he could eat such a meal without inadvertently revealing his identity, he could carry off his entire deception.

As Ghonkaba ate, he remained alert to his surroundings, and noted that Miami braves were coming to the bivouac area from one sector of the fort's wall. After eating, they returned there. So he assumed that this was a section of the defense assigned to them to man. Feeling relieved when he had emptied the gourd, he thrust it into the hands of a passing squaw, and headed toward that sector of the wall. Both French troops in buckskins and Miami warriors were on the firing platforms inside the log palisade, but they seemed to pay no attention to him.

Watching a squat dark-skinned Miami warrior, who was several yards ahead, Ghonkaba followed him up to the wall. His duties, it seemed, were simple. He climbed to the parapet, and as soon as he appeared, a Miami already stationed on the platform departed for his own meal. Noting how other Miami were acting, Ghonkaba climbed to the platform and sat down, wrapping himself in his blanket. Through a hole in the wall about three inches high and equally wide, he gazed out at the forest.

No activity was at all likely until the Virginia militiamen launched their attack. So it was unnecessary for him to study the forest incessantly, as the Miami braves who sat on either side of him were doing. Instead, he concentrated on his immediate surroundings.

The Miami had been assigned a large sector of the platform, and Ghonkaba was somewhat dismayed when he counted one hundred of them in place. Assuming that for each warrior on duty another was at rest, waiting to replace him, the tribe had two hundred men at Fort Duquesne.

Equally disconcerting was his discovery that the Erie had a sector that seemed to be similar to that occupied by the Miami. That meant another two hundred braves were assigned to the fort's defense.

From his position, he could see the gun turret occupied by the French and the surrounding support areas where their infantry were located. Counting laboriously, he estimated that the French had far more than a thousand troops—the garrison had already been strengthened by Quebec. Combined with those of their Indian allies, this gave the French a strength far greater than Washington's forces.

Ghonkaba found these figures unsettling. The French outnumbered the Virginia riflemen so badly that a full-scale battle inevitably would lead to the colonists' total defeat.

Having learned what he had been sent to discover, Ghonkaba was eager to be on his way. But he knew that now, of all times, he must exercise great patience. A false move would arouse suspicions, and to leave the platform too quickly would be a serious error. Therefore, he continued to sit stolidly for hour after hour, seemingly indifferent to anything except his view of the forest.

He wondered how he could leave the fort without directing attention to himself, but decided that since he was unfamiliar with the routines of the place and the system of establishing sentinels, he could not possibly plan his escape in advance.

The wait seemed interminable. Evening came, and most of the other warriors were relieved, one by one, and went below to eat. Ghonkaba had no interest in another Miami meal; he grew increasingly eager to be on his way. At last his patience was rewarded when a young warrior approached, grunted, and sat down.

Glad that the Miami were a surly, ill-mannered

people who didn't believe in much conversation, Ghonkaba grunted in return and slowly climbed down to the ground, in no apparent hurry to leave the area.

His sense of smell told him the squaws were serving bear-meat stew again, and he was glad that he would be spared the ordeal of trying to down another portion. He headed toward the rear of the bivouac area, intending to slip away. Then, suddenly, his luck changed.

Two Miami, the feathers in their scalp locks showing that both were war chiefs of different ranks, glanced curiously at this brave who seemed intent on leaving the area instead of stopping to eat supper.

Ghonkaba could feel their eyes boring into him. He felt that he had no choice, however, but to continue, and pretending to be unaware of them, he kept moving toward the main gate.

He caught a swift glimpse as they silently fell in behind him, their curiosity aroused.

This totally unexpected development required an abrupt change in tactics. Even if the main gate was still open, Ghonkaba knew that to use it now would be an admission that he was up to no good, and the Miami would organize a search.

Of all the traits he had inherited from Renno, perhaps the most valuable was his ability to think clearly and calmly in moments of crisis. This faculty had not come easily to him, but he had been painstakingly trained by Renno, who had taught him that the worst enemy he could face was panic. So, his mind working rapidly, he maintained rigid self-control.

Not only would it be necessary to avoid the main gate, but he knew that anyplace inside the palisade where campfires or sentry fires were burning was to be avoided at all costs.

His only hope was to find a dark area and under cover of night make a break for freedom. Only to a limited extent could he pretend that he could not speak. He could not hope to sustain such a pose, and it would not take the Miami very long to ascertain that he was not one of them.

It was imperative, Ghonkaba knew, that he give the two war chiefs no hint of his intentions. So he walked slowly, almost strolling, seemingly unaware of the interest he had aroused. He stayed far from the fire that burned intensely inside the main gate; in its glare, he saw that it was closed and barred. He concluded that all the other gates probably were shut for the night also. That meant he would be obliged to scale the wall, and he realized that his problem was compounding swiftly.

Far ahead, inside the rectangular-shaped fort, he saw an area that was completely dark. No fires burned anywhere in its vicinity, though dark shapes on the platform told him that the palisade was manned.

When he drew closer, he utilized his extraordinarily keen eyesight to good advantage and was able to see that this section of the wall was guarded by the French infantrymen. Looking up at the sky, he saw heavy patches of clouds that completely obscured the moon. Among occasional breaks in the clouds, he caught glimpses of stars filling the sky above the mountains.

Suddenly Ghonkaba felt a wild surge of excitement. In a patch of clear sky ahead, he saw the widespread wings of a great bird that soared higher and then suddenly swooped low.

The bird was a hawk, sent by the manitous who guarded and guided the destinies of the Seneca! Since his earliest boyhood, Ghonkaba had heard stories of miraculous events that had saved the life of Renno and of Ja-gonh, who had trusted implicitly in the hawks that had enabled them to escape from their foes. It was almost too good to be true, but the evidence spoke for itself: the manitous had sent the hawk to help him in this time of grave need.

Paying no further attention to the Miami war chiefs, Ghonkaba concentrated his full attention on the hawk. The great bird swooped lower, then flew a short distance off to the right, where it moved still lower as it flew in an ever-tightening circle.

Certain of his destiny, the young Seneca moved toward the section of the dark wall directly beneath the great, swooping bird.

When a break occurred in the clouds for a few moments, Ghonkaba caught a glimpse of something he had not seen previously: a definite opening in the palisade. The wall extended to the left and to the right of a spot directly ahead of him now, but no logs joined the two sections.

This, he realized, was not an oversight. The gap had been left deliberately so that sentries and others, familiar with the palisade, could enter and leave even under the most adverse circumstances.

What mattered beyond all else was that the hawk was showing him the gap. The wall was at its darkest in this area. He could have no better place to make a break for freedom, and would not have found it without the hawk's assistance.

His spirits buoyed immeasurably, Ghonkaba knew what he had to do now. Giving no advance warning, he suddenly broke into a run, moving at the top speed he was capable of achieving. As his moccasins pounded silently on the hard-packed ground, he drew his Miami tomahawk with one hand, and his stone knife with the other.

As he had anticipated, two French soldiers armed with muskets and bayonets were stationed at the gap, one on either side. Both were peering out at the wilderness beyond the fort's perimeters, and neither was aware of the fugitive who was drawing ever closer to them.

Wishing that he had his own perfectly balanced tomahawk, Ghonkaba let fly with the one he carried. His aim was remarkably accurate, and the weapon caught one of the French sentries in the back of his head. He crumpled to the ground instantly.

The second Frenchman was startled by the outburst of sudden, silent violence. He looked around in bewilderment for the assailant.

By that time, Ghonkaba was upon him, striking once with the stone knife, wielding it deftly as he brought it down with full force. It penetrated the body of the sentry and disappeared all the way to the hilt.

In a single, swift motion, Ghonkaba pushed aside the body and darted out of the fort. He was free now, but he knew his troubles were just starting. He knew that the two Miami war chiefs would be trying to explain the situation to the French commander of the sector. It was only a matter of time—moments, perhaps—before a manhunt would be organized and underway.

It was a custom of the Seneca to clear an area of at least one hundred feet in width beyond the boundaries of a stockade. This was done to prevent enemies from sneaking close to the palisade and, perhaps, mounting it unseen. The English had adopted the same technique. The French, however, had never bothered to learn it, and consequently, the forest stood only a few yards from the palisade.

Had the French followed the Seneca custom, Ghonkaba undoubtedly would have been captured.

Once he was in the sanctuary of the wilderness, he felt safe, even though his ordeal was far from ended. He threw himself to the ground, knowing that the firesticks of the white soldiers and the arrows of the Indians almost invariably were fired too high when a target was not clearly visible. Hugging the ground, he crawled forward slowly, blending in with his environment. It was almost impossible for the defenders to see him, and with each moment, his chances of escaping unscathed improved dramatically.

Now his long years of training took over. Seneca warriors began their education at the age of nine, and from then until they were awarded the feathers of a senior warrior after they reached their twenties—provided they saw no active combat before then—they learned how to maneuver, how to use the forces of nature to their advantage, rather than be forced to cope with a hostile environment.

The sound of musket fire from the rifle platform broke the silence. Occasionally a bullet whined overhead, but Ghonkaba knew that the enemy was firing blindly. He heard the whistle of arrows, too, but the Miami and the Erie, like the French, were firing wildly as they searched in vain for him. He would not have such a natural advantage indefinitely, however, and after he had crawled some three hundred feet, he rose and ran at full tilt, following a zigzag course so that he would make a more difficult target to reach in the unlikely event that a pursuer caught a glimpse of him.

At last he came to the banks of the Monongahela,

and knowing what needed to be done, he tied his moccasins together and draped them around his neck. Then, without hesitation, he plunged into the chilly waters and struck out for the opposite bank. The force of the stream, he knew, would carry him toward the fort, which was the last thing that he wanted, so he swam against its flow.

Again his lifelong training came to the fore, and he negotiated the river with an almost astonishing ease. When he reached the opposite shore, he knew he faced new problems. It was cold, bitterly cold, and he was already chilled from his exposure to the water. But he would have lost valuable time had he rolled in the grass to dry himself, and furthermore, he would have left unmistakable evidence for his pursuers. So donning his moccasins again, he began to run at a pace even more rapid than the ordinary Seneca trot.

The exertion restored the circulation of blood to Ghonkaba's numb, cold body, and soon he felt far better able to cope. He established a loping gait, his speed deceptively fast, and he headed straight for Colonel Washington's encampment. Thanks to the intervention of the hawk, Ghonkaba's safety now seemed assured.

Concerned about putting as much distance as possible between himself and any pursuers, Ghonkaba made no attempt to cover his tracks. That process, requiring great skill and infinite patience, would have been unduly time consuming. It was more important that he report to Washington than try to conceal his whereabouts indefinitely. Washington would have to decide what action the French were likely to take and what means he could employ to protect his own regiment.

Ghonkaba maintained his punishing pace through

the long hours of the night, and when daylight came, he knew he had left his pursuers far behind. He put his ear to the ground and listened carefully, but could hear no footsteps and no marching body of men. He had far outdistanced his pursuers, and his last doubt vanished. He knew now that he would be able to fulfill his complete mission.

When Ghonkaba reached the Virginia sentries, he was admitted through the lines without question. A short time later, he was taken before Colonel Washington, who was eating an aromatic fish chowder.

To Ghonkaba's delight, he was offered a similar meal, and as he ate ravenously, he told his story.

Washington and his staff listened without interruption. Only when he was done did the colonel speak.

"Would you say, Ghonkaba, that your estimate is high or low?"

"It is a conservative estimate, Colonel," the young Seneca said.

Washington turned to his staff and spoke incisively. "As I see it, our situation is simple—far too simple, unfortunately. The French and their allies outnumber this regiment by more than two to one. The odds may be as great as three to one—far too large for comfort. Next, there seems to be little doubt in Ghonkaba's mind that the enemy will follow him, and are sure to discover our presence."

"Then a full-scale battle looms ahead, Colonel," the operations officer said.

Washington smiled, but his pale eyes remained glacial. "We will have no full-scale battle if I can help it," he said, "at least, not for the present. As much as I would like to take a firm stand and give the French a drubbing, I do not look forward to being beaten by a much larger force. Therefore, we're going to retreat."

Most of the officers looked crestfallen, and several expressed their dismay.

"Before this campaign ends," Washington said, "even the most bloodthirsty among you will be satisfied. I promise you we'll get all the fighting that we need. But first we've got to equalize the odds."

"Just how do we do that, sir?" one of his battalion commanders asked earnestly.

A competent commander such as George Washington prepared for every contingency, and when faced with a crisis, already knew what had to be done. This was the case now, and Colonel Washington spoke with authority. "I intend to withdraw about ten miles up the river," he said. "As we moved downstream, I observed a high, rugged bluff on this side of the river that, with a strong fort built there, would offer us a splendid defense bastion. We shall begin our withdrawal tonight, in spite of the hour, and when we get there, we'll start to cut timber. We'll build our fort at once, and the French will have to attack."

Within a short time, the regiment was on the move, and by daybreak, the fort began to take shape. In later years, when Washington became the commander in chief of the American forces seeking independence, it was erroneously claimed that, in spite of his many virtues, he lacked a sense of humor. That claim was untrue, as every militiaman who accompanied him on this march could appreciate. His sense of humor was dry, to be sure, as everyone readily agreed who heard the name he gave the redoubt. Fort Necessity found its way into history books and achieved a measure of immortality.

When the sun rose, sentry lines had been established, and hunting parties had been sent into the forest on foraging expeditions. Washington was busy directing the building of the defense towers that would complete the fort when he was notified that a party of French and Indians had arrived on the opposite bank of the river.

Washington chuckled when he saw the amazement on the faces of the French scouts. Lowering his glass, he said, "We've given them something to think about by building this fort so close to Duquesne." As he watched the enemy party vanish into the wilderness, he predicted, "They'll be back. You can bet your last ha'penny on it. Colonel Proche will know that he must reduce our Fort Necessity, but I daresay he'll send to Canada for reinforcements to make sure that the job is done right, and that gives us time to strengthen ourselves, as well."

Sending for Ghonkaba, he explained the situation in detail, and then said, "I want you to go at once with a message to Governor Dinwiddie and General Ridley. They need to be told that the campaign here is taking shape more rapidly and more definitively than we had assumed, and that there will be a major battle. Tell them that we are badly outnumbered and that we need reinforcements. I realize that our other regiments have been committed to defensive positions, and that a decision to withdraw them would have its difficulties, but in order to prevent this force from very possibly being wiped out, we need all the help that they can possibly bring to bear. It is most urgent!"

Ghonkaba listened carefully, then repeated the directions to make certain that he understood.

Washington, taking a firm position, would remain at

Fort Necessity with his regiment and, if necessary, would fight the enemy—vastly superior in numbers to his own forces—without help from anyone. He hoped that the governor and Tom Ridley would have a large number of men to spare, but the doubt in his voice did not impress itself on Ghonkaba until much later.

Ghonkaba headed south and eastward without delay and called on all of his stamina and skill as he crossed the mountains. He had developed a great admiration for Colonel Washington and his riflemen. They were fearless yet cautious, and despite his initial reservations, he found them the equal of the Seneca in almost every way.

Perhaps what Renno and Ja-gonh had claimed was really true—that a difference actually existed between the English and the French. Ghonkaba had never given credence to the idea before, but now he had reason to pause and reflect. The militiamen of the regiment had uttered no complaint when they had traveled ten miles upstream late at night and then begun the grueling task of building a fort.

They had remained good-humored and high-spirited, and like their commander, they were prepared to face a vastly superior force unaided.

It was a matter to be pondered at length, Ghonkaba decided, and he thought of little else as he sped toward Virginia's capital at Williamsburg.

WAR CRY

Chapter VII

Good fortune smiled on Ghonkaba, and Brigadier General Tom Ridley already was in Williamsburg when he arrived there. The general was conferring with Governor Dinwiddie, and as a consequence, Ghonkaba was able to meet with both of them at the governor's small but handsome mansion.

Ghonkaba delivered an impassioned speech as he explained the military situation that Colonel Washington and his regiment faced. He omitted no detail, and his admiration for Washington and his troops was evident.

Governor Dinwiddie believed that all Indians were

natural actors, and his fleshy face was covered with a broad smile as he listened to Ghonkaba's recital.

General Ridley, however, was impressed by his cousin's sincerity, and by his sense of fellowship with Washington and his men. It appeared that a metamorphosis was taking place within the young Seneca.

The governor looked concerned. "This is very odd," he said. "Colonel Washington already knows the disposition of all our troops and must realize that all of our regiments are fully committed. I don't see how he could have forgotten."

Ridley cleared his throat. "Unfortunately, Your Excellency," he said, "I am sure he didn't forget. He's desperate for help, and is hoping against hope that we can rearrange our priorities."

"That's impossible," the governor declared flatly.

"I know," Ridley replied, and sounded sorrowful. Then he turned to the bewildered Ghonkaba. "We have a total of only four regiments," he said, "and in addition to the men who are with Washington, the remaining three are all assigned to various sectors. The protection of the people of our colony makes it impossible to withdraw men from those duties and send them to Washington. As he knows, he'll have to triumph or perish on his own."

No one was more surprised than the residents of Philadelphia to discover that their city, expanding little by little, had become the largest English-speaking community in the colonies.

Philadelphia was unique, perhaps because of the influence of the Society of Friends, which was introduced into the New World by William Penn, the colony's

founder. The city was graceful, its pace deceptively leisurely; in manufacturing and in shipping, however, it
led its nearest rivals, Boston and New York, by a considerable margin. Because the city offered only a few
inns, visitors were obliged to reside in homes where citizens took in boarders. Even the waterfront district was
sedate, and fewer saloons were to be found and far
fewer brawls occurred, than in other seaports.

The community did boast a large number of eating
places, and the meals they served seemed universally
good. Philadelphians, it seemed, took pride in their
cooking.

The Indians of half a dozen tribes, principally the
Conestoga, the Conoy, and the Unami, wandered freely
about, not restricted in any way. Again, this was a
result of the early policy of William Penn, who had
sought to establish friendly relations with the Indians
of the area. Administrators of the colony had continued
his practices. The Naturals, as the Indians were called,
stared respectfully at Ghonkaba as he made his way
through the broad, cobbled streets en route to the
headquarters of the militia to which he had been directed. The presence of a Seneca was highly unusual in
Philadelphia, but the members of other tribes, recognizing his war paint, accorded him the respect for his
nation that was universal.

Ghonkaba stubbornly knew what he wanted to do,
what he felt he had to do. His friend, Colonel George
Washington, was in serious trouble. He needed reinforcements in order to repel the French, but Virginia
could send him no assistance.

Therefore, he had to look elsewhere for help. Virginia's sister colonies had to provide him with aid, just
as one Iroquois nation would come to the assistance of

another in time of need. Ghonkaba could see no alternative, and he intended to leave no stone unturned in his attempt to gain men and arms that would enable Washington to turn the tide, to translate almost certain defeat into sure victory.

Ultimately, he found the military headquarters, and after explaining his mission to several subordinates, he was invited to sit with a panel that consisted of three colonels. He explained to them in detail the situation that Colonel Washington faced, and ended his account by asking for the assistance of Pennsylvania troops.

The colonels regarded him dubiously, and one of them shook his head. "What you're asking is a rather tall order. How does it happen that Virginia doesn't provide its regiment with relief?"

Feeling both foolish and apologetic, Ghonkaba explained that troops were needed for a variety of purposes in Virginia, and that they couldn't send any units to Washington's aid.

"That's all the more so here in Pennsylvania," one of the officers said. "The Miami occupy territory on our western perimeter, and the Erie lie to the north of us. Both are heavily populated, very strong nations, and we're obliged to keep our own militia close at hand in order to ward off attacks on our own people."

His statement summarized the position of the Pennsylvania militia. Increasingly disturbed and unhappy, Ghonkaba pleaded for help for George Washington. The regiment, as he knew, could not hold out indefinitely at Fort Necessity without reinforcements. The very thought that Washington might suffer defeat and be forced to give up Fort Necessity seemed intolerable, unthinkable to him.

The Pennsylvania colonels listened to him sympathetically, and one of them sighed. "I wish we could be of help to Virginia," he said. "I'm sure all of us feel as I do. But we'll be forced to rely on ourselves if the French and their Indians—particularly the Erie or the Miami—launch an attack on one of our western towns. I'm afraid we've got to look after ourselves because no one else is going to do it, and with our survival at stake, we must be selfish."

Ghonkaba tried hard to persuade them to change their minds, but his efforts were to no avail. It became very clear that, regardless of what happened to the beleaguered regiment, Pennsylvania would look out only for her own welfare.

The most the officers would do for him was to arrange for his transportation to New York by boat, instead of leaving him to cross the territory on foot. They also gave him a letter to Colonel Philip Schuyler, the deputy commander of the New York Colony's militia, who, as it happened, had close ties with the Mohawk, the largest of the Iroquois nations.

The atmosphere in New York was unique, unlike that in any other city in the colonies. The principal port of entry for immigrants from England, Scotland, and Ireland, as well as for the trickle that continued to arrive from Holland, Sweden, and the German states, New York was undoubtedly the most cosmopolitan of New World communities. Her people were obsessed with their own desire for greatness, and it was said that a New Yorker worked harder than the inhabitants of any other colony. People on the streets walked more briskly, and those who rode invariably appeared to be in a great hurry.

The personality of New York expressed itself in a number of ways. Its inhabitants were conscious of the current London styles, and both men and women closely resembled those of the capital of the Mother Country. The colony also not only supported the first theater ever built in the New World, but the demand for seats was so great that two additional theaters had come into being. The only other town that had even one theater was Charleston in South Carolina.

In spite of its relative cosmopolitan air, the presence of Indians was taken for granted, and Ghonkaba created virtually no attention as he made his way to the stone building that stood near the artillery battery at the bottom tip of Manhattan Island. Here, he had been informed, was the military headquarters of the New York militia. On his way, he passed a number of members of small Long Island tribes, whom he ignored. He was pleased, however, to encounter several Mohawk, and they exchanged warm greetings as they passed each other. It was good to see fellow Iroquois, and his feeling of being an alien was dissipated somewhat.

Schuyler, who would achieve lasting fame later as the senior major general of the American forces fighting for independence, was a wealthy landowner who knew the Mohawk intimately. He received Ghonkaba without delay and, much to the young Seneca's delight, was able to speak his language.

Ghonkaba quickly repeated the familiar tale of the plight of Colonel Washington. Colonel Schuyler listened in attentive silence, occasionally passing a hand over his ruddy face.

When Ghonkaba had finished making his plea, he looked hopefully at the colonel. Here, he thought, was an officer who understood the situation and needed no prodding.

To his astonishment, Schuyler hit his desk with a

heavy fist, striking it so hard that two quill pens fell out of the jar of sand in which they rested. "It's a damn shame, I know," he said, "but there is not a blasted thing in this world that I can do to help Colonel Washington and his men."

Ghonkaba looked at him in openmouthed astonishment.

Schuyler laughed bitterly. "I'll explain as best I can," he said, "but I certainly won't blame you if you don't understand. First off, in order to sign a recruit for the New York militia, we're obliged to promise him that he'll never be called on to serve outside the actual borders of New York Colony without his specific permission. That means that before we could dispatch a regiment of four hundred troops to Virginia, we'd need—in writing—the approval of every man in the regiment for such service. And that's just the first obstacle."

Ghonkaba looked at him in bewilderment, knowing the colonel wasn't joking.

"Suppose," Schuyler said, "that I feel as I do, that it would be an important development in the campaign against France to send at least a regiment—preferably two—to Colonel Washington's assistance. Under the laws of New York, I'd be obliged to certify to that need in a formal document that I would submit to the legislature of New York Colony. There—provided that what the politicians regard as more pressing business didn't intervene—the question would be debated. For one reason or another, there would be interruptions, a great many interruptions, while other business had to be attended to. So while the debate on whether to send the troops to the aid of Virginia was still before the legislature, many weeks would pass. The military fate of Colonel Washington would be decided by events in the field long before the legislature finally voted down the proposal."

Ghonkaba's perplexity grew, and he could scarcely believe what he was hearing.

"I know how you feel, young man, and I don't blame you in the least," Philip Schuyler said. "But I assure you that I don't exaggerate, and I swear to you that the request would be rejected."

"But why?" the young Seneca wanted to know. "How can one English colony refuse to go to the aid of another under such circumstances?"

"Virginia isn't very close to New York," Schuyler explained, "and several colonies between us and them act as buffers. New Jersey, Pennsylvania, Delaware, and Maryland, to be specific. The politicians who sit in the legislature are shortsighted, and they would refuse to believe that we, ourselves, would be in any danger because of what did or didn't happen in Virginia."

Ghonkaba tried to grasp what he was hearing. "If the Mohawk sent a plea to the Seneca for help," he said, "our entire nation would rise up as one warrior to come to the aid of the Mohawk."

"You're an Iroquois," Colonel Schuyler told him with irony, "and for that reason you're a primitive savage, with unsophisticated reactions to the world and its problems. You would automatically come to the aid of a sister nation just as she would aid you because both of you take your pledges seriously. In these colonies, however, it's a matter of each for itself, each standing alone and refusing to lift a hand to a sister colony, regardless of the circumstances."

Ghonkaba was so shocked that he was incapable of coherent thought.

"If you wish," Colonel Schuyler told him, "I'll introduce you to the commander of the New York militia and to the key members of several committees of the legislature. But I must be honest with you and tell you that you would be wasting your time and your efforts. You would only become more frustrated. Before any resolution is found, the Virginians at Fort Necessity will have fought a battle against the French and their allies, and the issue will already be resolved one way or the other."

Philip Schuyler thoughtfully provided Ghonkaba with passage from New York to Boston on a brig, which would cut down travel time considerably, and he sailed off to Massachusetts Bay.

The voyage in the crisp, late autumn air provided Ghonkaba with a brief respite, during which he reviewed his efforts, still stunned by the reception he had received everywhere. Not only had Pennsylvania and New York refused to come to the aid of Colonel Washington's beleaguered regiment, but even Virginia herself had declared itself unable to raise a hand for her sons. The explanations were varied, but they added up to only one thing, at least in his mind: the English colonies were selfish beyond belief, and every man was interested only in his own welfare.

Landing in Boston, Ghonkaba went directly to the house of General Strong. There he was greeted with great warmth by Beth, who was openly delighted to see him. In spite of his concern over the situation at Fort Necessity, he was equally pleased to see her.

Insisting that he stay as their house guest, she listened carefully to his tale and said, "I'm confident that Papa will be able to help you. I'm expecting him home for supper within the next hour. And, as it happens,

Sam Adams, whom you will remember, is coming for supper tonight, too."

Ghonkaba wanted to feel relieved, but after his reception elsewhere, he was dubious. "You really think," he asked, "that the general will agree to help?"

"I can't imagine any reason why he wouldn't," Beth said. "He's always preaching the doctrine of cooperation among the colonies. Now he will have a perfect opportunity to practice what he preaches."

When General Strong came home, he greeted Ghonkaba cordially. A few moments later, Sam Adams arrived.

Ghonkaba launched into his recital before supper in such great detail that they moved to the table and were halfway through the meal by the time he finished.

"I must ask you—for reasons of security—to write nothing about this entire matter," the general said to Adams.

Sam Adams accepted the desired censorship. "I don't believe in doing the French any favors," he said, and added, "Do I assume correctly that you're going to provide the Virginia regiment with the aid so lacking everywhere else, General?"

Kenneth Strong hesitated. Ghonkaba knew, even before the general spoke, that he, too, would find excuses to avoid sending troops to Fort Necessity. A knot of hard anger, forming in the pit of his stomach, seemed to grow within him.

"First of all," General Strong said, speaking for Ghonkaba's benefit, "we are many, many hundreds of miles distant from the frontier in question. Except under circumstances that are almost inconceivable, I cannot see how we could be expected to provide militiamen in any substantial numbers. That's basic to the problem you present me with. Then we must note that our militia is an organization made up of volunteers who contribute their time and their services for the defense of their colony. They receive only token pay, and it's a hardship for them to leave their homes. That is true for the defense of their own homes and families, to say nothing of traveling far away to participate in another colony's fight."

Ghonkaba glanced across the table and saw from Beth's expression that she, too, was steeling herself for her father's rejection.

"Massachusetts Bay," the general continued, "has the largest militia force by far of any of our colonies. We have a total of five regiments. Of these, four already have been summoned to active military duty in the present emergency. I have assigned two regiments to the Maine District, where they are keeping close watch on the Algonquian. The other two regiments are currently stationed on the western border of our colony, and there they will stay. Whenever we are at war with France, innumerable stories are heard to the effect that we're going to be invaded by soldiers marching down from Canada. There's no way of judging the accuracy of these reports, but I can't take any risks. Consequently, it is essential that I keep two regiments stationed on the western frontier."

"What about the fifth regiment, Papa?" Beth asked. "Do I gather that you haven't summoned them to the colors yet?"

"That's right," her father said. "They are still civilians, and I've had no immediate plan to call them to active duty. Most of the men in the regiment are recruits who've had little or no military training, and I'm reluctant to activate such a unit except in a case of the

direst emergency. They most assuredly would be useless on a campaign in the wilderness."

Ghonkaba had heard all he wished to hear, but he
couldn't resist saying, "When I left Fort Necessity,
General, Colonel Washington's riflemen faced a very
dire emergency."

General Strong regarded him soberly. "I'm sure they
are in grave peril," he said, "and I have in no way dis-
counted any of what you've told me. But the fact remains that a regiment of raw recruits would be of no
help. They might well cause a further, avoidable
disaster."

"How does such a unit gain military experience?"
Sam Adams interjected.

"There's only one way possible," the general replied.
"I've been intending to wait until this coming spring,
and then call the regiment to duty for a three-month
period of training. Then I'll send the unit back to civilian life again until it may be needed."

"Long before then," Ghonkaba said harshly, "the
corpses of the Virginia riflemen will be rotting in the
ground at Fort Necessity."

Kenneth Strong sighed and turned to Sam Adams in
appeal. "How can I possibly explain our basic situation? You understand it without being told. But how
do I explain to someone who isn't familiar with our
ways?"

Adams turned to the young Seneca and forced a
smile. "We like to think of ourselves as civilized men,"
he said, "and I'll grant you that in Massachusetts the
ways of civilization are strange indeed."

Beth, seeing Ghonkaba's scowl, was concerned. It
would be difficult, at best, to explain so that the warrior, whose loyalties were direct and who favored ac-

tion to meet the threat of an enemy, could understand a complex situation.

"Most of our citizens in Massachusetts Bay are immigrants or the sons of immigrants from England, Scotland, and Ireland," Adams said. "Some were French refugees who came here seeking religious freedom after King Louis XIV rescinded the Edict of Nantes, which had guaranteed freedom of worship to French Protestants. In any event, without exception, our people come from countries where military service has been voluntary. In times of great stress, some of the German states rely on conscription—or involuntary service—but the traditions in England and in France have been very firm. The man who joins an army or navy and hastens to the defense of his country does so of his own free will. Coming to the New World has been a jarring experience for a great many of our citizens. Here, military service is compulsory. Every man is required to make himself eligible to be called to duty in times of emergency, and the minimum period of service lasts for ten years, usually from a man's twenty-first birthday."

Ghonkaba was unimpressed. Every Seneca received military training from earliest boyhood, and it never occurred to any male of the nation that he would not defend his people.

"More often than not," Adams continued, "units of various sizes—regiments, battalions, or companies—are called to duty after one of our frontier towns is attacked and its residents scalped in an Indian uprising. Therefore, the men in a community are only too glad to serve. But the present situation seems to be very different. Though France has been maneuvering, it is widely recognized that no actual blows have been struck, and no battles fought. The need to strengthen our defense posture seems theoretical to a great many people. I have little doubt that the outcry would be very great if General Strong were to call an untrained, untried regiment of recruits to serve many hundreds of miles from their homes, rather than in defense of their own towns and farm communities. This may be difficult to understand, but it nevertheless is the present picture."

"You are right," Ghonkaba replied flatly. "I do not understand."

General Strong recognized the hopelessness of trying to explain the power of public opinion in a free state.

"It was in this very dining room," Ghonkaba said, his anger finally getting the better of him, "that I said I could see no difference between the English settlers and the French settlers. You two," he told General Strong and Sam Adams, "replied with many fine words. You explained that you English love freedom, while the French do not. You told me that liberty means so much to you, while to the French it means nothing. The words that you spoke were nothing but empty words! The French have answered the call of their country, and they are in arms and have built a great fort in the west. Colonel Washington, who is a warrior of courage and strength, tries to drive them from that fort. He needs men—many warriors—for the purpose. Pennsylvania and New York have refused to provide him with those warriors. Even his own land, Virginia, has declined to give them to him. Now Massachusetts Bay refuses, also."

"I'm afraid," Beth exclaimed, a defiant edge creeping into her voice, "that I'm compelled to agree completely with Ghonkaba. In a time of crisis, like the present, men are needed—not excuses!"

"A true warrior," Ghonkaba declared firmly, "fights for what he believes! He risks death for his beliefs. Colonel Washington and the militiamen of Virginia who are with him at Fort Necessity are true warriors. They stand alone. All others are cowards who wear false faces. They speak of freedom, but they do not fight for freedom. They cry out for liberty, but they do not raise their tomahawks to defend liberty." Unable to eat any more, or to tolerate the situation any longer, he pushed back his chair and rose to his feet. Only at the last minute did he murmur an excuse as he swiftly left the table.

Beth jumped to her feet and followed him, finding him already at the front door ready to leave the house.

"I admire you for taking such a strong stand," she said, "but I must beg you not to do anything foolish."

"I must do that which I think is right," he told her.

"I don't want you to be hurt," she pleaded, "and I do not want you to get yourself into trouble."

He was deeply touched by her concern for him, and he smiled. "Ghonkaba of the Seneca," he said, "has a skin as tough as the hide of an aged buffalo. I am sure no harm will come to me. Besides, I have been brought up to heed the words of Ghonka. It was my great-grandfather who said that no harm ever befalls a warrior who does what he believes is right. The manitous, who always know right from wrong, protect him from harm."

He felt a strong urge to kiss her good-bye, but he was too conscious of inhibiting elements. This was her father's house, and her father, with whom he was in violent disagreement, sat only a few yards away. So he bowed his head to her, extended his left arm in a stiff gesture of Seneca farewell, and made his way quickly down Beacon Hill.

Beth felt a great sense of personal loss as she watched his lithe figure descending the hill. For a moment she imagined that he had intended to kiss her, but she chided herself now for being a foolish romantic.

She sighed, closed the door, and returned to the dining room. She found her father and Adams finishing their supper. "Ghonkaba is gone," she said. "The explanation of why we must follow the other colonies in refusing aid to Colonel Washington was too much for him."

Sam Adams looked up slowly from his plate. He glanced at Beth, then looked fixedly at General Strong, his eyes shining. "I can't say that I blame the young fellow," he said. "I just wish that every man here in Massachusetts Bay and throughout the colonies had his conscience!"

Colonel Coulon de Jumonville, one of the most promising of General Montcalm's subordinate commanders, arrived in Fort Duquesne after marching an augmented regiment all the way from Quebec, a feat of no mean accomplishment.

Arriving there, he wasted no time in carrying out his orders to march on to Fort Necessity. He allowed his troops one week of rest, and then led them out into the field, along with some men from the Fort Duquesne garrison and every Miami and Erie brave whom he could recruit.

Exercising great caution in his approach to Fort

Duquesne, the French officer had gone to considerable lengths to avoid marching through the land of the Seneca. Actually, he had skirted the northern shores of Lakes Ontario and Erie before heading south, thus making certain that his presence would not be noted by the Seneca. He used the same caution now in his assault on Fort Necessity.

Under cover of night, after a two-day march during which the strictest secrecy was observed, he reached Fort Necessary. His troops were drawn into a semicircular formation around the bastion, with the Erie warriors on his left flank and the Miami on his right.

At dawn he attacked, and French infantrymen moved forward in waves, using the cover provided by the forest with the expertise of true frontiersmen.

The battle began as the first dirty streaks of light appeared in the dark sky overhead. A squad of Virginians assigned to a sector directly facing the river was dozing, and only the sergeant in command of the unit, acting as its sentry, remained awake. An experienced frontiersman, he sensed, rather than actually heard or saw, movement in the forests directly beyond the palisade. He peered out and at first could see nothing.

Then some shadowy, blurred figures appeared and began to move forward toward the cleared area.

The sergeant awakened his unit, man by man, cautioning each to remain silent. They made no sound but the readying of muskets for combat.

The squads on either side of the unit were alerted, and they, too, made ready for battle. The captain in command of the company stood inside the palisade, staring out into the darkness, and when he raised one hand, an expectant hush descended.

Then his arm swept downward sharply in a sudden arclike movement, and the rattle of musket fire revealed that the defenders were taking the initiative. The French had failed to catch Fort Necessity unaware.

But de Jumonville's men were in no way deterred by this unexpected development, and the entire line erupted as he sent a full regiment, bolstered by Indians, forward from the forest.

George Washington knew that the fight could not be won. Outnumbered by more than three to one, his small garrison was exhausted after months of unrelieved duty. Supplies of gunpowder, ammunition, and food were limited. Washington was determined, however, that the Virginians give a good account of themselves, and his regiment defended the fort with skill and courage. The defense was far more than Colonel de Jumonville had anticipated.

The defenders had their hands full. Washington recognized the urgent need for conserving ammunition, and as he went from one company to the next inside the palisade he cautioned his soldiers not to waste gunpowder or lead.

The Virginians had long claimed that they were the best marksmen in all the colonies, and the regiment soon proved that this was no idle boast. Keeping their commander's warning in mind, they made every shot count. The coming of daylight aided them, and they held their fire, shooting only when they saw living targets moving out of the forest into the clearing in an attempt to reach the stockade.

For several hours, the French made no progress and were held off by the Virginia riflemen's accurate sharp-shooting. Had Colonel de Jumonville traveled with any artillery, he could have reduced Fort Necessity with far fewer casualties. But he was compelled to continue to send his men forward in sally after sally in an effort to wear down the defenders.

By midday, signs were evident that the French tactics would lead to success. The defenders were growing weary, and with the entire regiment of riflemen engaged, no fresh reserves were available to throw into the fray. Every man knew all too well what was expected of him: he had to hold his position at all costs and, relying on his dwindling supplies of bullets and powder, make every shot count. As Washington saw the outlook, only one aspect was encouraging. The French and their Indian allies were suffering heavily, but his men were being spared because the enemy could not get at them. As a consequence, the defenders' casualties were remarkably light.

That situation could not last, as Washington was aware. As his men ran out of ammunition, they would be helpless, unable to defend themselves. Then they would be at the mercy of the French and the Indians, who would swarm over the fort's palisade. Washington knew that the Erie and the Miami would show no mercy and would engage in a grisly contest to see how many scalps each warrior could take.

The idea of a needless loss of life among his men was anathema to Washington, and as the day wore on, the ultimate fate of the beleaguered force became increasingly certain. Finally, when little more than an hour of daylight remained, company after company reported that their ammunition was virtually exhausted.

The Virginians had exacted as heavy a toll from the

enemy as they could, and their young colonel knew that the time had come to end the combat. With great reluctance, Washington gave the order to cease fire and to raise a white flag over the ramparts of the crude fort.

The rifle fire from the forest dwindled and soon stopped. Action on the flanks continued and arrows flew toward the palisade until French officers were able to restrain their Indian allies so that the cease-fire was observed by both sides.

The gates of Fort Necessity opened and Colonel Washington appeared, flanked by two subordinates, a flag-bearer who carried the banner of Virginia, and another who held aloft a makeshift white flag of surrender.

A group of French officers appeared from the forest, and the two groups came face-to-face in the clearing. As they halted, salutes were exchanged, and the commanders introduced themselves. Washington spoke in French, his voice thick with emotion.

"I am forced, sir," he said hoarsely, "to concede that I am able to fight no more. If your terms are reasonable, I am prepared to offer you my surrender."

Coulon de Jumonville looked at the young Virginian in admiration. As a professional soldier, he could not help but be impressed by the skill with which the defense of the crude fort had been conducted.

He faced a difficult problem, as well. If he took the regiment as prisoners, he would be responsible for transporting them all the way to Quebec, a march of many hundreds of miles through the wilderness that was sure to be extremely difficult. It would be impossible to keep them in the limited confines of Fort

Duquesne. He doubted how far his Indians could be trusted, and he certainly couldn't blame the Virginians if they tried to defend themselves against the savages, which meant that a series of brawls and battles could be expected all the way from Fort Necessity to Quebec.

It was far simpler, de Jumonville decided, to resort to a practice that was still followed in Europe and to grant the Virginians "parole." This meant they would be free to return unmolested to their homes, and in theory, at least, they would not engage again in combat in the present conflict.

"I am prepared, Colonel Washington," he said, "to grant your regiment parole."

"You are kind, Colonel de Jumonville," Washington replied with a candor that seemed most unusual to the contingent of French officers, "but I must make our situation plain to you. As I am sure you well realize, the defeat I have just suffered in no way brings the hostilities in which we're engaged to an end. Rather—since no war has actually been declared—I daresay this will be considered the start of hostilities when word of what has happened here reaches England."

De Jumonville, struck by the incisiveness of his foe's thinking, agreed.

"This regiment," Washington continued, "is made up of men experienced in fighting in the wilderness. It is no exaggeration to say that in my opinion they are the cream of the Virginia militia. Officers and men alike are unique in the colony, and perhaps in the New World. Therefore, it would be useless to obtain a pledge from them not to engage in further combat. The needs of war would force all of us, officers and men alike, to break our pledge. Therefore, I cannot accept parole if it depends on the promise that we will not engage in further combat."

It would have been easy for Washington, as de Jumonville realized, to accept whatever conditions were imposed upon him to march his regiment back to Virginia—and then to absolve the men from their pledge. But the young colonel was too honest for that, and the French commander's admiration for him increased. "I will refrain," he said, "from requiring any promise that you and your men remain noncombatants."

Washington bowed slightly in gratitude. "I crave one additional favor from you, Colonel de Jumonville," he said. "We are far from home and our food supplies, like our ammunition, are almost exhausted. I respectfully request that my men be allowed to keep their rifles and to use what ammunition they have left so that they may shoot game on the march back to our colony."

The request, though brash, was eminently reasonable, and Colonel de Jumonville concealed a smile as he replied, "I see no reason to refuse your request. I have only one demand in return—that your troops dismantle this post and render it incapable of being rebuilt before they withdraw."

Washington knew that the demand was fair, and he readily agreed to it. Then he drew his sword and extended it, hilt-first, to the French officer. "You have the honor, sir, of being victor in the first battle of the new war between our nations."

"And you, sir," Colonel de Jumonville answered graciously, "have the honor of having fought gallantly and well. Neither you nor your regiment has any cause to be ashamed of your performance on the field today." Almost impulsively, he returned the sword to his recent foe as an openhearted recognition of gallantry and courage.

Sick at heart, Ghonkaba headed home, traveling slowly across thinly populated farm districts, then through patches of dense forests. As he made his way to the sanctuary of the land of the Seneca, he decided to pause for several days to fish in local streams while he came to terms with the self-reproach he felt because of his failures.

He crossed portions of the hunting grounds of several other Iroquois nations, but he knew he was home when he heard Seneca drums announcing his arrival.

He sought out the first sentry whose territory he reached, and spoke to him bluntly. "Send a message to Ja-gonh, sachem of the Seneca," he said. "Tell him his son seeks permission to return home."

The sentinel's face showed no reaction as he beat out the message, and they heard it echoing and re-echoing in the distance.

Ghonkaba heard and deciphered the heartening return message. Dispatched with a speed that anyone other than a Seneca would have regarded as remarkable, it was very much to the point: "Ghonkaba, son of Ja-gonh, is always welcome."

Ghonkaba headed straight for the home of his parents.

He was not surprised to see almost the entire family gathered to greet him. No-da-vo and Goo-ga-ro-no were on hand with their daughters, as were El-i-chi and Deborah. So were Renno's sister, Ba-lin-ta, and her aged husband, Walter, who had originally come from Fort Springfield and who contributed to the family's white heritage. Ah-wen-ga, the first to see the young warrior, controlled her emotions with difficulty when she caught sight of her son. A hint of tears appeared in her eyes, but she curbed a desire to weep, and instead an expression of deep, fierce pride took the place of tears.

Ghonkaba went to her, bowed his head slightly, and extended his left arm in greeting. It would not have been seemly in the presence of others, even relatives, to embrace his mother.

Ja-gonh appeared from the inside of the building and exchanged a formal greeting with his son.

Ghonkaba was surprised and slightly shocked by his father's appearance. Ja-gonh, who always had been robust and hardy, looked wan and tired now, and Ghonkaba was struck by the thought that his father was working too hard, extending himself unduly, and ignoring his health.

The entire family moved to the circle around the stone-lined fire-pit, and Ah-wen-ga stated that they would wait until Renno appeared before they ate. He had been delayed, it seemed, by a messenger who had come from New York Colony by way of the land of the Mohawk.

No one questioned Ghonkaba. It was taken for granted that he would tell his story only when the Great Sachem appeared, and until then, everyone was willing to be patient.

The entire group rose to their feet as one when Renno at last approached, walking slowly, his ornamental headdress and buffalo cape in place.

Ghonkaba, standing rigidly with his left arm extended in greeting, was relieved to see that his grandfather appeared to be in good health, and noted particularly that his step was lively and firm.

Of all living members of the Seneca nation, and of the other Iroquois tribes as well, only the Great Sachem was entitled under almost any conceivable circumstances to forget protocol and break tradition when it served his purpose. Renno elected to cast reserve aside now, and embrace his grandson, hugging him fiercely.

His love was so great, so intense, that a lump formed in Ghonkaba's throat. He was relieved when his father asked that everyone sit and eat.

After the meal, Ghonkaba needed no prompting to relate his adventures, and omitted no significant detail from his story. He dwelt principally on his sojourn in Virginia and his two journeys to Fort Duquesne with Colonel Washington.

When he described what had befallen him on his espionage visit to the French fort when his life had been saved by a hawk, an electric current seemed to run through the family group. Everyone leaned forward eagerly.

Renno took the lead in questioning his grandson. When had he first become aware of the presence of the hawk? Had the hawk still been visible in the sky after Ghonkaba made good his escape from Fort Duquesne, or had the bird vanished by that time? How did he know that the bird was a hawk rather than an eagle?

Ghonkaba answered all the questions to the best of his ability, and his grandfather drank in every word. The young warrior was quick to recognize the significance that the members of his family attributed to the event. This was the first time since he'd become an adult that the manitous had given him any sign that he stood high in their regard. Both Renno and Ja-gonh had been younger when first visited by the hawk, but here, at last, was proof that Ghonkaba, too, had won the approval of the manitous and was cast in the now-familiar mold of leadership.

The rest of the young warrior's story seemed anticlimactic at first. But as he told of the predicament of Colonel Washington's regiment and of his own futile attempts to win support for him, the anger and disgust in his voice became increasingly evident.

"What I have known in my heart to be true has been proved true," he said. "As I have so long claimed, no difference exists between the French settlers and the English settlers. All men who have crossed the Atlantic to the New World are alike. They are selfish and greedy, thinking nothing of their responsibilities to their friends and their neighbors, and only concerned with their own welfare and their own riches."

Ja-gonh was on the verge of rebuking his son and countering his arguments, but a glance from Renno was sufficient to silence him.

The expression in Renno's eyes spoke volumes. Ghonkaba was young and felt unhappy because he had not been able to assist a good friend in need. Time would be needed to heal his wounds and to place the whole incident in perspective.

Ghonkaba became increasingly bitter and outraged. "I do not understand," he cried out, "why the Seneca and the other nations of the Iroquois help the English colonists when they will not help themselves! We should let them wallow in the mistakes of their own making. We should let them know the terror and degradation and death such as they are themselves inflicting on Colonel Washington and his regiment."

Ah-wen-ga, stirring uneasily, glanced obliquely at her husband.

Ja-gonh was aware of her concern and shared it. Her son, in his anger, was going too far; it was not his place to criticize or decry the alliances of the Iroquois.

No-da-vo sympathized with Ghonkaba, and so did Walter. Both seemed to understand the reasons for his upset and were ready to overlook his outburst.

Renno remained calm, seemingly unruffled. "In war," he said, "we often see injustice. Men of goodwill make mistakes, and their brothers die as a consequence. In my day, I have seen many wars and I have fought in more battles than I can recall. Out of this experience has grown only one certainty. Neither the manitous that guide the destinies of the Indian nations, nor the God in whom the colonists of all nations profess to believe, approves of war. When men fight and kill each other, they abandon the protection of the manitous and of God."

His family was startled, and Deborah, who had been married for many years to a clergyman, was particularly surprised by his vehemence.

"I could conceal the truth for a time from the son of my son," Renno said. "I could remain silent and several moons might pass, perhaps, before Ghonkaba learned the truth. But that is not the way of the Seneca and is not the way of Renno. The story you told about Colonel Washington of Virginia and his regiment of riflemen was not the last to be said on that subject. There's more that has happened than you know."

Ghonkaba grew very tense, and the light of the

cooking fire played on his taut face as he leaned toward his grandfather.

"The messenger I received only a short time ago was sent to me by Colonel Schuyler, whom you met. Schuyler is a fine man and a good officer. He is honest and true to his charges. So the word he sent me was dispatched in great sorrow."

Ghonkaba seemed to know what was coming. Clenching his fists, he hunched his shoulders as though to ward off a severe blow.

"Do not blame yourself for what has happened," Renno said gently. "You have done your best and have fulfilled your obligations. In time of war, no man can do more."

Ghonkaba drew in his breath sharply and, scarcely realizing what he was doing, held it.

"Colonel Washington and his regiment of riflemen," Renno said, "have been defeated by the French, together with forces of their allies, the Miami and the Erie. Colonel Washington was forced to surrender to his French opponent, a Colonel de Jumonville. You'll be pleased to hear, however, that the French have permitted the Virginians to return to their homes, and there seems little doubt that all of them will take up arms again before this struggle comes to an end."

Color drained from Ghonkaba's face as he slowly exhaled.

"Colonel Schuyler informed me of the sad plight of Colonel Washington," he said, "because the English colonists feel that even though winter is upon us, the French and their many Indian friends may turn on New England and New York. They want us to be prepared."

Rage now rendered Ghonkaba almost inarticulate.

"If I were the Great Sachem," he said, "I would tell the English to leave me alone and to go elsewhere for their aid. I would encourage them and the soldiers of New France to exterminate each other. I would not shed the blood of one Iroquois to assist them."

The members of his family were shocked. No man had ever spoken so bluntly or rudely to the Great Sachem.

Only Renno kept his sense of perspective. Of all those present, only he appeared to realize that his grandson had formed an admiration and close attachment to Colonel Washington of Virginia, and that he felt now that he had failed Washington—that if he had tried harder or acted in some other way, he could have procured the aid that the Virginia riflemen had so desperately needed. Ghonkaba's previous misconceptions about the English colonists had been reinforced now.

Renno started to speak, but his grandson gave him no opportunity.

Jumping to his feet, Ghonkaba snatched his tomahawk from his belt and brandished it over his head. In the firelight he looked like a fearful savage apparition. "May the God who watches over the destinies of the English colonies desert them," he cried, "as they deserted a brother-warrior of courage and strength at a time when he needed them." Not waiting for anyone else to utter a sound, he dashed off, soon disappearing from sight.

Goo-ga-ro-no's confidence in Ghonkaba was shaken, and her husband, stone faced and grim, obviously felt as she did. Walter and Deborah were greatly distressed, too.

Renno alone remained calm, and to general astonishment, he chuckled aloud. "Loyalty such as Ghonkaba demonstrates is a rare quality," he observed. "I am fortunate that he is my grandson."

Ja-gonh had difficulty in speaking, and when he replied, he spoke in a choked voice. "My son," he said, "has disgraced me for all time and has won for our family the permanent enmity of the manitous. He has openly defied the Great Sachem! He has denied the beliefs of his grandfather!"

Renno was still unperturbed. "He is young!" he said vigorously, as though recapturing a portion of his own exuberant youth. "He has much to learn, and life will teach him what he needs to know."

Chapter VIII

S trange tales drifted back to the main community of the Seneca in which it was reported that Ghonkaba, furiously angry and implacable, was seeking young, unattached senior warriors for a new army that he was forming. This force, it was said, would not abide by the treaties made over the course of the years by Ghonka, Renno, and Ja-gonh. Under no circumstances would this new force be allied with the colonials who were subjects of the King of England. Similarly, they would have nothing to do with France. They would dedicate themselves to one cause. They would fight for the recovery of all lands lost to white settlers by any Indian nation.

Ja-gonh and Ah-wen-ga knew from the outset that the strange tale was true. It was confirmed in the worst of all possible ways when a number of young senior warriors slipped away to join Ghonkaba's growing band. That was only the beginning of the time of trouble, however.

Soon thereafter, the sachems of the other Iroquois nations sent messages one by one to Renno. Some were baffled; others were indignant. All were upset because the grandson of the Great Sachem was traveling throughout the land of one Iroquois nation to the next, seeking recruits. Within a period of only a few weeks, his force reputedly numbered more than one thousand men. This made it large and powerful enough to obligate respect, particularly as it was made up entirely of Iroquois, with a core of Seneca. The warriors of no other Indian tribe could equal it as a fighting entity.

"Never in the history of our people," Ja-gonh said brokenly, "has there been such a rebellion as this. This undermines my fitness to lead the Seneca, and I must leave my post as sachem."

Renno shook his head. "Because Ghonkaba is young and foolish, it does not follow that his father, also, must be foolish."

It was impossible, even for the chieftain of the entire Seneca nation, to defy the word of the Great Sachem. All Ja-gonh could do was to lower his head in submission and ask, "What then shall we do?"

Renno, who had not lost his sense of humor, laughed lightly. "The sachems of the Mohawk, the Oneida and the Onondaga, the Tuscarora and the Cayuga, ask the same question. The governors and military chiefs of the English colonies are upset, and every day new messengers come wanting word on what we're going to do to halt my grandson and his force of warriors."

Not caring to repeat his question, Ja-gonh merely looked at his father.

"For the present," Renno replied serenely, "we will do nothing. Ghonkaba's activities have been far from orthodox, but as yet, he has broken no law of the Seneca or of our Iroquois brethren. He has not taken up arms against us or against our neighbors in the English colonies. He is ridding his soul of much anger, and it is good to know that he has the capacity to lead. Rejoice, Ja-gonh, that one thousand warriors follow him."

"I would be far more at peace within myself if I knew where Ghonkaba is leading them," Ja-gonh grumbled.

"We will find out in due time," Renno told him. "I cannot believe that anyone in the family of the great Ghonka—one who even bears his name—could have evil in his heart or in his soul. Our enemy is France, not the grandson of Renno! So we must be patient, my son, patient as always, and in due time, the manitous will reveal our destiny to us."

What no one in the land of the Seneca quite realized was that Ghonkaba had developed a plan that was both original and unique. None of the English colonies, it appeared, were able or willing to come to the aid of his friend, Colonel Washington. Therefore, he was going to lead his new brigade to Washington. This was Ghonkaba's concept of friendship, and he was pleased that he had thought of such an ingenious solution to the dilemma that Washington faced.

General Strong stared out his parlor window at the snow that lay thick on the Boston Common. "Now perhaps you'll believe me," he said, not turning his head, "when I tell you that the young Seneca warrior is a rebel and a hothead, and that he's bad medicine."

Beth, sitting before the hearth, continued to embroider the quilt she was making. Her hand was steady, and she did not miss a stitch. "I know very well what's being said about Ghonkaba," she replied, "and I know that he's engaging in some very unorthodox activities, to say the least. But still, I haven't lost faith in him."

"He has assumed command of a large and reckless band of desperadoes," her father said, his voice pulsing with anger. "And these men are no ordinary renegades. They're all young, but they're senior warriors of the Iroquois nations, and I doubt if any force in North America could defeat them in combat—except an army of their own people. I'd hesitate to send my regiments against them, and so would every other militia commander. If we didn't have enough to worry us, what with the war with France gaining in intensity, and Colonel Washington being forced to surrender near Fort Duquesne, this latest news is very discouraging."

"You seem to condemn Ghonkaba as a traitor, but he has performed no act of treason," his daughter replied firmly.

"He has made his rallying cry the termination of the Iroquois treaties of alliance with us, with New York, and with the other colonies. In brief, he has created an intolerable situation!"

"You miss my point," Beth said. "So far, he and his followers haven't taken up arms against us, against New York, or Connecticut, or any other colony. In fact, if I understand correctly, no one knows where Ghonkaba and his men have gone. They simply vanished into the wilderness."

General Strong snorted in anger and disgust.

"I believe I know him well," Beth said. "At least I know him sufficiently well not to have lost faith in him. When he performs an act of treachery against us or any other English colony, I will be willing to believe the worst about him. Until then, I can only urge you to relax and do what I'm doing."

Her father raised a sardonic eyebrow. "And what's that, pray tell?"

"I'm hoping for the best," she said firmly, "and I believe, with all my heart, that something good will come of all this."

Thanks to a network of alliances, the officials of New France were kept remarkably well informed of developments in the lands of the English colonies and their Indian allies. General Montcalm was elated by the stories of Ghonkaba's rebellion, and he expressed deep satisfaction when the rumors were confirmed.

"I've always said that luck plays an important role in determining the outcome of any war," he said, "and our new conflict with the British is no exception. We couldn't have predicted the defection of the grandson of Renno, but I can think of nothing that might happen in the lands of the Iroquois that could better serve our cause. Now we must act quickly and firmly in order to

179

make certain that we use these young rebels for our own good."

He spent an evening composing specific instructions, to be sent to Colonel Coulon de Jumonville. In order to insure a speedy delivery, he entrusted his letter to a scout of the Huron, the most talented and reliable of the tribes associated with New France.

Colonel de Jumonville was delighted when he received the communication, and the members of his staff cheered when he read portions to them. One fact puzzled him, however. "How on earth," he said, "does the general know that the Seneca and his men are moving through the wilderness toward Fort Duquesne?"

No one could answer his question, but his subordinates knew General Montcalm well enough to believe him without question. So sentries of the Erie and Miami were notified to keep a sharp watch for the Iroquois defectors, and less than a week later, a scout of the Miami, exhausted after a rapid trip through the wilderness, arrived at Duquesne with news.

"The force of Iroquois," he said, "is moving down the river called the Allegheny toward this fort."

"How many men do they number in their army?" the colonel wanted to know.

The scout shrugged. "There are many of them," he said.

"Five times one hundred?" de Jumonville persisted. "Eight times one hundred?"

Again the Miami revealed his inability to answer fully. "A brave who is alone and travels by himself," he said, "does not pause to count the numbers of his foes when those enemies are Iroquois. All I know is that I saw many hundreds of these warriors."

"Were they carrying large quantities of supplies?" de Jumonville then demanded.

The sentry pondered the question at length. "I think they carried almost no supplies," he replied. "I first saw them in the wilderness when they had sent out hunting parties in many directions. Now that winter is upon us, game is scarce, and the Iroquois would not rely on the efforts of their hunters to find food if they carried supplies of their own."

That observation made sense, de Jumonville realized, and, also, it fitted the circumstances of the young Iroquois party. Though the warriors had rebelled against their superiors, they had not—for whatever their reasons—raided the warehouses of the various Iroquois nations.

The French colonel reacted quickly and decisively, concentrating all his sentries and scouts on the Allegheny River approach to Fort Duquesne. He insisted that he be notified day by day of the location of the strange force.

What bothered him was the fact that they were headed in the direction of his fort, and he had no idea whether their intentions were friendly or hostile. In case they decided to make war on him, he had to disarm them before they could have an opportunity to attack. He could not know that the Iroquois hoped to bypass the fort, heading for a possible rendezvous with Colonel Washington.

When he learned that they were a scant two days' march from Fort Duquesne, he knew the time had come to act. So, accompanied by a small but expert force of fifty French soldiers, long accustomed to the ways of the wilderness, he set out to find and intercept the Iroquois. He took only a few Miami with him as scouts, using them, rather than the Erie, who were traditional enemies of the Seneca. His mission was extremely delicate, and he wanted to take no chance of offending the young rebels.

His scouts fanned out into the forests, and de Jumonville wondered whether they were completely wasting their time. But they eventually reported that the Iroquois were about ten miles due north.

The French colonel called in his scouts and proceeded in a direct line for the Iroquois, taking the precaution of raising and prominently displaying a white flag.

He couldn't know it, but the scouts of the column— most of them Tuscarora, who were especially adept at this phase of wilderness warfare—soon became aware of his presence. They saw no particular menace, however, in the handful of white men and Miami Indians. Ghonkaba, to whom they reported, was only curious.

So de Jumonville's force remained unmolested, and ultimately, he encountered the main body of Iroquois. He promptly made it clear that this was no chance encounter, but rather that he had been seeking the Iroquois.

Ghonkaba quickly summoned the leaders of the braves from the other Iroquois nations that were represented in his command. His instinct told him that the French officer intended to parley with him, and perhaps make an offer of some sort, and he wanted his colleagues to be represented at such a meeting. His hold on them was tenuous, and he was unwilling to take responsibility for making decisions on his own initiative.

The Indians felt a responsibility for entertaining the unexpected visitors, and their ingenuity was challenged.

But they met the issue neatly by sending out several hunting parties, and as luck would have it, one of these groups encountered a small herd of buffalo in a valley. They succeeded in slaughtering a cow and two calves, which would provide more than ample food for everyone. That night they all feasted on buffalo meat.

De Jumonville, wise in the ways of the Naturals, refrained at first from discussing the matters that had brought him deep into the uninhabited forests. He chatted pleasantly, confining himself to inconsequentials, until they had finished eating. Then he belched politely to show that he had enjoyed his meal, and launched into a speech, with one of his escorts translating into Algonquian.

He began by tracing the history of France in North America, and stressed the great friendship that Louis XIV, and after him Louis XV, had always shown toward Indians. As proof of his contentions, de Jumonville cited the amicable relations that France had enjoyed with the Huron, Ottawa, Algonquian, and Micmac.

His performance was smooth, polished, and very evidently impressed a number of his listeners. Ghonkaba, however, sat with his arms folded across his chest, his impassive face registering no feelings.

De Jumonville knew that Ghonkaba, as the leader of the expedition, had to be convinced of the rightness of the French cause, and he realized that his work was cut out for him. This was the son of Ja-gonh, the grandson of Renno, and no matter what had caused him to break so abruptly with his elders, he could be no fool, and it would be unwise to make exaggerated claims that could not be substantiated.

Ghonkaba listened cynically, telling himself that the

French were even more insincere than were the English. The fact that France had established alliances of long standing with tribes that lived to the north of the Seneca in no way impressed him. These nations, as he had been taught all of his days, were stupid and deserved nothing better than a relationship with the French.

At last de Jumonville came to the heart of his proposal. France, he said, was prepared to extend the hand of friendship to these young warriors, and was prepared, also, to prove in deeds, as well as words, that she meant what she said. "In the arsenal at Fort Duquesne," he said, "are many firesticks, as well as much gunpowder and much lead. For such an occasion as this, we keep many more arms than our own troops can be expected to make good use of. We will gladly provide every one of your warriors with his own firestick, which he may keep. We will also provide each brave with a blanket, a frying pan, a square of burnished steel that he may use as a mirror, and for all who command in the field, we will make you a gift of scissors, as well."

The eyes of many of those present shone with avarice, but Ghonkaba did not display any emotion. "The generals and colonels who represent Louis of France in the New World are generous, indeed," he said. "But it has been our experience that the French, like the English, demand a price for their friendship. When they are generous, they wish generosity in return. What does France want of us?"

He was playing right into the hands of Coulon de Jumonville, who quietly rejoiced because his carefully thought out plan was working perfectly. "We require nothing," he said. "We want nothing."

184

Ghonkaba looked at him blandly. Refraining from calling him a liar, the young Seneca merely remarked, "I have known many colonists in my life, but I have never known one who gave without receiving in return."

"In me," de Jumonville said, "you have encountered such a man."

"Firesticks are expensive," Ghonkaba persisted, "and the cost of bullets and gunpowder requires the expenditure of many of your francs, also. Surely those who are close to the King of France will object strenuously when they find that this money has been squandered."

The colonel shook his head emphatically. "Squandered? Never! It is the hope of King Louis—a hope that is shared by all of us who swear fealty to him—that one day all Indians in North America will be brothers and there will be no more war. We are working toward that goal, and all that we do leads us closer to it. This is made manifest in our readiness to supply you generously with the guns and ammunition that I already have offered you without any reservation."

Now Ghonkaba knew for certain that the Frenchman was lying. He had heard enough discussions between the English colonial authorities and had been present at enough sessions of the Seneca and Iroquois councils to know that the as yet undeclared war in the New World was the direct responsibility of France.

De Jumonville looked around the circle at the attentive faces of the young warriors who regarded him with steady gazes in the firelight, and decided that he had done all he could to accomplish his purpose. He would be wise to drop the issue and let the Indians come to the decision that he thought was inevitable. "The men of France," he said, "do not force their opinions on their friends, just as they do not force their gifts upon them. I will retire now to the camp that my Miami guides have established for me, and I will go to sleep. By morning, perhaps you will have made your decision, and then you can tell me whether you accept or reject the gifts that I offer." He rose swiftly before Ghonkaba could reply, and then withdrew completely from the scene.

The Iroquois continued to sit around the fire. "I think," said the senior warrior of the Mohawk, who was the head of his contingent, "that the French officer is an honest man. I think we should accept his offer."

"I have long wanted a good new firestick," the Oneida said quickly, "and I'm sure that all from my nation feel as I do."

"That is true," the leader of the powerful Tuscarora said. "It is also true that we have long coveted such weapons, which will make us the equal in combat of all who come to our world from across the great sea."

The Onondaga spoke slowly. "I see something strange about the offer we have received," he said. "I cannot quite figure out what it is. Perhaps Ghonkaba of the Seneca, who knows more of the ways of the white men than we do, can explain."

Ghonkaba realized he faced a grave crisis. All that held the expedition together was a sense of common purpose. The braves had joined him because they felt as he did, that they were being exploited by the English and the French alike. Much as he was disinclined to become too specific, he knew it was necessary to speak frankly. "We are far from our homelands," he said. "We are sitting in the wilderness near the land of the Erie. Why have we come here? I will tell you why. We, and the braves who have marched with us, are

186

tired of being fooled by those who have crossed the great sea in huge ships that resemble birds. The English have professed friendship with us, but they have taken our lands. The French have professed friendship for an equally long time with the Huron and Ottawa, the Algonquian and Micmac, but they have taken lands that belonged to those nations since the time of the grandfathers of our grandfathers. We have decided, in whatever wisdom we may possess, that the English and the French are alike. Both are insincere, both are selfish, both are greedy."

"I do not know whether the French colonel lies or tells the truth," the Mohawk declared. "The one thing that I cannot forget is that he has promised us firesticks and ammunition and gunpowder. He must deliver those things to us if he wants our friendship."

"Of course!" the Cayuga added eagerly. "Our friendship is of importance to him. We have much to gain and nothing to lose by going to the fort of the French with him, and there we will see for ourselves whether he keeps his word."

"It has been my privilege," Ghonkaba said, "to hear many negotiations between the English colonists and the Iroquois. To the house of Ghonkaba's father, and in the house of Ghonkaba's grandfather, have come many visitors who have negotiated treaties with us. I have been privileged, also, to see those treaties on paper. The men of England and of France are not content, as the Iroquois are, to reduce their treaty promises to mere words. They are inscribed on parchment paper, which they use as we use wampum, and these papers are signed by their highest officials. That is the way they do business."

"How does this affect the French colonel's promise of firearms?" the Tuscarora demanded.

Ghonkaba's shrug spoke volumes. "Who can say?" he replied. "But if the colonel is sincere in his declarations of friendship, he will wish to sign a treaty with us. Each of us, as the leaders of the braves of our nation who are present in our expedition, will be asked to sign, and the governor-general of New France also will sign."

The Iroquois were confused by his adamant stand.

"What does Ghonkaba expect of us, and what does he wish us to do?" the Mohawk asked.

Ghonkaba drew a deep breath. "I propose," he said, "that when we meet with the French colonel tomorrow morning, we speak with tongues as glib as his. I propose that we pretend to accept his offer, and that our behavior suggest that we believe his friendship for us is sincere. I propose that we march with him to Fort Duquesne, and that we accept the firearms that he offers us. If he is honest, at least to the extent of keeping his promise to us, we will be given the new firesticks that you cherish.

"Remember, my brothers, that we have made no promises to the French colonel in return for his gifts. Once we are in possession of the firesticks, ammunition, and gunpowder that he says he will give us, we will return to the forest—our real home."

His words were persuasive.

The following morning, Coulon de Jumonville was delighted when the Iroquois leaders informed him that they would accompany him to Fort Duquesne, and accept the gifts that he offered them. He was convinced that he had struck a major blow that would result in ultimate victory for the French cause. The young rebels' friendship would be won, and they would join forces with the French. One thousand vigorous, trained Iroquois would be a major addition to the French armed forces, and he doubted whether others among the Iroquois would continue to be loyal to Great Britain. General Montcalm would share his elation and undoubtedly would recommend him for promotion—his future was assured!

The Iroquois lived up to their reputation, impressing Colonel de Jumonville with the speed and ease with which they marched through the wilderness. Never had he seen Indians as disciplined or as efficient, and he began to realize the full significance of the coup that he believed he had pulled off.

Ghonkaba was secretly amused by the warmth of the reception that he and his fellow warriors received when they reached Fort Duquesne. This was his third visit, and he couldn't help contrasting his present reception with those he had received in the past. The first time he had come here, accompanying Colonel Washington, he had been barely tolerated as an ally of the English colonial. On the second visit, he had disguised himself as a Miami, and had barely escaped with his life. Now he was hoping to outsmart the French in the intricate game that the colonel was playing.

Somewhat to Ghonkaba's surprise, muskets were issued to his followers almost immediately after their arrival at the fort. The French were equally generous with gunpowder and with supplies of lead and bullet molds, as well as with blankets and other valued articles.

He made an inspection of the muskets, and found that the French had not stinted. These were not the latest model of weapons that the French infantrymen at the fort carried, but they were effective.

He realized that the French were very shrewd. It would be extremely difficult for any war chief of the Iroquois to persuade the recipients of these gifts to take up arms against France.

Because Ghonkaba did not trust the French, he was eager to leave Fort Duquesne as rapidly as possible. Therefore, once the gifts were presented, he immediately gave the order to return to the wilderness.

The abruptness disappointed de Jumonville, but he was too experienced in dealing with savages to reveal his reaction. Instead, he smiled, and his expression was merely politely regretful as he said, "I won't try to detain you if you must go, but I hope that you will remember France with affection in the future."

"We shall always be very grateful to you for these gifts," Ghonkaba assured him.

That same day, the Iroquois took their leave, marching off into the forests of the north. As Colonel de Jumonville saw them off, standing beside him was Lieutenant Colonel Proche, who had become his second-in-command. "I hope," Proche said, "that we aren't making a terrible mistake by giving muskets to these savages."

De Jumonville laughed. "A mistake? I think not! Did you see the faces of those warriors as they were handed muskets? All of them were positively overjoyed. We've neutralized a very potent force of exceptionally able warriors at a very low cost."

"I hope you're right, sir," Proche said, and kept his further doubts to himself.

De Jumonville reflected that his subordinate's lack of ingenuity would prevent him from rising any higher in rank. "Whether we'll ever be able to persuade them to join forces with us, I don't know," he said. "But I can promise you this much: they're sufficiently grateful that they'll never turn those muskets against us!"

Well aware that the gift of surplus muskets would cause consternation in the ranks of their enemies, the French made certain that word was quickly spread throughout the English colonies. Indian tribes who were allied with them passed the news along to tribes that were neutral, and in a remarkably short time, the word spread.

In Virginia, Tom Ridley expressed deep dismay. "I knew that Ghonkaba was a hothead," he said, "and that his judgment could be impaired, but I'm shocked by his association with France. I never expected to find him, of all men on earth, guilty of treason, and it distresses me that I'm related to such a man."

Colonel George Washington, however, remained calm. "I've come to know Ghonkaba well under adverse circumstances," he said, "and this news in no way changes my opinion of him. You needn't be ashamed of your relationship with him, General. He's committed no treasonable act yet, and I would be most astonished if he ever does."

"Are you suggesting that the stories are false, and that he and his followers didn't receive firearms from the French?"

"Oh, I'm willing to assume that they did," Washington replied. "But that doesn't mean they're going to aim the muzzles in our direction. I have no idea what Ghonkaba has in mind. I can't fathom the minds of Indians quite that well. But I'm certain that he and his band of young rebels will never actually join forces with the enemy."

"I hope you're right," Ridley replied fervently. "With Fort Duquesne still firmly in French hands, we now must find some way to wrest it from them. So far, no plan comes to my mind."

In Boston, General Strong was stunned, and immediately opened a lively correspondence with Colonel Philip Schuyler in New York. He made no secret of his feelings to his daughter.

"I hope you'll accept my judgments of character hereafter, Beth," he said. "Ghonkaba has not only robbed the Iroquois of almost one thousand of their best warriors, but has now formed an alliance of some sort with our enemies."

"You're leaping to conclusions, Papa," she retorted. "You do not know for a fact that he's made any kind of a pact with the French."

"The facts speak for themselves, unfortunately," General Strong replied harshly. "Louis of France never has been noted for his generosity, and his subordinates aren't in the business of giving charity to those with whom they've failed to reach an understanding. I can't imagine General Montcalm approving a gift to Ghonkaba and his renegades unless he had a firm agreement that they would enter the war on the French side."

"I find totally incomprehensible," Beth said flatly, "the idea that Ghonkaba would be that much of a renegade and would turn on his father and his grandfather."

"You have far greater faith in him than I have, then," her father answered, though his anger was diminishing. "I have made some concrete suggestions to Colonel Schuyler, and if he accepts my proposals, you and I will be going, once again, to the land of the Seneca in great haste."

Messengers traveled almost incessantly in the days that followed between Boston and New York; eventually, the militia of Massachusetts Bay and New York reached a meeting of the minds. General Strong immediately arranged for a journey to the land of the Seneca. The wilderness was still covered with snow and the weather was bitterly cold. "I'm afraid," he said, "that this is an emergency that transcends personal considerations. It won't be easy for you on the trail, Beth. I'll do the best that I can for you and try to shield you as best I'm able. But if you suffer hardships, as well you may, at least you'll know that it's in the best of all possible causes."

The young woman was curious about the course of action her father was taking, and had no idea why he was going to visit the leaders of the Iroquois League at the worst of all possible times for travel through the forest. But she knew better than to ask questions about official business, and she consoled herself with the thought that she would find out in due course.

The knowledge that Ghonkaba was at the root of the problem was unsettling, to be sure. But her faith in him did not waver. She considered it inconceivable that he would be a turncoat to the cause of his father and grandfather, and that he would actually join their foes.

The trip was made on horseback, with packhorses carrying supplies for both the travelers and their mounts. The seventy-five cavalrymen assigned as escorts were, without exception, good riders, and in spite of the difficulties caused by the cold and snow, the party made reasonably good time.

Game was so scarce as to be virtually nonexistent, but General Strong had prepared for that possibility. He carried ample supplies of fresh meat for the escort and, in fact, had more than enough for the return journey as well.

He was solicitous of Beth's welfare on the trail, as were the officers and men of the escort, and she suffered no ill effects from the journey. The difference in the appearance of the wilderness in winter was startling, and she could not help but contrast it with its appearance when the foliage was full and lush. What surprised her, however, was the absence of Indians. She commented to her father that apparently the Indians stayed at home in this season.

But he smiled as he contradicted her. "On the contrary," he said. "When a group as large as ours is abroad, you can wager that the Indians through whose lands we travel are well aware of us, and are keeping track of our movements. But their sentries are keeping out of our sight, that's all."

Beth marveled at the cleverness of the braves, and wondered how they managed to conceal themselves when the trees and bushes were bare and only the evergreens appeared to offer any substantial cover. She decided that she didn't really know a great deal about the ways of Indians.

It seemed strangely comforting to her when she heard the throbbing drums of the Massachusetts, then of the Mohawk, and ultimately, of the Seneca, announcing the progress of their party. They received a warm greeting in spite of the inclement weather. Lodgings were found for the cavalrymen, and although the

Seneca were none too familiar with horses, their warehouses were easily converted into barns to shelter the animals.

No-da-vo, acting as Beth's escort, took her to the same small house she had occupied previously, and there she found Deborah, once again, waiting for her. They impulsively embraced.

"You have no idea how glad I am to see you again," Deborah said. "I've been so eager to talk with you."

"No more so than I've been," Beth replied. "Is there any word from Ghonkaba?"

Deborah shook her head. "We've had no direct word, if that's what you mean. In fact, we have heard nothing new about him or his companions since the spread of that disgraceful story that they accepted arms from the French."

A beacon of hope seemed to pierce the gloom in which Beth had been immersed. "You mean the story is false?"

"No," Deborah said. "I'm sorry to tell you that it's anything but false. Renno is never one to listen to what an English lawyer would call hearsay evidence, so he has investigated in his own way. I don't know the details, but I do know that he has confirmed the story, and it's true—all too true—that Ghonkaba, the Seneca who went with him, and the other Iroquois who joined them, truly did accept gifts of muskets, ammunition, and gunpowder from the French."

Beth was so shaken that she didn't know what to say.

Deborah showed her the fire burning in the small house. "You notice," she said, "that as is customary, the fire is located directly below an opening in the ceiling. Unfortunately, that's as close as the Seneca come to having chimneys in their houses. The system works splendidly, as long as you keep the animal skin coverings over the windows tightly closed. Any time you open them and admit a breeze, however, the smoke will fill the inside of the building, and then you'll have to go out-of-doors until it clears. So although it's hard to distinguish daylight from night, and you rob yourself of seeing anything that's going on outside, I assure you that it's much wiser to keep your windows tightly covered. The same is true of the skins covering the entrance, of course."

Deborah drew nearer to Beth and put an arm around her shoulder. "I can imagine what you're thinking about Ghonkaba, and I'm sure you've been grieving," she said. "But don't feel badly."

Beth turned to her questioningly, but did not dare trust her voice to ask aloud.

"I have known Renno for more than sixty years," Deborah said. "I've know Ja-gonh since birth, and I held Ghonkaba in my arms when he was an infant. I've been married to El-i-chi for more than a quarter of a century now. I know the family, and I know the quality of men they are. I tell you this because I don't care what evidence seems to condemn Ghonkaba. I refuse to believe that he is a renegade and a traitor!"

Beth caught her breath and a hand crept to her throat. "I'm so glad to hear you say that," she exclaimed. "My father is convinced that he's become an ally of the French, and in spite of my own convictions as to his character, I was beginning to wonder."

"If Ghonkaba lives," Deborah said gravely, "you can be sure that he'll clear his name."

"If he lives?" Beth found it difficult to speak the words.

"I don't know what action the Seneca may be planning to take against Ghonkaba and his followers," Deborah said, "any more than I know what your father is planning to do with the Massachusetts Bay militia. But I can tell you that they view the problem as a very serious one. El-i-chi confides in me in almost all things, but in some he becomes completely a Seneca and withdraws. And this is one of those occasions. I have no information that I can give you, nor does his mother. This is a time when we are completely put aside. The men of the nation, the men who decide its destiny, are determining Ghonkaba's fate."

Chapter IX

General Strong looked first at Renno, clad in his war bonnet and cape of office, as the Great Sachem sat before him in the council lodge of the Seneca, then at Ja-gonh, who was in a pose identical to that of his father. Perhaps the dim light of the lodge was responsible, but the face of neither revealed any emotion whatsoever. Father and son appeared to be statues carved out of rock. This was all the more remarkable, Kenneth Strong ruminated, because they were actually white men and had no Indian blood at all. But their reactions were those of Indians, not of Englishmen.

"Nothing can be more harmful to a cause," the general said, "than the defection of a major combat unit in time of war—no matter what the cause of the defection. The disease can pass from one brigade or regiment to another with great rapidity and ease. It's like the plague that spreads its terror before even the best of physicians can bring it under control. I have been in touch with the colony of New York, and they have agreed to a plan that will enable them and Massachusetts Bay to take prompt steps to correct this volatile, dangerous situation."

Renno did not move, and his voice was expressionless. "What action do you propose?"

"I will send a reinforced regiment, really a full brigade, into the field immediately," General Strong said. "Colonel Schuyler will do the same, and we will send these units to meet the Iroquois rebels, engage them in combat at the first opportunity, and inflict a severe defeat. We are agreed that they must be crushed, and we are prepared to perform that distasteful task, although it grieves us to prepare for battle against warriors whom we have regarded as our comrades in arms."

Ja-gonh busied himself lighting a pipe with a coal that he took from the perpetual fire in the council chamber, and the general suspected that he was trying to conceal his emotions.

Renno had no need to engage in any such subterfuge, and was completely in control of himself. He held up a hand to demonstrate his disapproval of the scheme outlined by the general.

"My heart has been heavy," he said, "because I have feared that the military chiefs of the colonies would reach just such a decision. I know that if they go

200

into the field to punish Ghonkaba, they will destroy him."

General Strong felt desperately sorry for him and for Ja-gonh. He understood what these proud men must be suffering.

"Ghonkaba is flesh of my flesh," Renno said. "My blood, and the blood of my son, flows in his veins. All that I have done in more than eighty summers of my life is destroyed if it is true that he has turned against his people, his nation, and his family. But I find it impossible to believe that he is a traitor to the Seneca. The fact cannot be denied, nevertheless, that he has defied us, and has robbed us of nearly one thousand of our best warriors, who are badly needed in the fight with the French that looms ever nearer."

"The words of my father are true," Ja-gonh intoned, in stating his complete agreement.

"When a child disobeys his father," Renno said, "the father does not ask others in the tribe to punish the boy. He does not go to other tribes for help, nor does he go to the colonists, who are his neighbors and friends. He attends to the matter himself, and inflicts the punishment that he decides is best. So it is when the boy grows to manhood."

General Strong thought he knew what was in Renno's mind and silently marveled at the moral courage of the Great Sachem. He wondered if he would have the strength to propose and carry out the plan that evidently had been brewing for some time in Renno's thoughts.

"Like my father before me," Renno continued, "for many years I have held the trust of the people of all of the Iroquois nations. They have made me their Great Sachem and have entrusted me with the welfare and well-being of all of our nations. Now the authority that binds together the people of the Iroquois is threatened. It is threatened from within. Principally by one who is not only a Seneca, but is one of my own personal brood. I must punish Ghonkaba myself. It is not right that the task be turned over to the soldiers of the white colonists."

Ja-gonh was calm, his expression grim, and it was evident that he agreed with the harsh decision of his father.

"This is not the season of the year when warriors should march through the wilderness," Renno said, "but in a time when the life of the Iroquois League is threatened, we must ignore the weather and do what we must. An expedition will be formed immediately. It will consist only of Seneca warriors. Even though some warriors of other Iroquois nations have joined Ghonkaba in his foolish error, I will not ask for help from my brother nations. This is a problem that concerns the Seneca—and the Seneca alone will be responsible for solving it."

One of the secrets of Renno's continuing success over the course of a long and distinguished life, Kenneth Strong realized, was his deep, unshakable pride in the Seneca nation.

"I have delayed in the formation of this force," Renno went on, "in the hope that Ghonkaba and his foolish comrades would come to their senses. This they have not done, and now you rightly demand that their corps be disbanded. So be it! The Seneca avengers will prepare for an immediate journey to seek out their stupid sons. They will be commanded by Ja-gonh, because it is his place to punish him whose blood flows in his veins and to inflict discipline upon him. Second in command of the expedition will be No-da-vo, the husband of my daughter. He, too, has been disgraced by the conduct of Ghonkaba, and must wipe clean the record, as footprints are wiped from sand so they no longer show."

General Strong was astonished by the inflexibility of Renno's will. It would have been easy enough for him to assign the task of commanding the punitive force to a competent Seneca war chief who was not related to him. But he demanded that his son and his son-in-law live up to the highest standards of his nation, standards that he set for himself.

Ja-gonh was not surprised by his father's decision. He had no idea of the plans in Renno's mind, but they would be typical of him and of the traditions of the nation. Ja-gonh knew that, as the father of Ghonkaba, it was his own duty—his right—to force his son into line or to suffer the consequence. In this case, the consequence meant death on the battlefield, at the hand of his own father. The demands of the Seneca were unyielding, and this, as Ja-gonh well knew, was the quality that made the nation great. It gained strength from its refusal to compromise with principle, no matter how repugnant the task to be performed.

By the time General Strong and Beth departed, their presence no longer being required in the land of the Seneca, the expedition to seek out the rebels and force their capitulation was well under way.

Beth knew nothing of the plan until her father mentioned it to her at their supper fire on their first night in the wilderness on their return journey. She was aghast when she learned of it.

"I've thought of Renno and Ja-gonh as civilized men," she said heatedly, "probably because they're descended from English colonials. But they're not! They're savages, more barbaric than the pure-blooded Seneca who can trace their ancestry through generation after generation."

"You're badly mistaken," her father told her gently. "You have no idea what this decision has cost Renno and is costing Ja-gonh. Can you imagine how difficult it will be for Ja-gonh to order his Seneca to open fire on the rebels? He has far greater strength than I'd have. If I were wearing his moccasins, I assure you I'd lack the will and the courage to carry through a decision like that."

"Then why would he and Renno torture themselves? Or do they enjoy it?"

"On the contrary. They grieve even harder than I would grieve in like circumstances," General Strong said.

"I feel so desperately sorry for Ah-wen-ga," Beth remarked. "It must be dreadful for her to know that her husband is setting out with an expedition to kill their son. I think knowledge like that would drive me mad."

"I'm sure that Ah-wen-ga will be required to use every fiber of the courage that is within her, and the self-control that she has been taught since birth. But you miss a point of great significance, Beth. It's facing up to a crisis like this that makes the Seneca great. I can think of very few nations in human history that have shown similar strength. I can imagine a leader in ancient Sparta making such a decision, and until Rome became corrupt under the emperors, a Roman leader might make the same decision. But beyond that my mind boggles. Don't you see the effects that this terrible incident will have?"

Near tears, Beth only shook her head.

"The Iroquois will be so impressed," her father said, "that they will accept the leadership of the Seneca without question. The Indian nations that are allies of the French will be overcome by fear. The French will be impressed, just as we will, and it's bound to hurt their spirits, as it will work to help ours."

"But what a terrible price to pay," Beth murmured. "I'm almost sorry that you told me, Papa, although I'd never have forgiven you if you hadn't. For Ja-gonh's sake and Renno's, as well as for Ghonkaba's, I can only pray that the incident somehow turns out well, though I can't for the life of me see how that is possible."

Snow glistened in the pale, blue-white light of a dying moon on the cornfields. It was bitterly cold, and the seasoned Seneca warriors had slathered grease on their bodies, hands, and faces to ward off frostbite as they prepared to begin their long march in search of their sons, brothers, and cousins who had followed Ghonkaba.

When No-da-vo reached the house of Ja-gonh, his brother-in-law awaited him. Together they walked a short distance to the house of Renno, where the Great Sachem received them. He was wide-awake, in spite of the early hour; he had shaved on either side of his scalp lock, and the familiar streaks of green and yellow war paint were smeared on his face. It was bitterly cold in his room, but he did not appear to be aware of the chill. He sat on the ground, his arms folded across his chest, and when his son and son-in-law entered, he inclined his head a fraction of an inch in greeting to them.

"The expedition that will find and punish Ghonkaba is ready to depart," Ja-gonh told him.

A faint gleam appeared in Renno's still-piercing blue eyes. "May the manitous watch over you," he said, "and may you succeed in this most difficult of missions."

Ja-gonh and No-da-vo were grateful for his blessing.

"I need not tell you," Renno said, an unexpected quaver appearing in his voice, "to exercise great caution. Ghonkaba is near and dear to you, just as he is to me. When you find him and his misguided followers, if it seems at all possible to defer action, do not plunge into battle. Give them to understand that you want to parley with them. Remind him of his debt to me, to you, and above all, to his people. Tell him that I bear him only love in my heart. Tell him, also, that his deeds when he accompanied Colonel Washington to Fort Duquesne have added to the respect which I always have felt toward him."

If he was being lenient in his treatment of his grandson, Ja-gonh could not blame him. The miscreant was, after all, his own son.

"Only if Ghonkaba proves obstinate will you persist in your drive against him. Then—but only then—will you attack him. If you are forced to attack, you will show him, and those who follow him, no mercy. Every rebel who under those circumstances fails to return to the fold, regardless of his reason, must die."

Ja-gonh bowed his head to show that he understood and would obey.

"I place only one restriction upon you," Renno said. "In the event that you are compelled to fight, keep in mind that your opponents are Iroquois and that, therefore, they serve the same gods and the same manitous that we serve. Therefore, none will be scalped, and he who takes the scalp of a rebel will be required to face me upon his return. I swear that I will not deal leniently with him."

No-da-vo was relieved. It was horrible to contemplate the possibility that Ghonkaba would be killed by the force headed by his father and his uncle, and thereafter would be scalped by some member of the expedition.

"I will do my best," Ja-gonh said huskily, "to persuade Ghonkaba and his followers to see the light of day as we see it, and to return to their proper place beside their comrades."

His father made no reply; the interview was at an end. Ja-gonh and No-da-vo rose in unison, extended their left arms in farewell, and took their leave. Nothing in their manner or Renno's revealed that all three were grieving.

No-da-vo went off to join the warriors, who were still assembling, and Ja-gonh stopped at his house to pick up his weapons.

Ah-wen-ga awaited him there, as he had known she would, and they looked at each other in silence, with neither speaking. Memories flooded them, and they recalled the difficulties and dangers they had endured during their courtship, the good times and the bad they had known in the many summers of their married life together.

Had Ah-wen-ga chosen to bid her husband farewell publicly, neither would have shown emotion, and no physical contact would have been made. But in the privacy of their home, the rules of Seneca conduct were suspended. Ja-gonh stepped forward, took his wife into his arms, and held her close.

Ah-wen-ga clung to him, unmindful of the grease he had smeared on his skin, and a dry sob welled up in her and escaped. Ja-gonh held her still more tightly.

"May the manitous bring you back to me in safety," she said.

He smiled at her. "Never fear," he told her. "I will return."

"May you show mercy to Ghonkaba, and may he return with you," she whispered.

His reply was firm, and he was compassionate but unyielding. "May the manitous grant him the wisdom of opening his eyes to the error of his ways," he said. "Then I can return with him at my side with a clear conscience and an easy heart."

Ah-wen-ga nodded vigorously, ashamed of her momentary weakness. Her faith in her husband was all encompassing, and she knew he would do everything in his power to protect their son.

The departure of a large number of warriors ordinarily was a festive occasion for the women, the elders, the girls, and the junior warriors, as well as the smaller children. But this was no ordinary venture. The punitive expedition was unique in the long history of the Seneca nation, and so not one person ventured outside the palisade to see them off.

It was very quiet in the house of Renno after they had left. Deborah came in to build up the fire in the main room, and enjoying a special concession made to her because she was not a Seneca by birth or early training, she cooked breakfast indoors because of the raw weather. She baked corn bread, placing the meal on red-hot stones to cook, and after cleaning several large fish that El-i-chi had caught the previous day by making a hole in the ice, she proceeded to fry the catch.

El-i-chi soon joined her, and they exchanged a swift glance. No sound came from Renno's room, and both were concerned about him, knowing how trying his farewell to Ja-gonh and No-da-vo must have been. At last when the meal was ready, Deborah called him.

Both were surprised to see that he had covered himself with grease, making it plain that he was planning to go out-of-doors after breakfast. This was not part of his usual routine, but he might choose to explain later and tell them his destination.

His step was firm, his appetite was hearty, as usual, and he ate in a companionable silence.

The Great Sachem was a law unto himself, and no Seneca would dare to question him. But Deborah was still as much a New England colonist as she was a Seneca wife. "Where do you think you're going in this cold, Renno?" she demanded at the close of the meal.

Her daring amused him, as it always did, and he grinned at her. No matter what his rank, she was not impressed by it. "I intend to walk into the forest," he said.

It was evident that he was reluctant to say anything further, and El-i-chi would have let the matter drop. But Deborah was far more persistent than her husband. "It's far too cold," she said, "for a man of your age to wander into the wilderness. You've been fortunate so far this winter, and you've been healthy. But you don't want to take any unnecessary risks and catch the ague."

Renno's smile showed that he had taken cognizance of her warning, but that he chose to ignore it.

"There's a small clearing deep in the forest that I have known ever since I was a boy," he said. "I intend to go there."

El-i-chi understood at once, and his curiosity was satisfied.

But his wife still found herself unable to restrain herself and, in spite of her many years of marriage to El-i-chi, was not satisfied. "Why do you persist in taking needless risks?" she asked.

Renno realized that he would have to offer her a full explanation. "When you lived in Fort Springfield as the wife of a clergyman," he asked, "where did you go when you faced a grave problem that you could not solve yourself?"

She was bewildered but answered truthfully. "Why, to church, of course."

Renno nodded solemnly. "Ever since I was a small boy," he said, "I have gone to this clearing to pray to the manitous when a crisis in my life has occurred. It is my wish to go there this morning."

Deborah subsided meekly. "Would it be too much to ask you to wear the woolen sweater that I knitted for you, then?" she wanted to know.

Renno chuckled aloud. El-i-chi grinned, because, as he said to his wife, "It does not become the dignity of the Great Sachem to dress like an English colonist. The buckskin shirt that Renno wears is enough to protect him from the cold, especially as his skin shines with the grease of an animal."

Deborah's sniff was eloquent, and she devoted herself to frying more fish for herself.

Renno donned his elaborate headgear and cape before he ventured out. Carrying only his tomahawk and a pair of sharp, double-edged knives, he set out at once through the forest.

The few Seneca whom he encountered before he left the town greeted him quietly and then hastily stepped out of his path. They, like the members of his own family, were aware of the tension he was suffering on this eventful day.

At one time, Renno required no more than an hour's brisk walk to reach the little clearing in the forest that he favored. Now, however, the combination of his age and the snow and ice underfoot slowed him, and two hours passed before he reached the spot. It was just as he remembered it, and he looked around slowly, then stood erect, raised his head, and looking up at the sky, spread his arms wide.

"Hear, O manitous," he called in a loud voice. "Listen to the pleas of one who has been faithful to you and has lived according to your bidding and your will all of his days." He prayed fervently and long, asking the manitous to intercede with the gods of earth and sky, sun and moon, fire and water, to protect and shield his son and his grandson.

He continued to pray loudly at great length until his voice grew hoarse. Concentrating his entire being on the concepts that he was putting into words, he lost all consciousness of his surroundings, as so often happened to him when he came to this clearing. At last he finished his prayer and stopped speaking.

Only then did it finally occur to Renno that his long, earnest prayer had totally exhausted him. His head drooped, his arms and legs felt like lead, and he was overcome by a strong desire to sleep. He gave in to the urge. A bare spot in the clearing, where the sun had melted the snow, was dry. He stretched out and soon drifted into sleep. He knew he was secure, that he was protected by Seneca sentries and by his own sixth sense of impending danger in the wilderness. So he fell into a much deeper sleep than he otherwise would have done.

Gradually, even though he was sleeping, his vision seemed to clear, and he saw himself sitting in the very clearing where he slept. He knew then, in some way he could not fathom, that he was dreaming, and it seemed very natural when a rustling sound of dead leaves told him that someone was approaching in that dream.

He smiled in happy anticipation when he recognized the solid, burly figure of Ghonka, his father. In some inexplicable way, this was not Ghonka as he had been at the end of his life, when he had been foully murdered by a Huron, but was Ghonka of earlier years, when he had been in his prime. On his head he wore a bonnet identical to Renno's, and around his shoulders was draped a feathered buffalo cape that was just like Renno's, too.

One aspect of Ghonka's appearance was puzzling. Although he was very real and instantly recognizable, he seemed quite transparent: Renno could look through him and see the bare trees and the snow and the color of the evergreens.

He dreamed that he saw himself rise to his feet, and he and his father extended their left arms in a Seneca greeting.

"I have come to you, my son, from the hunting grounds that lie on the far side of the great river because of the need to exchange thoughts with you."

"I am grateful to you for this favor, my father," Renno answered. "I am sorely troubled, and my heart lies heavy within me."

"You grieve," the great warrior said, "because your

grandson—who bears my name—has defected and appears to deny the very essence of those things that make the life of a Seneca worth living."

"That is so, my father," Renno replied, "and I apologize to you with my whole heart for encouraging Ja-gonh to give your name to his son. You have the greatest name in all Seneca history, and your memory is revered by all who knew you. Small children are taught tales of your exploits, and you will be known and loved as long as the Seneca nation endures. I regret that your name has been soiled by your young descendant."

Ghonka held up a heavy hand to stem his son's flow of words. "Fear not, Renno, and may your mind be at rest," he said firmly. "Ghonkaba is impetuous, but his heart and mind are sound. He continues to wear the yellow and green war paint of his ancestors, and that paint will not be smudged with dirt. It is regrettable, of course, that he behaves in such a way as to seem to bring disgrace on our family and on our nation."

Renno took a deep breath and dared to ask, "How does my father know these things?"

Ghonka gave no sign that he even heard the question. "Every young warrior," he said, "goes through a period in his life when he rebels against the authority of his elders and the teachings of his tribe. That is the way of the young. That is an ordeal through which every warrior must pass, as surely as the adolescent boy passes the tests that enable him to become a man. He who bears my name will emerge from his present ordeal in such a way that credit will reflect on you and on Ja-gonh, as well as bring additional glory to my name."

Renno's heart beat more rapidly. "How does my father know these things?" he asked again.

"The manitous guard the secrets of those who have crossed the great river into the land of our ancestors," Ghonka said. "They guard these secrets well. I am not permitted to reveal how it is possible for me to foretell the future."

Renno opened his mouth to ask yet another question, and then closed it again firmly. His father had spoken, and that—as always—was the end of the matter.

Ghonka cocked his head to one side as though listening to something in the distance.

Renno strained hard, but in spite of his magnificent hearing, no sound was audible.

"Another, who has been waiting to see you, is eager for words with you now that you have opened your heart and your mind to communication with us," Ghonka said.

As Renno watched in astonishment and dismay, the figure before him gradually became fainter and finally vanished from sight. He felt great regret that he had been unable to bid farewell to Ghonka.

He had no time, however, to dwell on that, because another figure began to take shape before him, and he was elated when he recognized the familiar figure of Betsy, his wife. She, too, looked years younger than she had when she had died; she was in the prime of life, lovely and charming, vigorous and brimming with the femininity that made her so different from every other woman Renno had ever known.

He stared at the apparition, and then overcome by emotion, he started toward her.

Betsy held up a hand to halt him. "Come no closer,

my dear," she said. "If you do, I will be obliged to vanish at once. Strict rules apply to my appearance, and they must be obeyed to the letter. I have applied many times for this privilege, and it has only now been granted to me, so let us not abuse it."

Renno halted, his arms hanging limply at his sides. "I love you," he said simply. "I have loved no other woman in all of my days, and I long for the time when we will be reunited for all eternity."

"That time is not at hand yet," Betsy told him. "Your span of life in the land of the living is not yet ended, and you have functions to perform there. But don't worry, my love. The day will come when we will indeed be together again for all eternity. Time passes swiftly on your side of the great river. But when you have crossed it, you will discover, as I did, that time is meaningless."

Renno continued to stare at her, deeply shaken. Her blond hair shimmered, her pale eyes glowed, and she never had looked more desirable. "You have kept your suntan," he said, and was annoyed with himself for making such an inane remark.

Betsy's peal of laughter echoed across the clearing, and the sound was precisely as Renno had remembered it. "I knew that you would notice that," she said. "I made a small wager with Ena that you would mention it."

"You have seen my mother?" he asked anxiously.

Betsy nodded gravely. "Like all of us who love you, and who have crossed the great river, she waits patiently for the day when you will join us. Until that time comes, however, she begs you, just as I do, to enjoy your stay in the land of the living. You have everything that any man could want. Everything that any man could ask. You have great powers and un-limited authority. Your name is even greater than that of Ghonka, your father, and no man is more proud of your accomplishments than he is. You have won the affection, as well as the respect, of your people. Enjoy these last years that you spend with them."

"It is difficult to relish life," he said, "when the joy is blotted out by the thoughtless escapades of Ghonk-aba, the son of my son."

Betsy's smile was tender, and she indulged in a familiar gesture that he remembered well, brushing back a lock of her hair with two fingers. "How well do I remember," she said, "when I held Ghonkaba, my grandson, in my arms. He was only a baby then. Today he is a grown man and a senior warrior."

"I regret that he is also foolish," Renno replied. "He has caused heartache for those who are related to him and love him, and he threatens to bring disgrace on our heads."

Betsy shook her head. "This he will not do!"

She seemed to be repeating the assurances that Ghonka had given him, and Renno was reluctant to question her too closely, not wanting to be rebuffed again. But he could not resist asking, "You are sure?"

"I have come to you today," Betsy said, "because the grief in your heart is so heavy. I wish to relieve you of a terrible burden. Trust in the manitous as you have always trusted them, and they will continue to shield you and those whom you love. Ghonkaba has a great destiny to fulfill. It is a strange destiny, and he will walk a path far different from that taken by Ghonka and Renno and Ja-gonh."

Again Renno was very curious, but was afraid to

question her. What she meant by the strange or un-orthodox path that Ghonkaba would follow was beyond his comprehension, but he consoled himself with the thought that in time the mystery would be revealed to him.

Renno then looked at her longingly. "When will we two meet again?" It would not be seemly for him to admit how very greatly he missed her.

Not until Betsy smiled did he realize that her image was beginning to fade. "I am near you always," she said, her voice so faint that it was barely audible.

"Wait!" Renno cried, clutching at thin air. "Wait!"

His words echoed through the clearing—and Betsy, like Ghonka, was nowhere to be seen.

Renno, awakening suddenly from his dream, was alert at once, with the sleep vanishing from his system as surely as the apparitions had vanished. He was in the clearing, just as he had dreamed. Jumping to his feet, he examined the snow where Ghonka and Betsy had stood. He could find no marks on the smooth, white surface, nothing to show that anyone had been there.

Reflecting on his dream, going over it again in full detail, step by step, Renno was uncertain of how real it had been. He knew one thing for certain. He would obey the precepts of the manitous as Betsy had related them to him, and under no circumstance would he mention his dream to anyone. Not to El-i-chi and Ba-lin-ta, nor to Ja-gonh, his son.

It was enough, he thought, that he had enjoyed an unbelievably rare privilege, and he wanted nothing to interfere with the possibility that he might be granted a similar opportunity in the future. As he reflected on the two visits he had received in quick succession, he became increasingly convinced of their reality. He had dreamed infrequently in the past, but such dreams as he had ultimately proved to be valid, without exception, and he had sufficient faith in the manitous to know that they would not play tricks on him.

Consequently, he had no need to worry about Jagonh's expedition and the fate of Ghonkaba. Why, then, was he still so deeply concerned? He could not answer that question. The mysteries of life and death, of the afterworld, and of the world in which he lived, remained unfathomable.

Colonel Jared Carpenter, a lean, tough woodsman who lived in the wilderness north of the frontier town of Schenectady, was the commander of a regiment of New York militiamen. Although he had not had occasion to lead his men into battle in the current crisis, he had already acquired a considerable reputation. Quarrelsome by nature, Carpenter clung to the belief that no Indian could be trusted; this attitude had caused an endless series of needless disputes with his nearest neighbors, the Mohawk and the Oneida, as well as with the Seneca.

He was an experienced and competent military commander, however, a veteran of long standing who inspired confidence in his subordinates. Therefore, in spite of his shortsighted approach to the Indians, he retained his position as a district commander for the New York militia, even though the proximity of his position to the Mohawk caused much friction.

Colonel Carpenter traveled to Massachusetts in order to meet Kenneth Strong there after the general's return from the land of the Seneca, and they sat down together in a room within the old log fort, overlooking the Connecticut River, that protected the town from surprise attacks.

"The Seneca," General Strong said, "have rejected our offer of a punitive expedition to neutralize Ghonkaba and his followers."

"It seems to me," Carpenter said harshly, "that we should each send a regiment into the field, regardless of what the Seneca think. The young fool is dangerous, and he's got to be silenced."

"The Seneca," the general replied, "are planning to take care of him themselves. They're sending an expedition of their own to silence Ghonkaba and his followers, and to break up their unit."

The New Yorker scowled. "Did they put any promises in writing?"

"I saw absolutely no need for that," the general said. "Renno and Ja-gonh told me of their intentions, and I have no reason to doubt their word."

"You're more trusting, then, than I am," Carpenter said, still scowling.

Kenneth Strong looked at him unblinkingly. "Massachusetts," he said, "has been dealing with Renno of the Seneca for more than fifty years, and in all that time, he has always kept his word to us. Never once has he broken it."

"Maybe he's reliable because he's not a Natural by birth," Colonel Carpenter said. "So it's possible that he'll gag his grandson and hog-tie him before any real harm is done. God knows somebody has to do it!"

"I'm sure Renno will do whatever is necessary," the general said. "He's painfully aware of the need to neutralize the Iroquois rebels, more than we are."

"I shudder," the colonel said, "when I think of the potential harm those young Indian idiots can do. Their stance outside the fold will help to rob the other Iroquois of their desire to fight. No man is going to plunge into battle with fervor when his brothers and cousins and sons are facing him on the opposite side of the field."

"I believe you're taking an overly gloomy view," Strong told him. "To the best of our knowledge, the rebels haven't enlisted under the French banner."

"Then it's only a matter of time before they do!" Colonel Carpenter retorted. "You can bet the French didn't hand out muskets and ammunition to them because they admired the Indians' war paint!"

"Since the Seneca intend to handle this problem themselves," the general said, speaking quietly but firmly, "we have no choice, and we'll simply have to sit back and see what happens. We can't afford to antagonize the leaders of the Seneca nation and of the entire Iroquois League by acting hastily on our own."

"I'll tell you this much," the New Yorker said forcefully. "If I got my hands on Ghonkaba, I'd hang him from the nearest strong tree. And if the Iroquois didn't like it, I'd simply tell them I was sorry, but that was an expression of the way we civilized people in the colonies feel."

"Then it's fortunate for our cause," General Strong said, "that Ghonkaba is beyond your reach. We face a long and difficult war in the years ahead. Of all the wars we've had with the French, this promises to be the most difficult and prolonged. So we'll need the unflagging support of the Iroquois for a long time. It seems to me that a policy of justice, tempered with mercy and understanding, will serve us far better in the long run."

Jared Carpenter held his ground. "Ghonkaba is lucky," he said, "that he hasn't fallen into my hands. I'd make an example of him in no time at all!"

Chapter X

The expedition under Ja-gonh's command, twelve hundred strong, all of them veteran Seneca warriors, streaked through the forest toward the south. Several scouts found a salt lick and brought down a number of deer, enough to give the entire expedition fresh meat for several meals.

When they came to the land of the Erie, the scouting patrols were strengthened, but their traditional enemies were nowhere to be seen. It was possible, even probable, in the opinion of Ja-gonh and No-da-vo, that the Erie were aware of their presence, but wisely chose to look the other way. No tribe would willingly challenge such a sizable force of Seneca.

At last the unit arrived in the western lands that Virginia claimed, and there Ja-gonh slowed their pace. It was essential, he felt, to locate the rebels as soon as he could, but he didn't want to alarm them, either, by approaching them too rapidly.

Ghonkaba and his warriors knew nothing of the expedition's proximity until one night, while they were eating a meal at their campfires beside a swift-moving stream, a sentry hurried into the camp. He was a Seneca, and Ghonkaba assumed from his speed that he carried information of importance.

Ghonkaba looked up from his meal in concern, and the other leaders, each one representing an Iroquois nation, stopped eating, too.

"An expedition from the land of the Seneca is drawing near to us," the scout said. "It is commanded by the sachem of the Seneca, and the war chief, No-da-vo, is his deputy."

Ghonkaba knew immediately that any unit commanded by his father, with his uncle second in command, could be no ordinary expedition. "Where are they going, and what is their goal?" he demanded.

The sentry looked stricken. "I thought I was well hidden," he said, "but the scout—who was my instructor when I was a junior warrior—knew of my presence instantly. He beckoned to me and gave me a message that he asked me to take to you. The sachem of the Seneca is searching for us."

The leaders of the renegade group looked at each other in consternation. "What does he want with us?" the Mohawk asked.

"He did not say, and I did not inquire," the sentry

told him. "But it seems to me that an expedition larger than ours, made up only of Seneca, would march through the wilderness for only one purpose. They're on the warpath, and they intend to teach us a lesson."

In spite of their traditional impassiveness, the young Iroquois without exception were upset, and quite clearly were deeply concerned.

Ghonkaba, who felt as his comrades did, nevertheless was more adept at hiding his feelings. Certainly, this was a moment when it was necessary for him to assert his authority. "All of us remember that, as children," he said, "whenever we disobeyed the commands of our parents, we were sent into the woods and forced to remain there overnight, without food or water. Now we are men, senior warriors. We are too old to be punished like children."

The prospect of facing his father and his uncle in a direct confrontation sent chills up and down his spine, but he didn't care to mention that. "It seems to me that we must lose ourselves in the wilderness without delay."

His comrades agreed, rapidly and heartily.

"Pass the word through the camp," Ghonkaba said. "Put out campfires and remove all signs that we made our bivouac here. We must prove now that we are experts in avoiding detection. We must make ourselves invisible as we put greater and greater distance between us and the warriors of the sachem of the Seneca."

The rebels needed no urging; however, it was a waste of time and energy. Their efforts would have been effective if the rebels were followed by English or French colonials, and perhaps would have been effective against such nations as the Algonquian or Micmac.

But they were being followed by the wisest, shrewdest, and most experienced of all warriors. What was more, these were the men who had taught the young Seneca all that they knew.

So it was all too easy for Ja-gonh's scouts to pick up the trail of the fleeing band and to keep track of them wherever they went.

Ghonkaba tried to joke, in order to help keep spirits up, but his companions failed to see any humor. They had been floundering, unable to determine their next move after they had accepted the gifts of firearms and ammunition from the French and had left Fort Duquesne. Now, Ghonkaba told them, their goal must be throwing the Seneca veterans off their trail. After that, they could try again to find Colonel Washington's troops.

The rebels tried every trick they knew to put more distance between themselves and their pursuers, but finally they gave up and faced reality. They halted, established sentry outposts, and prepared for whatever might befall them. They did not have long to wait.

An emissary from their pursuers appeared and demanded an immediate interview with their leader. He was taken to the campfire of Ghonkaba and his companions, and the young Seneca was badly shaken when he recognized a senior warrior. He knew him well, and had been his frequent companion on hunting trips.

But the older Seneca gave no sign that he recognized his former friend. "I bring you the words of Ja-gonh, sachem of the Seneca," he said. "Hear them, O Iroquois, and ponder them well. Ja-gonh demands the right to appear before your entire company and to address you. If you do not agree, he and the Seneca who accompany him, all of them appointed to their posts by Renno, the Great Sachem, will be obliged to make war upon you and to force you to relinquish your arms."

Ghonkaba tried delaying tactics. "What is it that Ja-gonh wishes to say to us?" he demanded.

The Seneca messenger regarded him sternly. "The sachem of our people did not confide in me, as you should know. When he is ready to speak of what is on his mind, he will speak. Until then, no man knows what he will say."

Ghonkaba smarted under the rebuke and felt like a junior warrior put into his place. "Give us time," he said, "to discuss the message you have brought and to give you our decision."

"I will wait," the elder warrior said coolly and withdrew into the forest out of earshot.

The discussion was brief and succinct. "As I see the problem," the Oneida said, "we have little choice. We must fight. We know what Ja-gonh will say if we listen to his words. He will demand our surrender, and when we return to the lands of our own nations, we are certain to be punished."

"That's true," the Mohawk added gloomily. "We have broken a fundamental law of the Iroquois, and we would be required to pay for what we have done."

The Tuscarora and Onondaga agreed, and the Cayuga raised his voice timidly.

"Perhaps we should surrender now without waiting to hear an address by the sachem of the Seneca. Perhaps we should throw ourselves on his mercy."

The others promptly howled him down.

Ghonkaba said to him, "If we do as you suggest, we will be admitting our guilt, and it will be like standing up before our entire nations and admitting that we were wrong to rebel."

"We would be robbed of our manhood!" the Oneida declared fiercely, and the others were unanimous in their agreement.

The messenger was summoned, and when he reappeared, Ghonkaba spoke for all when he said, "We are not children who are rebuked by their elders when they stumble or make an error in judgment. Therefore, we have determined not to hear the thoughts of the sachem of the Seneca."

The older warrior looked slowly around the semicircle at the upturned faces of the rebels. "You have not forgotten the alternative, I hope," he said. "Then you and all of your comrades will be attacked by the force that is commanded by the sachem of the Seneca and his brother-in-law."

Ghonkaba folded his arms and, unable to look at the messenger, gazed steadily into the small fire that burned near his feet. "So be it!" he exclaimed.

"So be it," his comrades echoed.

The die was cast. The messenger raised his left arm in farewell and withdrew quickly.

No longer having a choice, Ghonkaba summoned all his comrades and brought them up-to-date on developments. Without exception, they knew they would be forced to defend themselves against a force of seasoned Seneca veterans in the morning.

The atmosphere hardly resembled the customary spirit of an Iroquois camp the night before a battle. No one looked forward to combat, no one rejoiced at the opportunity to exercise his manhood, no one boasted of the scalps that he would add to his belt.

The high hopes that they had entertained when they

joined Ghonkaba had vanished. The young warriors were trapped now, with the realization that they had maneuvered themselves into this untenable position.

Sentry lines were set up, and the young warriors, their resolve shaken, but aware that they had no alternative, settled down for an uneasy night's rest before the battle that inevitably would begin at dawn.

Ghonkaba rolled himself in his blanket, stretched out on the ground, and pondered the hopeless situation. He had erred, and not only had caused grave problems for himself, but had involved hundreds of fellow Iroquois. He still felt that he was right in his assessment of the English and French, that both were selfish and took advantage whenever they could of the Indians' gullibility.

On the other hand, he should have known that he could not with impunity defy the traditions of his people. The arm of the Seneca was long, and Seneca justice was swift and sure. Now, thanks to his folly, hundreds of fellow Iroquois would face almost certain death. He knew how methodical the veteran Seneca were, how remorseless his father and his uncle could be in battle.

So he had no illusions. Thanks to his mistake, scores of warriors, the cream of the younger generation of Iroquois, would die before the sun set again.

Eventually, in spite of Ghonkaba's abiding concern and his deep gnawing guilt, he became drowsy, and after a time, he drifted off to sleep.

Ghonkaba, who seldom dreamed, first realized that he was dreaming when a bulky figure materialized before him, and he saw a square-shouldered Indian warrior, with a thick barrellike chest and aquiline features. His dark skin glistened, and the gaze of his black eyes was so penetrating that Ghonkaba had to avert his own gaze. Belatedly, the young man realized that the visitor in his dream was wearing an elaborate bonnet and a feathered buffalo cape that resembled the symbols of his grandfather's exalted rank.

"You are Ghonkaba," the older man said in the tongue of the Seneca, his voice deep and commanding.

"I am," the young man whispered.

"Do you know me?"

Ghonkaba thought hard, and after a time, he guessed the man's identity. "You are my ancestor," he said hesitantly.

The older man nodded as he folded his arms across his chest. "That is true," he said. "I am the father of your grandfather. I am Ghonka, whose name you bear."

The young Seneca was thrilled beyond measure. For the great Ghonka to appear before him in a dream was a privilege that far exceeded his wildest expectation. "You do me great honor," he exclaimed, but his voice seemed faint.

Ghonka's expression remained unchanged. "I have not appeared before you in your sleep in order to honor you, young namesake," he said. "On the contrary. I have come because you are in danger of bringing dishonor on our family and on the Seneca, whom I love as I could love no other people on earth. Already there are those who believe you have acted to bring disgrace and dishonor on the Seneca."

Ghonkaba was so abashed that he didn't know what to say, so he remained silent.

"Thanks to your folly," his great-grandfather said, speaking as though he were pronouncing sentence, "many of our Iroquois comrades may die by the time the sun god rises high overhead tomorrow."

"I know," Ghonkaba said, and again unable to meet the piercing gaze of the older man, he covered his eyes with his hands.

"I formed the Iroquois League with good friends from the Mohawk, Oneida, Onondaga, Tuscarora, and Cayuga, when I was your age," Ghonka said severely. "We fought side by side against many Indian nations and against the French. We covered ourselves with glory as we accompanied our good friends, the English colonists, into battle. My son, Renno, has carried on the tradition that I started and has walked in my footsteps. Ja-gonh, his son, does the same. Both have brought great glory to the Seneca, to the Bear Clan, and to our own family. You have chosen a different path, and because of your choice, many young warriors may die tomorrow before they have a chance to reach their prime in life. If this tragedy occurs, the manitous, who have looked upon you with favor, will turn their backs on you. You will know disgrace and suffering such as you cannot imagine. I appear before you to tell you these things so that I may warn you against committing these follies when daylight comes."

Ghonkaba was badly shaken. Never had anyone addressed him so severely, and he was jarred to the very marrow of his being. "What can I do, Great Ghonka," he cried, "to avoid this fate and these terrible afflictions?"

For the first time, a somewhat softer note appeared in the voice of the warrior who had founded the family's fortunes. "Only one choice is open to you," he said. "You and your companions have elected to fight the Seneca of Ja-gonh, my grandson. If you do, you

231

will suffer a defeat so severe that it will be remembered for all time. In only one way can this catastrophe be avoided."

"How?" Ghonkaba pleaded. "Tell me, and I shall do exactly as you bid me!"

Ghonka studied him for what seemed like a very long time before speaking again, and when he raised his voice, it was unyielding. "As a Seneca warrior," he said, "you have the right to challenge the leader of the force that will attack you to personal, individual combat. If you fight him, the two expeditions will have no need to meet in battle. The winner of this combat will win the day for his comrades. He who loses will lose the day for his comrades."

Ghonkaba was horrified. The prospect of meeting his own father in hand-to-hand combat was contrary to every loyalty he had ever felt, and the mere idea was too terrible even to contemplate. "Surely there must be some other way," he said. "Surely in your wisdom you know of some honorable choice that I can make!"

Even as he spoke, the figure of Ghonka became fainter.

"Wait!" Ghonkaba begged. "Do not leave me now. Stay and help me in this hour of crisis!"

The figure of Ghonka disappeared, and immediately Ghonkaba was awake.

He realized that his face and body were bathed in cold sweat. Rivulets of perspiration ran down into his eyes, blinding him, and when he moistened his lips, they tasted salty.

His dilemma, he realized, was frightful. If he persisted in the present plan, he and his comrades would fight a battle they could not win. The outcome was already ordained, and in that event, his name would suffer disgrace forever. If he should escape death—and he suspected that the manitous intended to spare him so that he would suffer a worse fate—he would be drummed out of the Seneca nation. He would be regarded with contempt by his former compatriots and by their brothers of the other Iroquois nations. He would be forced to spend the rest of his days as a scorned outcast, unable to hold up his head in the company of fellow Indians.

His alternative was to meet Ja-gonh, his father, in individual combat. It would be easy, he supposed, to pretend to fight, to give up the struggle, and allow his father to kill him. But that would solve no problems. Everyone who witnessed the event would know that he had lost deliberately, and a new pair of champions would be summoned to represent the two sides in combat. If he fought Ja-gonh, he would have to do his best to win.

Ghonkaba knew he had no real choice. Regardless of the outcome, regardless of the strain it would place on him, and presumably on his father, he had to meet Ja-gonh in individual battle, which only one of them would survive.

With his decision made, Ghonkaba was stunned to discover that morning was fast approaching. The first streaks of dawn were appearing in the sky, and the whole camp was stirring. Young warriors were taking their places in the wilderness, finding what hiding places they could at this season, and they needed no instructions as they awaited the onslaught.

Consulting no one, Ghonkaba strode forward to the limits of the perimeter that his men occupied and cupped his hands.

"Hear me, O Seneca," he called loudly. "Hear the

words of Ghonkaba, son of Ja-gonh, and grandson of Renno."

His own men, stunned by his action, stared at him in silent curiosity. He could not see their foes in the forest, but a faint rustle in the dead leaves, here and there, told him that his words were heard.

"It is wrong," he called, "for brother to fight brother, and cousin to fight cousin. It is wrong that many should die and many should be maimed because of a dispute within my family.

"My quarrel was with Ja-gonh, my father, and it is right that I face only him. So I challenge him to personal combat. If he wins, the Seneca expedition will triumph and the losers will do their bidding. If I win, my companions are free to do as they wish."

He paused, taking a deep, shuddering breath, and his palms felt clammy. "Does Ja-gonh, sachem of the Seneca, hear my words?" he shouted. "Let him respond to this challenge!"

Ja-gonh and No-da-vo, already sick at heart, listened in wonder to his words.

"He's right," No-da-vo said. "He has found a way to avoid terrible bloodshed. But in order to spare warriors of courage on both sides, a terrible penalty must be paid. Ja-gonh, do you have the strength to meet your own son in personal combat?"

Ja-gonh was tight lipped, his only sign of emotion. "I must accept his challenge," he answered sadly. "No other way is open to me. As sachem of our people, I am compelled to make this sacrifice.

"I ask but one boon of you," Ja-gonh continued. "If I fail to survive this effort, or if I kill Ghonkaba, but am myself injured, I leave to you the awful task of telling Ah-wen-ga what has occurred. This is one time in which there will be no need for you to give strict regard to the truth. She is a wife, and she is a mother, so speak to her with words that will give her the least burden to bear."

"I will do as you request," No-da-vo assured him.

Ja-gonh then cupped his hands, and shouted, "Ja-gonh, sachem of the Seneca, accepts the challenge of Ghonkaba to personal combat!"

He stripped to his loincloth. The day was bitterly cold, with a hint of snow in the sky above the mountains, but he shook his head when No-da-vo somberly offered him a gourd containing grease.

"I will not spread the oil on my body," he said. "I have no need for it."

No-da-vo had no need to ask his reasons. In a free-for-all fight to the death, every small advantage was precious, and it was customary for a Seneca, as for members of many other tribes, to grease their faces, bodies, and limbs prior to combat. Ja-gonh wanted to take no advantage against his son and was indifferent to the possibility that Ghonkaba would be anointing his own body with grease. The gesture was as reckless as it was bold, and No-da-vo, who would have liked to persuade him to reconsider, knew better than to interfere. The duel to be fought was so unorthodox that no one should stand between father and son. He wished for some other way to solve the problem, but could find none. Either the blood of father or son would be spilled before peace was achieved.

Meantime, Ghonkaba's comrades surrounded him, regarding him in silent admiration. Only a warrior of almost superhuman courage would offer to fight his own father—the leader of his tribe, as well—in order to spare the lives of others, and they did not know what to say.

The young warrior stripped to his loincloth in a silence that seemed to grow heavier by the moment. Someone offered him a container of grease to protect his almost nude body, and the entire company was surprised when he refused. "Ordinarily I would anoint myself," he said, "but I am fighting him who sired me, and I want to take no unfair advantage of him."

When he was ready, he was handed his tomahawk, a superbly balanced weapon, and a long, metal knife with a bone handle, which he slid into his belt. These were the only weapons he was allowed.

A clearing near the two encampments in which there was little snow was the natural site for the combat, and there the warriors of the two opposing expeditions gathered. The atmosphere was heavy and somber, unlike the carnivallike air that often prevailed at such fights. Everyone present knew that he was witnessing an occasion that would be remembered in the annals of the Seneca and of the Iroquois for all time.

Relatives gazed at each other across the open space without giving any sign of recognition. No greetings were exchanged, and the rebels stirred uneasily as they approached the scene. They knew they were responsible for this dreaded confrontation, but they could do nothing to halt it.

Ja-gonh appeared, and although he wore neither his elaborate bonnet nor his cape of office, he walked like a true sachem, his body erect, his head high. In middle age, he had strong, sinewy muscles in his arms, shoulders, and back, and his legs resembled the trunks of trees. By any standards, he was a formidable opponent. He took no notice of the braves who surrounded the clearing, and he moved into the open area, lightly swinging the deadly tomahawk that he carried in one hand.

Many who saw him wondered if he intended to hurl it the moment that Ghonkaba appeared. That was his right and within the rules of the encounter, and judging from his demeanor, he was prepared to do whatever was necessary to win the struggle.

Unsmiling, Ghonkaba approached the open space slowly, walking with a heavy tread. His legs felt as though they were encased in sheaths of heavy metal, and his heart pounded so hard that he felt a singing sensation in his ears.

He caught sight of Ja-gonh, also unsmiling, unyielding, and felt like bursting into tears, something he had not done since he was a boy of three summers.

Memories almost too painful to recall flooded the young warrior's mind, filling him with a bittersweet nostalgia. He remembered being taught to hunt by Ja-gonh, and recalled vividly how he'd been instructed in the mysteries of tracking deer and other wild animals. He remembered Ja-gonh's painstaking, careful lessons in how to make himself invisible in the wilderness, how to survive in this very special world that the Indians called their own. When he had been hurt, his father, while soothing him, had taught him to sustain his injuries like a true Seneca warrior. When his behavior had been mischievous, Ja-gonh had punished him for his transgressions. But not once in all the years of the young warrior's childhood and adolescence could he recall his father having lost his temper.

Under no circumstances, Ghonkaba knew, could he raise a hand against this man.

Ghonkaba threw down his tomahawk with such

force that the cutting edge bit into the frozen ground and the weapon was securely fastened there. Then, in almost the same motion, he snatched his knife from his belt and drove it, too, into the ground, point first.

Ja-gonh watched him, his impassive face revealing no emotions.

Ghonkaba's eyes met his father's, and they looked hard at each other, neither of them wavering.

Standing with his arms hanging at his sides, Ghonkaba spoke loudly in a hoarse, but clear, voice. "Hear me, O sachem, and heed my words, my brothers of the Seneca and of the Iroquois. I proposed a duel between me and Ja-gonh as a way of preventing the shedding of much blood. But now, in the moment when I come face-to-face with Ja-gonh in combat, I cannot face him. My arm will not obey my will, and I cannot use a tomahawk, a knife, or any other weapon against him. If I have failed my brothers, I am regretful. But I would offend the manitous, and the gods themselves, if I raised my hand to strike him who sired me."

It was very quiet now in the wilderness. More than two thousand braves were gathered, but no one spoke, no one moved.

"I do not expect to escape unscathed and unpunished," Ghonkaba continued. "I issued my challenge in a fair fight, and I am willing to take the consequences. Therefore, my father, deal with me as you will. If you take my life, I ask only that you do it swiftly so that I may be relieved of the burdens of remorse that I feel."

Ja-gonh took a step toward him, and even the hardened No-da-vo drew in his breath and held it.

Ja-gonh's face revealed none of the inner turmoil he was suffering. Grasping the bone handle of his tomahawk firmly in his right hand, he raised his arm slowly above his head.

Even though only warriors accustomed to battle were present, an almost visible shudder ran through the assemblage.

Then, suddenly, Ja-gonh dropped his tomahawk to the ground, flinging it from him as though it were a living rattlesnake. He plucked his wicked double-edged knife from his loincloth and deliberately threw it to the ground as well.

Taking another step forward, he raised both arms, put them around his son, and embraced him.

Critics of the Iroquois—especially the Seneca—who have claimed that these nations were noted for their cold-hearted lack of human feelings, are badly mistaken. A low sound, like that of a collective sigh, swept through the gathering as the warriors watched. Some found the scene too painfully emotional, and turned away. Others stared in fascination at father and son, knowing that a legend was in the process of creation.

Ja-gonh continued to embrace his son. No-da-vo had a duty to perform and stepped forward. "Inasmuch as a challenge to individual combat was issued by Ghonkaba, and then was withdrawn, I proclaim Ja-gonh, sachem of the Seneca, as the winner. Under the rules of our people, sacred for all time, he will name the condition that the losers must obey, and they will heed his words."

Ja-gonh released Ghonkaba, who took half a step backward, his fists tightly clenched, his head bowed.

Ja-gonh surveyed the warriors, looking across to the far side of the clearing where the young rebels had congregated. "Hear me, my son," he said, "and hear me, O Iroquois who have followed Ghonkaba into this wilderness. We are warriors, all, and it is presumed that you are at home in the forests, and know where you are and what you are doing. But you and Ghonkaba, together, have traveled into a strange and remote wilderness that is alien to all of us."

Listening intently to his father's words, Ghonkaba knew he was right and was amazed by his own response.

"You carry firesticks given to you by the French. So I will issue all of you a fresh challenge. Let any warrior who considers himself expert in the use of a firestick stand forward. I will confront him with any warrior from my command, chosen at random, who will use the bow and arrow of our ancestors, and I will wager that he who wields the bow and arrow will prove to be the better shot. I will even grant you the right to name the terms of the wager. Let him who is expert stand forward!"

Ghonkaba well knew that he himself was proficient in the use of firearms, but his father's challenge did not apply to him. He had been taught the use of rifles, muskets, and pistols when he was a small boy. But he was unusual among the company in that respect. Therefore, he remained silent and allowed the drama to unfold.

"My fellow Seneca, and fellow Iroquois," Ja-gonh said, "you have allowed yourselves to be duped by the wily French. We have only narrowly averted a great tragedy."

The young warriors looked at each other uncertainly. The sachem of the Seneca was no ordinary man, and they were willing to listen to him, willing to be convinced that he was telling them the truth.

"The French," Ja-gonh said, "spent but a small

amount of gold for the muskets, the lead, and the gunpowder they have given you. Perhaps the sum of money they have expended does not seem trivial to you. But I have lived for many moons in the land of the French, and I know I speak the truth. Their king lives in a great palace, a single building large enough to hold all the members of an Iroquois nation. So I do not exaggerate when I tell you that they do not miss the gold that they have spent on these firesticks that they have given you."

His listeners were more than receptive now. He could sense that they were gradually becoming convinced of the authenticity of his words.

"What did the French gain for the expenditure of their paltry gold?" Ja-gonh demanded. Then, in a thundering voice, he declared, "They have completely disrupted their foes. The Iroquois, the one group of nations on whom the English colonists can depend for help in their war with the French, are in turmoil. It would be impossible for us to provide the English with warriors today, because we are engaged in an absurd fight among ourselves. All this the French have accomplished! Unless we act firmly and swiftly to reverse the tide, they will win the war. When we are enslaved by them—and make no mistake about it, we shall become their slaves—we can look back upon your mistake as the incident responsible for their great victory."

Ghonkaba slowly raised his hand, continuing to look at his father, and then turned to face his comrades. Raising both arms, he cried, "My father, the sachem of the Seneca, is right in all that he says. I was wrong. Very wrong. I almost caused a great catastrophe through my stupidity. The manitous have taken pity on me, and thanks to the intervention of my grandfather's father, my eyes are open at last."

Ja-gonh and No-da-vo wondered what he meant by the reference to Ghonka, but were willing to bide their time. This was not the moment to interrupt.

"I place myself under the authority of the Seneca, and I swear fealty to my people and to their sachem. What he commands, I will do. What he forbids, I will avoid." Ghonkaba turned again and faced his father.

Ja-gonh reached out and grasped him by the shoulder, his manner approving. "You have heard the words of Ghonkaba, who led you into the wilderness," he said. "Let all who would follow his example step forward now and join with my company as we march, once again, to the north. Let those who would go their own way depart at once, and let them never again come within sight of any living Iroquois!"

His meaning was very clear, and without a single exception, the rebels capitulated. A few of them started toward the opposite side of the clearing, moving rather hesitantly at first, but within moments, a full-fledged stampede was under way.

Ja-gonh had accomplished a near-miracle. Not only had bloodshed been averted, but the dissidents had returned to the fold and would march off to war beside their brothers in the Iroquois nations.

Chapter XI

A stranger in the land of the Seneca, unaware of the drama that had just unfolded, would have assumed that the seasoned veterans under Ja-gonh's command had just won a great victory. All the Seneca turned out to greet the warriors, and the mood was festive. Bonfires burned brightly in the fields outside the palisade, and sides of buffalo and venison were roasting for the feast that would be enjoyed by all that night. Squaws wore their best doeskin dresses decorated with porcupine quills, and the unmarried maidens donned their newest rawhide headbands. Junior warriors were allowed to wear war paint in honor of the occasion, and smaller children also participated in the holiday. The elders and the medicine men marched out in full regalia to greet the returning warriors, and as the drums throbbed, beating a lively tattoo, the returning braves marched through the gate and into the town.

Ah-wen-ga and Deborah stood together a short distance inside the gate, both of them inconspicuous.

But Ja-gonh, marching at the head of the combined units, his intricate bonnet instantly marking his presence, noted them at once. His eyes met his wife's, and the most subtle of communications passed between them. Only another Seneca versed in the delicate subtleties of human relationships would have perceived that they were speaking to each other silently.

All is well, Ja-gonh was reassuring her.

May the manitous be praised, Ah-wen-ga's eyes said.

Directly behind the sachem marched No-da-vo, dour and solemn as always.

Third in the procession was Ghonkaba, whose step was light, and who acted as though the weight of the world had been removed from the burden that he carried. He caught sight of his mother, and broke tradition by grinning at her openly. Not for him was the impassivity so typical of the Seneca.

Ah-wen-ga's eyes looked suspiciously bright and moist. She turned to Deborah and said something.

Deborah, not being a Seneca by birth, was free to react as she pleased, and she laughed aloud, clapped her hands, and blew Ghonkaba a kiss.

The young warrior was mortified, but at the same time delighted. His foolhardy escapade had not robbed him of the sympathetic love and understanding of either his mother or his great-aunt, and the opinions of both meant a great deal to him.

The procession disbanded quickly, and the participants became busy greeting their wives and parents, and relating the events that had led to reconciliation between the veterans and the younger warriors.

Ja-gonh's work was not yet done, and instead of going to Ah-wen-ga and Deborah, he headed straight for the council lodge, with No-da-vo and Ghonkaba close behind him.

In the lodge, Renno, in full regalia, sat in front of the ceremonial fire, with the principal medicine man on his left and El-i-chi on his right. Other medicine men were gathering, as were the war chiefs and elders of the nation.

As his first order of business, he ordered that all the French muskets be confiscated and placed under guard in a central storage area. Then he turned ponderously to the principal matter before him and the council.

Ghonkaba's trial was about to begin in earnest. The council of the Seneca intended to pass judgment on him.

Renno's face showed neither relief nor pleasure when he saw his grandson, hale and hearty, standing beside his son. Showing no emotion, he appeared as impersonal and remote as were the medicine men and the war chiefs who sat behind him.

Ja-gonh halted, raised his left arm in greeting, and respectfully extended a salutation to the Great Sachem of the Iroquois.

Not waiting for a response, he launched into a recital of the incidents that had led to the reconciliation with Ghonkaba and the rebels.

The elders leaned forward; the war chiefs and the medicine men, forgetting their impassivity, were deeply impressed.

When Ja-gonh had finished, No-da-vo picked up the recital and related a number of additional details.

When he, too, had finished speaking, Renno directed his gaze toward Ghonkaba, his pale eyes so penetrating they seemed to pierce the young warrior to his marrow. "Stand forward," the Great Sachem commanded.

Ghonkaba obediently moved two paces closer to him.

"What caused Ghonkaba to change his heart and his mind? He was determined to fight his father and the veterans of the Seneca to the death, yet he made an offer that prevented bloodshed. What caused him to do this?"

Ja-gonh and No-da-vo had asked the same question in a variety of ways but had received no satisfaction. Ghonkaba had been reluctant to reveal the mysterious experience that had resulted in such a great change in his attitude and behavior.

Now, however, he had no hesitancy in speaking freely. Putting the elders, the war chiefs, and the medicine men out of his mind, he concentrated on his grandfather, seeing no one else in the lodge. Then he cleared his throat.

Ghonkaba revealed that during the night before the battle was to take place he had dreamed a curious dream, and that in it, he had been visited by the father of his grandfather.

Renno instantly leaned toward him and raised a hand, jabbing a forefinger. "Describe this man to me," he commanded. "Tell me all you can remember about his appearance."

Ghonkaba obeyed, and recalling the wraith vividly, he described his visitor in infinite detail.

Renno was unyielding. "Now tell me about his voice," he insisted. "Describe it for me."

Ghonkaba tried so hard to recapture the sound of the visitor's voice that beads of sweat dotted his forehead.

Renno was satisfied at last. "It is true," he said. "I believe that you were privileged to enjoy a visit from the great Ghonka in your sleep. Relate to me the substance of your talk with him."

Every word of that encounter was engraved on the young warrior's mind, and he had no difficulty in repeating the conversation word for word.

Not a sound violated the stillness of the council lodge when he had finished. Renno, obviously very deeply touched, adjusted his feathered bonnet, then folded his arms. Apparently he needed a few moments to gain control of his emotions, even though his face revealed no feelings.

"When this meeting of the Seneca council comes to an end," he said, "I wish the medicine men to accompany me to the place where the Great Faces repose. There, I wish to offer thanks to the manitous, and most of all, to Ghonka, my father, for intervening. To him belong the credit and the glory for the happy ending to the unprecedented rebellion of the young."

Ja-gonh lifted his head and spoke. "At last I know what transpired to change the heart and mind of Ghonkaba, my son," he said. "I, too, am grateful to Ghonka, my grandfather, and I will come with you to the place where the Great Faces rest, so that I, too, may thank Ghonka, my grandfather. But there remains a problem that can be solved only by the living."

Everyone stared at him. Ghonkaba knew what was coming, and braced himself.

247

"It is true," Ja-gonh said, "that not one warrior of the Seneca or of any other Iroquois nation has suffered death or injury as a result of the incidents that have caused us so much turmoil. But the rebellion of my son, and its consequences, which included his attracting a following among those of his own age in our own and other lands, created great turmoil. It was necessary to send a strong expedition to conquer the rebels and bring them to their senses. Our allies, the English colonists, have been badly upset by these events. Their good opinion of the Iroquois, and particularly of the Seneca, has been damaged. We cannot hold our heads up with pride."

Most of his listeners nodded from time to time, confirming the validity of his words. But Renno sat motionless as though carved of stone, listening, but in no way reacting.

Ghonkaba, watching him closely, marveled at his ability to conceal his reactions so completely, even from these, his close relatives and his intimate lifelong associates.

"The manitous stayed my hand and prevented me from killing my son," Ja-gonh said. "But it is not right that he should go free and unpunished after the upset and the turmoil he has caused."

"That is true," No-da-vo said in a low voice.

Others in the assemblage agreed, too, and there seemed to be little doubt that the entire leadership of the nation was of one mind.

Only Renno remained reserved, choosing to keep his own counsel.

"I freely admit to my father, the Great Sachem of the Iroquois, and to my brothers of this council," Ja-gonh said gravely, "that I am not able to make a decision that will make it possible for me to act in this matter. I have prayed to the manitous for their help and guidance, but they have not elected to help me. So, with the approval of the council, I must abdicate my responsibilities and ask my father, the Great Sachem of the Iroquois, to decide in my stead, what punishment is to be inflicted upon Ghonkaba, my son, for his transgressions."

At a gesture from Renno, No-da-vo stepped forward and polled each member of the Seneca council in turn.

The vote was unanimous. All were in favor of turning the problem over to Renno, who now looked into the fire and spoke softly. "My blood," he said, "flows in the veins of Ghonkaba, my grandson. When I look at him, I see my own reflection—as I looked when I was his age—returning my gaze. I have led this nation and all the nations of the Iroquois for many years. We have enjoyed many successes. But I cannot pass judgment on my own flesh and blood with a clear mind and a clean heart. Always, I would fear that I was too lenient because Ghonkaba is my grandson. Or I would worry that I would try to overcome that problem, and that I would be too stern and too strict in my judgment. If Ja-gonh, my son, who is your sachem, cannot determine what is to be done, it is not right to burden me with that responsibility."

His listeners were surprised and upset by his words.

"The manitous have made it plain," he went on, "that they are keeping close watch over those who are descended from the great Ghonka. Ghonka, himself, has shown us his favor by appearing before my grandson. I do not wish to offend the manitous, or my father, by passing judgment upon my grandson. But I cannot leave the task undone, nor can I allow him to go unscathed." He looked at Ghonkaba, his gaze uncompromising.

The young warrior quailed inwardly, but in spite of himself, he could not help but admire his grandfather.

The Great Sachem beckoned to Ja-gonh. "You will form an escort," he said, "and you will travel to Boston. You will take Ghonkaba with you. There you will hand him into the custody of General Strong, the commander of the colony's militia. He is a fair man, a just man, and a wise one. He knows the Seneca and our ways. You will give him the authority to deal with my grandson as he sees fit and to inflict such punishment on him as he deems appropriate. This is only fitting, because the people of his colony, together with those of the other English colonies, were imperiled by the rebelliousness of Ghonkaba. They who shared the danger shall have the satisfaction of sharing also in the punishment!"

In the silence that followed, Renno wrapped his cloak of high office more closely around him, rose, and left the council chamber.

Ghonkaba, taking his place in the procession that filed out of the lodge, was of two minds. He was relieved, knowing that his grandfather could have inflicted severe punishment on him for his rebellion. On the other hand, he had no idea whether General Strong would be severe or kind in his treatment. One thing he did know, and his blood raced more rapidly at the thought: no matter what his fate, no matter what might befall him, he would soon see Beth Strong again.

Kenneth Strong sat behind the desk in his study

looking out at the melting snow on the Boston Common, and puffed reflectively on a *segaro* imported from the Spanish West Indian Islands. He listened attentively, but without comment, as Ja-gonh, seated opposite him, explained the strange mission that had brought him to Boston.

"I realize," the sachem of the Seneca said, "that my father's decision—made without consultation with you—places you in a strange and somewhat embarrassing position. So if you don't want to accept responsibility for Ghonkaba, or if you don't know how to treat him, I'm relying on you to be candid. All you need do is to tell me that you can't accept the responsibility, and I'll report accordingly to my father, and we'll find some other solution."

"Not at all," General Strong replied. "I'm slightly perplexed as to how to proceed, but it strikes me that the least I can do for good friends and loyal allies is to relieve you and Renno of an impossible burden. I believe that Ghonkaba probably can be rehabilitated. What are your thoughts on this?"

"I quite agree with you," Ja-gonh replied. "He was rebellious, as all young men are, but I never saw anything vicious in his attitude, and he certainly meant no harm. I believe he sincerely regrets causing the problems that he created. You may want to talk to him yourself about all this."

The general shook his head. "On the contrary. I feel that the less discussion I have with Ghonkaba about his transgressions, the easier it will be to work out a tenable arrangement with him."

A tentative half smile appeared on Ja-gonh's face. "You accept the assignment, then, impossible though it may seem to be?"

"Of course!" Kenneth Strong said heartily. "There's been no question about it since you first outlined the problem."

"I'm indebted to you," Ja-gonh said soberly, "as is my father."

"I think not," the general said. "If this plan works out, as I hope it will, Massachusetts Bay will again be indebted to the Seneca. I must concede, however, that the events of the past few months have strained relations between the colonies and all the Iroquois because of the uncertainty created as to your reliability, and I am grateful beyond measure that the matter has been concluded."

While the two men conferred, Ghonkaba sat in the drawing room with Beth Strong. She had asked him what had happened, and he told her the story, in full, of his ill-fated expedition and its ignominious end.

It was not easy for him to speak freely, to admit to her that he had been misguided and foolish, but he forced himself to be candid.

He looked at Beth and was surprised when he saw a hint of tears in her eyes.

"You seem to be ashamed of yourself," she said softly, "and act as though you've committed a great wrong. You're badly mistaken. What you've done is a wonderful thing that required great courage and a demonstration of real character. If I were you, I'd hold my head high. You have every reason on earth to be proud of yourself!"

Ghonkaba knew she was sincere, but it was plain that she did not understand, and he explained the situation in which he now found himself, telling her about his grandfather's decision and the reasons behind it.

She clasped her hands together. "I can't speak for

my father, of course, but I think I know how his mind functions, and I'll be very surprised if he does not react as I have. There's no need, really, for you to worry."

Ghonkaba was heartened by her attitude. She was the first person he had encountered who made him feel like holding his head high.

Impulsively, Beth reached out and placed a hand on his arm. "I just want you to know," she said, "that no matter what my father decides, I am standing with you, and I am proud of what you've done. I hope you'll share that pride with me."

"It seems to me," General Strong said to Ghonkaba, "that you have paid quite fully for your mistakes. But your grandfather and your father don't agree with me, and I've consented to do what I can to help you rehabilitate yourself—in your own eyes, as well as in theirs. I want to make several things clear to you. You are not my prisoner. I intend to treat you as an associate who will, at the appropriate hour, stand shoulder to shoulder with us in the war against the French. Is that agreeable to you?"

Ghonkaba assented instantly. "It is, General," he replied. "Not so long ago I would have had to refuse your generous offer because I could see little reason for sympathy with the English colonies. But my attitude is beginning to change now, and I have committed myself to the cause of the Seneca and the Iroquois League. I am willing, therefore, to act in whatever capacity you may choose for me."

"Good!" the general replied. "When spring comes and the armies go into the field, I'm sure there'll be use for you. As I've told you, I feel you've already paid heavily for your admitted transgressions, which, frankly, I reviled as they were occurring. You've now started on a new career. Look at it in that light."

Ghonkaba did as he was bidden, but time hung heavily on his hands. General Strong was occupied with administrative affairs of the militia, and Beth was busy writing letters. In fact, she spent so many hours each day at the task that Ghonkaba saw very little of her. One afternoon he voiced his curiosity.

"I'm doing volunteer work for Sam Adams," she informed him. "He developed this wonderful idea, and it's worked out even better than I thought it would. He formed a Committee of Correspondence and he encouraged the formation of similar committees in all the other colonies."

Ghonkaba was still mystified. "What do these committees do?"

"We exchange information," Beth explained. "We keep each other informed on political matters, on military affairs, and on anything that we think will interest the people of a sister colony. Sam writes the initial letter for Massachusetts Bay, and then I copy it—again and again. In fact, if I may be so immodest as to say so, I have tried, with some success, I think, to improve some of those letters in the process of copying them! We're now corresponding with eight other colonies on a regular basis, so that gives me a great many letters to write."

Ghonkaba thought privately that these efforts were a waste of time, but he was too polite to say so.

Beth sensed his skepticism. "I know of nothing that has proved as valuable to all the English colonies as the committees," she said. "We've been accustomed to going our separate ways, all of us. Through the work of the committees, we're finding we have a great many interests in common, particularly now that we're preparing for an all-out war with France. Here!" She gathered papers from various piles on her desk and thrust them at him. "This is a copy of the letter that I'm currently sending out. And here are some replies we've received. You're at least somewhat familiar with affairs in New York, Pennsylvania, and Virginia, so these letters from the Committees of Correspondence in those colonies will show you what we're doing."

Ghonkaba read the communications and, in spite of his dubious attitude, was deeply impressed: what Beth had told him was true; the developments in one colony in the military and political spheres affected the other colonies as well.

What he found especially enlightening was the concern among all the committees for the Iroquois and the war effort. Without exception, the writers had repeated the latest stories about Ghonkaba's rebels—and each expressed the hope that all would be straightened out to the satisfaction of the Iroquois, and to the benefit of both the tribes and their colonial allies.

Ghonkaba came to regard these letters as extraordinary, and realized eventually that his conclusions about the English colonies were totally false. He had been mistaken in his assumption that they were indifferent to the fate of the Iroquois nations. On the contrary, they showed deep concern and an abiding interest in the welfare of the Indian tribes. What he had considered a lack of interest had been caused by poor communications.

As he had already started to learn, these English

colonials were very different from the French. Their attitudes, their sympathies, the very way they approached their problems of day-to-day living, were very different. Sam Adams had thought of a simple device that had brought the English colonies together and was knitting them into a unified whole. Until now, Ghonkaba had paid little heed to the newspaper editor, thinking him a rather shallow and slovenly person. Now, however, he recognized his genius. If the colonies continued to depend upon each other, they were far more likely to win the war with France, and Adams's contribution was easily as important as what any general could accomplish on the battlefield.

Ghonkaba was troubled because the style of living that he saw in the Strong home was too easy and luxurious. No one hunted in the wilderness for meat to put on the table, and no one went fishing; neither Beth nor the maids grew crops and scoured the forests for herbs and wild vegetables. Instead, Beth went marketing several times a week in the open stalls at the bottom end of the Common, and Ghonkaba, who accompanied her one day, was astonished to see meats and vegetables, fruit and fish laid out, ready to be purchased, cooked, and eaten.

Even the preparation of meals, though complex, was made easy for them. A large stove was located in the kitchen outbuilding, behind the main house, where one of the maids prepared three meals a day, cooking in pots and pans that fried or boiled or performed other strange conveniences that seemed part of the luxurious way of life that he basically scorned.

When a man wanted new shoes, he went to a bootmaker, just as a tailor provided him with suits, and a haberdasher was responsible for his shirts, stockings, and underclothes.

Once the young Seneca overcame his astonishment at the complexity of civilization, he began to feel increasingly restless. Sensitive to his moods, Beth asked one day, "Something is troubling you—what is it?"

"Life in a city is too easy, too soft," he replied. "This war will be fought in the wilderness, and I, as a Seneca brave, will engage in it. I pray to the manitous that I am not being robbed of my strength, and that I will be able to give a good account of myself when the time comes."

Beth, bewildered, questioned him further and at last understood. "I don't think you need be overly concerned," she told him. "When the time comes, you'll be able to do your part."

"But when will that time arrive?" he wanted to know. "I ask the general this question every day, and he just tells me to be patient. It is the way of my people to show patience. But my situation is not that of other Seneca. I feel that I must prove my worth, and this I cannot do spending my days in a warm house, eating my fill, and sleeping in a soft bed every night."

Beth made an effort to improve his spirits. "For whatever this is worth," she said, "I understand how you feel, and I sympathize with you."

He looked at her, saw her blond hair gleaming in the light of the fire blazing in the hearth, became aware of the intense concern in her eyes, and he was deeply moved. "Why does it matter to you what becomes of me?" he asked. "What difference does it make to you?"

Beth was incapable of replying to his question, and her face became almost scarlet.

The realization dawned on Ghonkaba that she was

far from indifferent to him. He had hoped that she was learning to care for him, but had not really considered it seriously because he preferred not to be disappointed. But even one unaccustomed to certain aspects of colonial civilization could not be totally blind to what was going on.

As an honorable man, a Seneca warrior of standing, only one further request was possible. "Do I have the permission of Beth Strong," he asked, "to pay court to her?"

Beth became even more flustered and struggled for self-control. "If I were alone," she said, "if I answered to no authority other than my own, I would grant you that right freely, and with all my heart. But I cannot forget that I am the daughter of a major general, and knowing my father, I am certain that, if you go to him with your request, he will reply that you must first fulfill your obligation to the Seneca."

Ghonkaba's hopes had soared briefly when she had first started to respond, and then his heart sank. She was right, he knew, and her father would be justified in demanding that he prove his worth before he was granted permission to court Beth. He bowed his head. "I will wait," he said, and never had it been so difficult for him to speak a few words.

Colonel Jared Carpenter of the New York militia, sent to Boston on a liaison mission to plan the coordination of the activities when the spring came, was immediately closeted with General Strong.

Scarcely had they reviewed the international situation—both of them unhappy because England, continuing to procrastinate, had not yet declared war on

France—when Colonel Carpenter spoke his mind with typical bluntness.

"I gather that you have the young Seneca rebel, who created all the trouble, under your wing these days?"

"I do," Kenneth Strong admitted. "As a matter of fact, he's living in my house until we go into the field. He'll be enormously useful to us as a guide and scout, no matter where we're forced into action."

Carpenter raised an eyebrow. "Do you actually intend to use this renegade as a scout for your regiments?" he demanded. "How can you possibly trust him?"

"If I'm any judge of character," the general replied, "I know very well that I can trust him."

"I hope you'll pardon me for saying so, General," Carpenter declared, "but I think you're behaving like a damn fool. You can lose one hell of a lot of valuable lives if you've misjudged this Natural."

A debate with a man as bigoted and as firm as Jared Carpenter was a waste of time, and General Strong tried to change the subject. He started to discuss the mobilization tables of various colonies that had been consolidated.

But Carpenter was not to be denied his say. "Please turn the whole problem over to me," he asked. "And I will promise you that I'll make short work of it. In no time at all, there will be no problem."

"What do you have in mind?" the general inquired, knowing the probable answer.

Colonel Carpenter's smile was thin lipped. "First off," he said, "I'll haul the rascal off to New York in chains, making damned sure that he can't escape. Once I cross the colonial borders with him, I'll string him up promptly enough!"

259

"You're joking, of course," the general said.

"The hell I am!" Carpenter struck his host's desk smartly with the open palm of his hand.

"For one thing," Kenneth Strong rebuffed him, "Ghonkaba now sincerely regrets the furor he created and is eager to make amends for it. For another, he's the son of Ja-gonh, the sachem of the Seneca and the grandson of Renno, the Great Sachem of all the Iroquois. Do you think we would endear ourselves to either of them if we hanged the young man?"

Carpenter's shrug was eloquent. "You surprise me, General," he said harshly. "You're as bad as Schuyler and some of the others who are always inclined to favor the Indians. I say to the devil with the Seneca and with the entire Iroquois League! We can't really rely on them, and they're worthless to us."

General Strong disagreed violently, but he could see nothing to be gained by becoming involved in an argument. He had intended to invite Colonel Carpenter home for noon dinner, but he hastily changed his mind. The presence of Ghonkaba would be sure to create trouble, and he didn't want the young Seneca to be unduly exposed to needless problems.

One thing was certain: it never would be possible to assign Ghonkaba to a position as a liaison officer dealing with the New York militia. It would be wise to keep as great a distance as possible between him and Jared Carpenter.

In all the years of Ah-wen-ga's marriage, she had never taken advantage of her position as Ja-gonh's wife or as Renno's daughter-in-law. Nor had she ever used her status as the daughter of Sun-ai-yee, the late sachem of the Seneca, for her personal benefit. But the present situation was so far beyond her control and so worrisome to her that she finally decided—with great reluctance—to go to Renno and discuss the matter with him.

Applying a sootlike substance to her eyes, and daubing her lips with red berry stain, Ah-wen-ga changed into her porcupine-quill-beaded doeskin dress, and biding her time, went to Renno's house at an hour when she could expect to find him at home and alone.

She arrived in time to see her father-in-law engaging in an activity that few Indians knew about. He was writing quite rapidly and with great dexterity in a large leather-bound book, using a quill pen and a jar of ink. She halted, then asked timidly, "Do I interrupt at a bad time?"

Renno looked up from the pages he was inscribing and smiled at her. "This estimate of the strength of the Iroquois forces can wait. I'm honored by this visit, my daughter."

"I'm honored that you've chosen to receive me, my father," she replied carefully, and bowed her head low when he motioned for her to sit. As she sat opposite him, she felt his pale eyes, so similar to her husband's, yet so much more penetrating, boring into her.

"You have not come to pay homage to me, I know," Renno told her, "and since I sat before your fire last night and ate the food that you prepared, you know I am in good health and in sound spirits. Therefore, you have come to me because you are troubled. What brings you here, my daughter?" He, like Ghonka, his father, always brought problems into the open without subterfuge.

261

"Many years ago," Ah-wen-ga said, "the goddess of fertility, who has been so bountiful in the crops that she has given to the Seneca, determined in her wisdom that Ah-wen-ga was to bring but one child into the world. Well do I remember the jealousy in my heart when Goo-ga-ro-no, the sister of my husband, had three children, all daughters. I was sorely troubled, and my own father having left the land of the living and crossed the great river to join his ancestors, I went to Renno with my problem."

"I remember the occasion well," Renno said, and those who knew him only as a harsh and uncompromising ruler would have been surprised by his gentle tone. "I told you to be content, my daughter, because your one child would outshine all other Seneca of his generation. This I believed at that time, and this I still believe."

"I, too, believed it with all my heart until Ghonkaba behaved like one who eats the wild grasses that grow near the elm trees and loses his wits. Then, my belief returned to me when Ghonkaba came home with Jagonh and his rebellion was at an end. Now he is being punished for his transgressions and must live in Boston, to be banned from the land of the Seneca until he performs deeds of valor. But there are no conditions that will make possible such deeds and win him the respect of his people once again. Is there not any way in which the Great Sachem can mitigate this punishment? I do not question the wisdom of the Great Sachem, and I do abide by his will. It is just that the uncertainty of waiting is most difficult for me. I do not want it to deprive me of reason, as I sometimes fear that it might!"

Renno considered the anxious mother's concern, and

her plea. He was sympathetic to her, and as a parent himself he wished that it were possible to grant her request. But finally he gazed at her stolidly and in the kindest of tones told her with evident great regret that the punishment unfortunately must stand. It would be improper for the Great Sachem to show favoritism for a grandson.

Ah-wen-ga bowed in acceptance of his judgment, and withdrew. Her continued patience was extremely difficult in the weeks that followed. In vain, she awaited a great battle that would enable Ghonkaba to rehabilitate himself, but no such engagement took place. Worry continued to keep her sleepless night after night, and she came to fear that her son and his problems would be forgotten, lost in the maze of larger and more pressing issues.

That, however, was not the case. Only General Strong knew how often Colonel Carpenter petitioned for custody of Ghonkaba in order to deal with him summarily.

The general, in fact, was beginning to regret his willingness to take charge of the young brave. No military action was possible until the colonial high command could discern the intentions of General Montcalm, and until then, Ghonkaba had little to occupy him. This meant that he and Beth were thrown more and more into each other's company, and the general thought he could see a romance beginning to develop under his nose, while he could do nothing to counteract it.

Then, late in March, when the bitter New England winter was drawing to its close, a totally unexpected break occurred. General Strong received a letter from Colonel Washington in Virginia. The young officer-surveyor-farmer had learned of Ghonkaba's presence in Boston from a liaison officer, and was requesting the transfer of the Seneca to his own staff. Washington wrote,

He impressed me very favorably during his period of service with me, and I am eager to renew our relationship. Therefore, I will be eternally obliged to you if you can see fit to send him to me.

This, a relieved Kenneth Strong thought, was the perfect solution of how to deal with Ghonkaba. He spoke to him that same day, and was pleased to learn that Colonel Washington's enthusiasm was reciprocated. "He is a commander of great wisdom and courage," Ghonkaba said, "and I will be honored to work with him again. I know he will win many battles against the French."

General Strong wrote a candid letter to Colonel Washington, and after acceding to the request, he outlined, in detail, the reasons for Ghonkaba's presence in Boston. Knowing that the Seneca would make far better time than would any messenger he might send with his reply, the general gave the letter to Ghonkaba to deliver himself.

The night before Ghonkaba's departure, the general retired to his study to attend to some letters, and Beth was left alone in the drawing room with the young Seneca.

"I'm pleased for you," she said. "I know how relieved and happy you must be that you're going to have some action at last."

"I have had a long wait with nothing to keep me occupied, as I'm sure my grandfather anticipated when he decreed my punishment," Ghonkaba replied. "I have learned a great lesson, and that is one of the reasons why I'm glad I had this experience. I've had another reason, too." He hesitated, took a deep breath, and averted his gaze as he blurted out, "I've had this wonderful opportunity to get to know you better."

She felt blood racing to her face and was annoyed by her lack of self-control, but he paid no attention to her state. When dealing with a serious subject, he concentrated on it completely. "It is good," he said, "that I shall be occupied for a number of months with Colonel Washington in the coming campaign. We have not spoken of our feelings, even though each of us has recognized them. Now I think the time has come for us to weigh our situation carefully."

Beth was unprepared for his candor.

"If the daughter of the commander of the militia were to marry a Seneca brave," he continued, "her life would be complex and she would face many difficulties. So would he. So it is wise to ponder on this matter and to decide whether a marriage is worth the great effort that would be necessary."

She didn't care to reveal that actually she had been thinking of little else lately.

"My grandfather and grandmother faced the same problem," Ghonkaba told her, "and for them it worked out very happily indeed. But I am sure that they were required to exercise patience and wisdom and self-control countless times over the years."

His consideration touched her deeply.

"It would not be fair to you, or to me," he added, "if I were to ask you now to marry me. This is not a question that can be settled quickly or easily. When I return from Virginia and I have won enough honors— as I hope to do—in order to be restored to my rightful place in Seneca society, then I will propose to you. Until then, just know that I love you. I have not fallen in love with you easily, or because I wished to. It happened to me, and I could do nothing to prevent it."

"I feel the same way," she murmured.

"I know," he said, "and for that reason, perhaps it is just as well that we're going to be separated now. It is better, far better, that we separate for a time so that we may think clearly and reach a decision that could affect us for the rest of our lives."

She was reassured as well as pleased by the maturity that he displayed.

Ghonkaba moved a step closer to her and, with a touch remarkably gentle, cupped her face in his hands and kissed her.

Beth felt an almost overwhelming urge to throw her arms around his neck, draw closer to him, and prolong their kiss. But she knew that it would be wrong to tempt the fates. They might lose the control they were both exercising and live to regret the consequences.

So she stood with her arms at her sides, and when he released her, she took a backward step.

Ghonkaba saw that her eyes were damp, and his heart immediately went out to her even more. This was real love, apparently, and he marveled at his own feelings.

With Toshabe, the Erie prostitute whom he had visited fairly frequently, he had felt very much at ease, able to communicate without difficulty. But this was a far different emotion. He no longer cared about himself. His entire being was directed toward satisfying this young woman who had come to mean so much to him.

"I know you will do well in Virginia," Beth told him, "and I'm sure that our problem will be solved properly. By the time you've completed your service there, we'll know what to do."

Chapter XII

Colonel George Washington was in bivouac with his regiment not far from Williamsburg, and was delighted when Ghonkaba appeared after his long, rapid trek through the wilderness.

They shook hands, both demonstrating warmth as well as admiration, and Washington said, "I needed you as a scout, and now that you're here, I'm ready for any action that may develop!"

"I was not expecting to hear," Ghonkaba replied bluntly, "that you think well of me after the way I failed you."

Washington was puzzled. "How did you fail me?"

269

"When we last saw each other at Fort Necessity, you sent me back to Governor Dinwiddie and General Ridley with a plea for reinforcements. I was unable to persuade them to supply you with the troops you needed to avoid a surrender."

Washington smiled faintly and shook his head. "It was not your fault," he assured the young Seneca, "that no troops were forthcoming. None were available. But General Ridley has told me how eloquently you begged on my behalf. I've also heard from the militia in Pennsylvania, in New York, and in Massachusetts that I had an eloquent, persuasive advocate, and all three colonies have apologized profusely because they were not able to send help. So dismiss that matter from your mind. You did far more than duty required."

Ghonkaba was pleased but thought, nevertheless, that the colonel was exaggerating. He appreciated the officer's candor when Washington went on to observe, "Though I understand that there was some question as to your breach of authority in the Seneca nation, that has no bearing on me and I am entirely willing to overlook it."

Washington was now fully occupied with a pressing matter. "You've arrived here just in time," he said. "We're expecting Major General Edward Braddock and his corps of British regulars to arrive in Williamsburg any day now, after quite a delay."

Ghonkaba brightened. "They're coming here?"

"Yes, unfortunately," Washington said. "Governor Dinwiddie corresponded with him, and General Braddock, instead of waiting until he arrived in the New World, estimated the situation here for himself, and then made up his mind how best to deploy his troops.

Apparently he decided while still in England that he would come directly to Virginia. What he has in mind, I don't really know—but I'm uneasy."

Ghonkaba looked at him with curiosity.

The colonel explained. "France has been waging an undeclared war for almost a full year. We—and our sister colonies—have adopted the attitude of waiting until the French make a move before we try to counter it. I'll grant you this leaves the original initiative up to them, but under the circumstances, it does seem to be the best posture we can assume.

"We outnumber them only when you add our Iroquois allies to our total manpower, and we are best advised to assume the defensive, rather than strike out on our own."

That was the approach also of the Seneca, and Ghonkaba approved of it.

"I don't know whether General Braddock agrees with that philosophy," Colonel Washington said, revealing his uneasiness, "but we'll soon find out. He wrote to the governor and General Ridley from London, stating that he was going to bring his troops directly to Virginia, so it appears that he has some specific plan of action in mind. We'll find out soon enough. Certainly, he has had ample opportunity in these past months to prepare such a plan. I know of no other good reason for the prolonged delay in his departure."

A few days later, British navy troop transports arrived at the peninsula across from the Norfolk harbor, and there General Braddock and his regulars, two thousand strong, debarked and soon began their march inland. When word was received at Williamsburg that they would arrive in the town within a very short time,

Governor Dinwiddie, General Ridley, and Colonel Washington, together with their staffs, went to the parade ground. Ghonkaba was present as a member of Washington's staff and tried to make himself inconspicuous as he stood among the young officers.

Lively music was heard in the distance, and soon the newcomers came into view, preceded by a regimental band, resplendent in scarlet uniforms.

Edward Braddock, a husky, red-faced officer, dazzling in the scarlet and gold of a major general, rode at the head of his troops on a handsome white stallion. Behind him were grouped the officers of his staff, also mounted, and then, on foot, came the two thousand troops.

"My reaction is that he's a martinet," one of Washington's officers observed softly during a lull in the playing of the fife and drum corps. The others nodded, and even Ghonkaba could see what he meant.

The troops had marched several miles, but every bronze helmet was burnished, boots were polished so thoroughly that they looked like glass, and the brass buttons on the red-coated figures shone. The white webbing that crisscrossed their tunics in the front and rear had been scrubbed clean. Without exception, the regulars were immaculate.

Colonel Washington shook his head in wonder. Never before had he seen troops polished and primped to such absolute perfection.

The Redcoats marched like automatons, and when the brigade adjutant ordered them to halt, they stopped as one man.

The sight was impressive, but Ridley and Washington exchanged quick glances. It appeared to Ghonkaba that they were worried; he suspected that they had their doubts about the general's ability to fight according to wilderness principles.

Governor Dinwiddie was invited to inspect the honor guard, and when he went through the timeworn ritual, Ghonkaba was overwhelmed by the precision. Muskets were raised and lowered to precisely the same level in unison; never had he seen troops like these. Many of the colonial militia were made up of splendid fighting men, and this was particularly true of Washington's regiment of riflemen. But for impressive appearance they couldn't compete with these regulars. If their performance equaled the superficial aspects of their splendor, Ghonkaba reflected, it would be a pleasure to go into battle side by side with such troops—and under those circumstances victory would seem to be assured.

Governor Dinwiddie took General Braddock off to his residence for noon dinner, having invited General Ridley and Colonel Washington to the meal, as well.

Tom Ridley considered the time ripe to inquire, "It appeared to us that you were coming with a campaign already worked out. Am I right, General Braddock?"

Sipping from a goblet of claret, his favorite wine, Edward Braddock smiled condescendingly. "Of course, my dear Ridley," he said. "I make it my business to prepare in advance for every move. I've decided that we're going to march on Fort Duquesne. By 'we' I mean my regulars, of course, but with as many regiments of your militia as you can muster, and also any Indians who happen to be allied to you, provided they're worth using."

It was plain that he had little regard for any fighting men except his own regulars. His attitude was insufferable, but neither Ridley nor Washington could express himself because Braddock outranked them.

Governor Dinwiddie, under no such restriction, raised one eyebrow and said, "I'm somewhat surprised, to put it mildly. May I ask why you want to attack Fort Duquesne?"

Braddock's expression and tone of voice made the answers self-evident. "The military reports from General Ridley state that Duquesne is a key to the American West," he said, "and what's more, you made one futile attempt to drive the enemy out, and failed. For the sake of overall morale, as well as to raise civilian spirits, I have determined that a victory over the French will be most salutary."

Colonel Washington started to speak, thought better of it, and refrained.

General Ridley, however, was becoming so irritated that he could not remain silent. "We may be playing directly into the hands of the French if we attack Duquesne," he objected. "It's a difficult nut to crack, and it's far easier to defend the fort there than to topple it. What's more, I think you'll find that up in Quebec, Montcalm will be delighted!"

General Braddock indicated his skepticism. "How so?" he asked.

Washington could restrain himself no longer. "We here in Virginia," he said, "together with our colleagues in Pennsylvania, New York, and Massachusetts, the other major colonies, are trying to avoid providing the French with a basic initiative this coming spring. With all due respect, General Braddock, I fear that we'll be doing exactly what Montcalm must be hoping we'll do if we try to take Fort Duquesne now. I happen to be the officer who failed in the attempt to reduce it, and I'll tell you flatly, we would have our hands more than full."

"There's a world of difference, Colonel," General Braddock replied loftily, "between your colonial militiamen and the professional soldiers who wear the uniform of the king. You'll see that we shall topple Fort Duquesne in short order."

He was so positive, so firm in expressing his opinion, that it seemed impossible to discuss the strategy further, much less to argue against his position.

To the consternation of Tom Ridley and the horror of George Washington, Edward Braddock prepared for his campaign against Fort Duquesne precisely as if his target were some French city on the continent of Europe. "There's no difference between military tactics on this continent or the continent of Europe," he said rather disdainfully. "Apply sound principles, and you win battles."

The two colonial officers poured out their troubles to Governor Dinwiddie, and he in turn tried in vain to reason with Braddock. "I think, General, that you may be discounting the influences of the wilderness. I've spent years in Virginia, and I've watched our militia go out on many campaigns, but in no way do their activities resemble what you're planning."

Braddock was firm but patient. "Your Excellency," he said, "I mean you no disrespect, but I strongly urge you to concern yourself with problems of civilian government. I owe my success to principles that I've always followed in the field, and I assure you that they shall succeed again."

Dinwiddie saw nothing that he could do to force the general to change his plans. Appointed military commander in chief on the authority of King George II, he had the authority to make his determinations final. Going over his head would require a petition to the Crown itself—a long, laborious process that undoubtedly would create great ill will, and probably would result in little effect on the actual situation.

"I want a supply train," Braddock ordered, "similar to what I'd need if I were attacking the French fortress of Lille." It was necessary to obey his whim, so scores of four-wheeled carts were provided, each pulled by a team of mules, and in these were loaded food and medical supplies, ammunition, blankets, cooking utensils, and tents. The wagons contained everything that the troops' officers thought would enable the men to survive the inhospitable wilderness.

Even the order of march that Braddock wanted was unorthodox. Colonel Washington's regiment should have led the corps because the militiamen were familiar with the territory, and were experts in wilderness lore.

General Braddock decreed that the expedition would be led by his fife and drum corps, followed by his two thousand regulars. Washington's regiment of Virginia riflemen, which he obviously considered an inferior force, would bring up the rear. He had decided against bothering to enlist the aid of any Indian tribe. "Savages can't be expected to fight as civilized men do," he explained contemptuously, "and they might be too difficult to control. Therefore, we'll not bother with their services."

"I'm afraid, Tom," Colonel Washington said in confidence to General Ridley, "that this campaign may be disastrous."

"We've done our best to convince Braddock of the difference between campaigns here and in Europe," Ridley said, "but now he's going to have to find that

out for himself. Meantime, keep your powder dry—
and salvage what you can!"

When Ghonkaba was presented to Braddock, the
general made it plain that he wanted nothing to do
with the Seneca, though the brave had a startling command of the English language and was introduced as
General Ridley's cousin. In the general's view, all Indians were barbarians.

Ghonkaba was very distressed by Braddock's attitude, but Colonel Washington managed to calm him,
explaining that the Virginians would rely on such information as he gleaned for them, even if the regulars
did not.

Early in the morning on the day that the expedition
started out toward the northwest, the fife and drum
corps struck up a lively air, and the companies of regular army troops did their best to maintain their ranks
as the open area began to give way to the forest.

The Virginia riflemen, spreading out, took cover
among the trees as they always did. Behind them at the
very rear of the line of march came the supply wagons.

Ghonkaba was stunned when he observed this, and
he immediately sought out Washington. "Is the English
general mad?" he demanded.

"Well, I'll put it this way, Ghonkaba," Washington
said. "General Braddock knows what he wants and refuses to take any advice."

Ghonkaba was aghast. "The music-makers," he said,
"advertise the presence of the whole column in the
forests. The English troops, instead of wearing buckskins, are wearing their brilliant uniforms, and instead
of spreading out, are trying to maintain the appearance
of a single marching line. As for their unprotected sup-

ply wagons in the rear, their presence is an invitation to the French to cut them off."

"I'm aware of everything that you say," Colonel Washington replied, "and I agree with you totally. Unfortunately, I'm a colonel and the commander of a militia regiment. General Braddock has told me that, in his eyes, I should be demoted by two grades and rank no higher than a major. He ignores everything that I say to him, just as he's ignored the urgent advice of General Ridley. Even the governor has had no effect on him."

"Only today," Ghonkaba informed him, "I was told by some local Indians that three Erie warriors were seen in the vicinity. That means that the spies and scouts for Colonel de Jumonville must be fully aware of the English intentions. What do you think de Jumonville will do when he learns of this?"

Washington laughed harshly. "It requires very little imagination to figure out exactly what he'll do," he said unhappily. "He'll rely heavily on the main bodies of the warriors of both the Erie and the Miami, and he'll kill as many of those poor devils from England as his sharpshooters can bring down!"

"What can be done to prevent such a catastrophe?" Ghonkaba demanded.

"I can't answer that question," Washington said, "but we certainly will be obliged to do everything in our power to hold our losses to a minimum, and to take as heavy a toll of the enemy as we can."

As Ghonkaba moved alone to a position far in advance of General Braddock's column, he could hear the fifes playing and the drums beating. The insanity, in which he was himself participating, was almost too much for him to bear, and he once again revised his opinions of the English versus the French.

French soldiers were wise, he decided, just as the English colonists were wise, and both groups adapted well to prevailing conditions, learning the mysteries of the forest. The English, however, were headstrong, stubborn, and appeared to be stupid beyond belief. He had created enough trouble for himself by defying the English allies of the Iroquois and wanted nothing more to do with them, and now it seemed that his instincts had been right. Braddock might be a great war chief in the land of his birth, but here, in the wilderness, he was a tragic laughingstock.

The corps followed the now-familiar route, marching generally westward to the banks of the Monongahela, and then following the powerful stream to the north toward Fort Duquesne. As they penetrated deeper into the wilderness, Ghonkaba's apprehensions increased. The fife and drum corps continued to play its daily serenades, while the Redcoats marched on as though on a broad, paved road that led to the castle of Lille.

Eventually, Ghonkaba began to discover signs of enemy forces, and each night he faithfully reported his findings to Colonel Washington.

"The colonel was right," he said, "when he told me that the French would rely on the braves of both the Miami and the Erie. This they have done, and hundreds of men of both nations are in the forest. Also, the French are well represented."

"How many men do you estimate are gathered under the enemy banner?" Washington wanted to know.

Ghonkaba thought carefully. "I would need another two or three days," he replied, "to confirm this, and I am not sure that we shall have that much time. But I would estimate more than one thousand troops and a thousand braves. In those figures I could be mistaken, of course, by several hundred men, but I don't believe I am."

"In that case," Washington said, "we have something of an advantage at the moment."

"We hold no advantage," Ghonkaba said.

Washington informed the commanding general that enemy forces were gathering in the forest, ready to pounce.

Braddock listened briefly but ignored the information. "I've seen no sign of them," he declared abruptly. "I haven't heard their band, and I have yet to observe their troop formations."

"I assure you, General, you won't see or hear either," Washington told him. "Soldiers fight here in a far different manner than in Europe."

Braddock's face reflected his lack of patience with uninformed military men who failed to understand the universality of warfare.

Two days later, the corps lined up in its customary formation for the day's march. The fife and drum corps struck up a stirring air, and the British infantrymen fell in behind them, maintaining rows as rigid and as straight as the forest would allow. The Virginia riflemen were nowhere to be seen, because their commander declined to expose them to unnecessary risks, and the supply wagons, as always, stretched out at the rear of the formation.

Cooking fires had been extinguished, and the bivouac area was left behind. The day's march was under way.

But as the musicians were playing, a strange phenomenon occurred. Arrows flew from the left and the right of the marching men, and instantly the martial music came to a discordant halt. According to the report that Washington submitted later to Governor Dinwiddie, one musician in three immediately fell to the ground, mortally wounded.

Almost simultaneously, the rattle of small arms fire broke out at the rear of the column from the left, the right, and from directly behind the wagons. Here the technique was different—and chilling. French sharpshooters, expertly concealing themselves in the forest, picked off the drivers of the carts, and as these men died, the wagon train came to a halt.

Men in buckskins soon appeared and disappeared with the wagons, one by one. Even in this maneuver, the French demonstrated their skill and cunning. No two wagons were hauled off in precisely the same direction. They merely vanished into the wilderness, and the bodies of the drivers were thrown onto the ground.

Edward Braddock did his best to compensate with raw courage for his bad judgment.

Without hesitation, he formed his British regulars into the customary "hollow squares" that they used when fighting a battle. Then, riding rapidly through the forest, so that all his men could see him, he ordered them to open fire.

His men were bewildered by the command, since they were fighting an unseen enemy. But they, too, did their best and, standing shoulder to shoulder, sent volley after volley crashing into the forest. Their efforts had little effect, and death continued to take its heavy toll on their ranks.

Perfect targets in their glittering helmets, with their

brass buttons in bold relief against their uniforms, they succumbed to French marksmen and to the Erie and Miami warriors.

Yet their ranks did not break. When a man fell, those on his left and those on his right closed ranks and kept the hollow square intact. These disciplined troops had been taught well and didn't panic.

Only later, long after the battle ended, could the extent of the damage suffered by the corps be known. Out of two thousand men, fourteen hundred were casualties—most of them killed outright. Rarely in the history of the British army had such a slaughter been inflicted on troops in the king's uniform.

The French cunning knew no bounds: the first of the English to be destroyed were the company-grade officers, the captains, lieutenants, and ensigns who were in immediate command of the troops. Without them, their men were rudderless, not knowing what to do next.

Staff officers were prime targets, as well, but no one attracted as much fire as Braddock himself. French sharpshooters and Indian warriors alike directed their fire at him, but for some time he seemed to live a charmed life.

His horse was shot out from under him, but he immediately mounted another, the gelding of an aide who had been killed. Again he lost his horse, and again he transferred to another. Standing in his stirrups, he waved his sword and repeatedly shouted, "Hold firm, lads! Hold firm!"

The superstitious Erie and Miami attributed superhuman qualities to the English commander. The French, being better educated, concentrated instead on trying to bring him down, and eventually his luck ran out.

Two bullets smashed into his head simultaneously, jerking him to a standing position like a puppet being manipulated on a string. He died instantly, but even in death he showed both courage and grace. Still clutching his sword in his hand, he slumped forward in his saddle, but somehow retained his seat.

When this was called to the attention of Colonel de Jumonville, he ordered his troops to cease their attack on the general, so it happened that Edward Braddock ended the battle as he had begun it, seated in his saddle, his feet securely fastened in their stirrups.

While the battle developed, and disaster after disaster was piled onto the British regulars, Colonel Washington and his Virginia riflemen were busy trying to avoid being overwhelmed themselves. The young colonel hardly could feel satisfaction in seeing his prophecies come true. On the contrary, his heart sank, and his one hope was to minimize the losses that his colleagues were suffering.

His troops, requiring no instruction in the basics of frontier fighting, used whatever natural cover they encountered. They spread out, with no two men within arm's reach of each other, and they remained close to the ground. Ignoring the snow, they stretched out prone and held their rifles on propped elbows.

Ghonkaba found himself fighting alongside the regiment, and became part of it. The battle had erupted just as he returned from scouting the enemy positions and giving a report to Washington. Now, chin down, he took up the fight beside the Virginians.

Unlike them, he preferred his bow and a quiver

filled with arrows to a long rifle. But his technique and theirs were identical.

When they saw a flash of fire from an enemy musket or watched an arrow speeding toward them, they located its source as best they were able. Then they waited until another shot was fired, and this enabled them to pinpoint the source. From there, it was relatively simple for the militiamen to dispose of a foe with their own rifles, or for Ghonkaba to accomplish the same result with his bow and arrow.

The toll of the enemy they exacted was not spectacular but was steady. The casualties inflicted on the French and on their Indian allies mounted even as the slaughter of the regulars continued.

Their officers issued no orders and none were needed; every man knew what was expected of him and did his part.

Colonel Washington behaved as did his subordinates. Ghonkaba, who was close enough to the colonel to see him and observe his movements, marveled at his fierce dedication to duty.

His sword remained in its sheath, and he, like the lowest-ranking private soldier in the regiment, used a long rifle to accomplish his ends. He fired shot after shot at the enemy, and the deafening silence at the receiving end of his fire proved that he had struck his mark.

Ordinary mortals would have grown weary and sickened by the incessant fighting and the death hovering over the battlefield. But the regiment was not composed of ordinary men. These were militiamen trained in the most exacting of schools, the frontier, and they knew that they had to triumph or die.

Ultimately, de Jumonville's aides called his attention

to the heavy casualties being inflicted on the French forces by the invisible regiment. He immediately concentrated his attention on wiping out that stubborn pocket of resistance, and ordered both his French troops and the Erie and Miami to direct their fire at the area of the forest where the Virginians were concealed.

Now the regiment truly came into its own. For each blow it received, it delivered two in return, and it struck with the force and fury of a heavy sledgehammer. The fire of the riflemen was almost incredible; they seemed to sense the presence of the enemy in the deep woods, and their bullets sought out their foes and disposed of them.

Ghonkaba matched the riflemen shot for shot, inflicting casualty for casualty. As the sole Seneca on the battlefield, he felt it was essential to uphold the honor of his people and the martial glory of his nation. This he did, performing with such precision and skill that Colonel Washington was additionally impressed. In his report after the battle, when he singled Ghonkaba out for notice, Washington wrote,

Never before have I seen an Indian warrior as skilled in the use of a bow and arrow as was this Seneca, whose feats matched those of our best regimental sharpshooters.

Time passed so swiftly that only a few noticed that the sun now stood directly overhead. The remnants of the British corps, still not understanding wilderness warfare, nevertheless continued to demonstrate courage, and their feeble, sputtering fire responded to the continuing French attack. But the Virginians were forcing the French to pay a heavy price for their victory. The price was so high that Colonel de Jumonville decided to break off contact with the foe while he remained a victor.

The French ended the battle as suddenly as they had initiated it. They withdrew swiftly, still under cover, and their Indian allies skillfully continued to hold the Virginians at bay before they, too, retreated.

Colonel Washington, well aware of the enemy maneuver, debated whether to follow and continue to inflict heavy losses. He decided to hold his present position. The survivors of the British corps were too dazed and battered to be of any use, and the riflemen of his own regiment were much too weary to pursue the foe.

For the rest of his days he regretted that he did not have a thousand men in reserve. With a force of that size, he knew, he could have cut the French to ribbons and reduced their victory to a defeat as shattering as that inflicted on General Braddock.

When news of the battle reached England, it was regarded as a major defeat, and the entire nation felt humiliated by the crushing loss that Braddock had suffered. A different view of the combat was taken, however, in the colonies, where people tended to regard the combat as a victory for the Virginia riflemen against overwhelming odds. Washington's reputation as a military leader was made secure, and his accomplishments against the French in the forest were in large part responsible for the offer he received, years later, to become commander in chief of the American volunteers who were fighting for their independence.

Thanks to Washington's generous praise, Ghonkaba also emerged as a hero of consequence. Those who failed to realize why he was the lone Seneca in the fight assumed that the prowess he demonstrated was in keeping with the nation's high standards.

Everyone close to him rejoiced. General Ridley immediately dispatched a report to the land of the Seneca. When Renno read it, he promptly announced that the ban against Ghonkaba was ended. His grandson, he decreed, had earned the right to rejoin his people, holding his head high.

In Boston, Beth Strong offered a prayer of thanksgiving for Ghonkaba's safe deliverance, and she wept tears of relief, mingled with joy, as she realized that his rehabilitation was far more complete than he had ever imagined it could be.

Chapter XIII

The disaster suffered by Edward Braddock had immediate repercussions in both America and in Europe. The royal governors and militia chiefs of the individual colonies seized on Braddock's failure—and the relative success of Colonel Washington—to send a new petition to London urgently requesting help in the form of troops, warships, and arms.

England, shocked by the death of one of her leading generals, declared war at last on France. And so began what became known as the Seven Years' War, which, in actuality, already had been fought in North America for a whole year.

The fact that England, at last, had entered the war created several upheavals, not the least of which was the "quiet revolution" in Parliament. One result of that was the fall of the Duke of Newcastle's government. The clamor for William Pitt to head a wartime coalition government was irresistible, and the House of Commons succumbed to the public will.

In a typically shrewd maneuver, Pitt brought Newcastle back into office as prime minister, the nominal head of the government—giving him the time-consuming task of resolving political disputes in the Commons—but reserving for himself the conduct of the war.

Having awaited such an opportunity for a long time, Pitt took the plunge with fervor and energy. He was the first government minister to arrive at work each morning, and lights burned in his office until late at night. As he gradually restored order out of chaos and obtained badly needed momentum in many fields of endeavor, he called a closed-door meeting of his top-ranking generals and admirals.

As the first Englishman of his generation to think in global terms, he shared his vision with the military leaders. "We have made a gross error," he told them. "We have concentrated our full attention on Europe, and we have led ourselves into the fallacious belief that victory or defeat in the war with France depends on what happens here. That is not so."

The admirals and generals, jarred out of their complacency, exchanged glances around the table.

"As you know, gentlemen, we are engaged in a contest with France—one in which no holds are barred—for domination of the New World, and for domination of India. The war will be lost or won in North America and in India, not in Europe."

Several of the young, more progressive officers in his audience smiled to hear him echoing what they had long contended.

"Together, you and I are going to alter our past policies and practices—for the better, with success rather than stalemate or defeat in mind. We are going to do whatever is necessary to gain total control of North America and total control of India. I charge you, here and now, with the responsibility for evolving campaigns that will achieve these goals. Hang the expense! We're fighting for our lives and for the future of our children's children. We'll spend whatever is necessary to achieve victory!"

The military men responded promptly and enthusiastically to Pitt's challenge, and in a remarkably short time, plans began to emerge from their drawing boards. Pitt remained open minded to all suggestions, and approved of idea after idea.

As the future began to take shape, Pitt sent a strange request to the high command of the army. He requested that an officer—one of sufficiently high rank to deal with men of consequence—be detached from the military and assigned to his office. The officer chosen, he stipulated, should be accomplished in diplomacy, as well as in the arts of warfare. Because he would be traveling, and separated from his family for a very long time, it was preferable that he should be a bachelor.

Two days later, Colonel Townsend Whiting presented himself at William Pitt's Whitehall office. Tall, debonair, and independently wealthy, this second son of an earl had managed, in spite of his relative youth, to carve a brilliant career for himself in the army. At thirty, an age when most officers were still captains, he had achieved a rank three notches higher, based on sheer ability.

Pitt, who was familiar with his background, was pleased with the high command's selection.

"I hope you enjoy traveling to distant places, Colonel," he said, "and that you don't require luxuries in your transportation and in the places you're sent."

Whiting smiled broadly. "I'm quite sure I'll survive wherever you may send me, sir," he said confidently.

"Good!" Pitt exclaimed. "I'm sending you to America, specifically to visit all thirteen of our colonies there. I want you to meet with the governor of each, with the ranking militia officers, and the most prominent of the local civilians. In every instance, I'm authorizing you to reveal some of our future plans, and I'm requesting you to urge them to be patient but steadfast until we can organize properly and send them the help they so badly need."

Townsend Whiting, listening intently, nodded understandingly.

"The reason for your mission," Pitt continued, "is all too apparent, I'm afraid. The colonies have been neglected, and are in danger of falling to France. The French have a first-rate army on hand under an extremely competent general, Montcalm, and they're supporting him with a powerful naval squadron. That means that the colonies can be easily overrun and defeated. It is most important that they take steps to protect themselves and to hold out until we can dispatch appropriate assistance.

"You may pass along the word," Pitt continued, "that we have learned a great deal from the Braddock debacle. We're going to send troops to America—as many troops as their militia leaders think they need in order to not only repel the French, but to conquer New France. These troops will be knowledgeable in the use of firearms, but they'll be subjected to special training in forest fighting after they arrive in America. They'll be commanded by the most efficient generals I can find, those who are dedicated to the cause of victory and are single minded enough to pursue that goal to the exclusion of all else. Furthermore, they will be supported by as many squadrons of warships as it's necessary for us to build and to send. You'll be given all of this in writing, to be sure, but I'm going over it with you now to make sure that we preclude misunderstandings."

"Your message is very clear, sir, and very heartening," Colonel Whiting replied.

"As one who believes that the Almighty is inclined to help those who help themselves, I am also prepared to provide the colonies with such sinews of war as they may require," Pitt added. "If they will list their needs, they can forward them to me through you. Specifically, I'm prepared to provide them with muskets, ammunition, gunpowder, and such supplies as blankets, cooking utensils, and medical needs. I understand that each colony prefers its own uniforms, so they will supply those for themselves. After you've visited all thirteen of the colonies, select your own headquarters. Preferably, it should be a city on the seaboard with easy access to shipping so that you can be in constant communication with me, and then we'll establish appropriate liaison."

"Will I operate alone, sir, or will I have assistants?" Whiting asked.

"That's completely up to you," Pitt assured him. "Tell me your needs, and they'll be met."

"If it's all right with you, Mr. Pitt," the colonel said, "I prefer to work by myself, at least at the outset, when I am going to visit the several colonies. I can go from place to place more quickly, and it will be more efficient if everything is channeled through me alone. Later, of course, when the colonies begin requesting war material, I may need the help of a staff."

"When the time comes," Pitt said, "let me know your requirements. Keep in mind throughout your assignment, if you will, that I am determined to win this war—not only for the present, but permanently. This is the fourth time in a century that France has tried to take our colonies from us, and I intend to end her threat to our security for all time!"

A messenger from the land of the Seneca arrived at the house of General Thomas Ridley in Williamsburg, where Ghonkaba was staying as an honored guest. The courier carried a communication written by Ja-gonh, in his own hand, relating not only his joy, but the great pleasure of Renno at the record that the young warrior had achieved in the battle with the French. Accordingly, Ghonkaba soon prepared to return to his homeland. He was unprepared for the reluctance he felt as the time to depart arrived.

Colonel Washington came to the Ridley house as a dinner guest, and Ghonkaba found himself explaining his feelings to his friend.

"Colonel," he said, "I have never had a brother, but I feel that you, and also the men of your regiment, are in many respects my brothers."

294

"We are not related by blood," Washington told him, "but our relationship surely is almost as close as any blood ties would be. We were drawn together by the ordeal we went through in the forest, and our survival is a triumph we will long savor."

Ghonkaba's parting from Washington proved to be a severe wrench. Each clasped the other's wrist, after the fashion of Indians, as the colonel declared, "I hope the fates will make it possible for us to serve together again in the future."

"I will pray to the manitous that we will be reunited in war," Ghonkaba replied, "and when we next are together, I shall pray that we have enough men and enough arms to win the victory that has not yet come within our grasp."

The following morning, he and the Seneca messenger set out for home. They traveled at a rapid clip, making even better time than Ghonkaba would have been able to accomplish alone. This was possible because in their infrequent rest periods, they took turns acting as sentries. By using this technique, the warrior who was not on sentinel duty was able to sleep soundly, thus renewing his energy and making it possible to run with greater speed through the forests.

They observed the customary precautions when they came to the land of their enemies, the Erie, and they readily eluded several patrols as they made their way northward. Ultimately, they reached the land of the Seneca, and Ghonkaba realized how much his status had changed for the better when he heard the beat of the drums heralding his arrival.

This welcome news was confirmed by the large, demonstrative throng that gathered near the palisade.

The family was represented by No-da-vo, whom

Ghonkaba saluted formally. In returning the salute, No-da-vo maintained the stolid appearance befitting a Seneca war chief who took pride in his ability to conceal his true feelings, but the light in his eyes gave him away. Ghonkaba realized how proud his uncle was.

In the gathering that cheered as he came through the gates, he caught a glimpse of Toshabe, the captive Erie with whom he had made love on occasion, and he was pleased that she, like so many others, was raising her voice as she shouted his name. Apparently he was more of a hero than he had realized; certainly it was unusual that a woman such as Toshabe would greet him so warmly.

As was proper, Ghonkaba went straight to the house of his grandfather, to whom he owed primary obedience. There, to his delight, the entire family was gathered. He raised his arm in greeting to Renno, who returned the gesture, then beckoned and embraced him.

Turning next to his father, Ghonkaba again extended his arm, and Ja-gonh replied in kind and then dared to smile at him openly. The greeting was warmer than the young Seneca had expected.

Then he turned to his mother, and Ah-wen-ga's reaction made it immediately apparent from whom her son had inherited his oddly rebellious nature. Tradition meant nothing to her; her son, who had been in disgrace, had returned honored and welcome, and she gathered him in her arms. In the warmth of her embrace, Ghonkaba knew that he had truly come home.

The meal that evening consisted of all of Ghonkaba's favorite dishes, prepared by the women of the family, and after they had eaten, he obeyed Renno and told, in full detail, the story of what had happened in the famous battle with the French.

The men of the family, long accustomed to war, listened attentively. Renno was silent and didn't miss a single word; neither did Ja-gonh. El-i-chi and Walter were equally attentive. No-da-vo shook his head repeatedly. "The English general," he exclaimed in disgust, "must have been a very stupid man."

"That is what I thought," Ghonkaba responded, "but my good friend, Colonel Washington, convinced me that I was mistaken. Imagine what might happen if one of us found himself in Europe, and was placed in command of an army there. He would fight as we have always fought in the forests of our own world. Is that not so?"

His listeners nodded in agreement. Renno, who knew the direction in which his grandson was leading the conversation, smiled in pleasure. Ghonkaba, at last, was maturing and was living up to his high promise.

"If we used the techniques of our own brand of fighting," Ghonkaba continued, "we would suffer a defeat in Europe as severe as the general, called Braddock, suffered in the wilderness west of Virginia. Europe and this world are very different, and they cannot be judged by the same standard. Each must be judged by itself, and those who live and fight must acclimate themselves to their surroundings."

"He who has learned that lesson," Renno said, "has learned much. I congratulate my grandson on his new-found wisdom."

While the women cleared away the gourds and washed them, Renno lighted a pipe and it was passed from one warrior to another. This was the first time that Ghonkaba had been allowed to participate in the

297

ceremony. It was the supreme accolade, the sign of his total acceptance as a man and as a warrior of stature.

"It may be just as well," Ja-gonh remarked contemplatively, "that General Braddock was killed and that his men were slaughtered. Knowing the English, it seems to me that a shock like this was required to teach them a lesson."

"That is so," Renno said. "Now they will know what our friends, the colonists, have learned from us—that the wilderness is cruel to those who do not understand it and try to fight it. But it is a comfort and a help to those who use it as it should be used."

"Perhaps," Ja-gonh suggested, "we will hear from our friends in Massachusetts or in New York before long, and they will ask us for our help in the war."

"We have waited for many moons, and the request has not yet come," El-i-chi commented. "Never have I known such a strange war."

"Cousin Tom Ridley believes, and Colonel Washington agrees with him," Ghonkaba put in, "that the tempo of the war soon will increase rapidly. The French will wish to take advantage of the victory that their force won against the British regulars, and the dominant question now is: at which colony will the French strike?"

"If I were the commander of the French," Renno declared, "I would not hesitate. I would attack Massachusetts." He pointed a long forefinger at his grandson. "Tell me why," he demanded.

Ghonkaba, knowing that he was being tested anew, drew a deep breath. "The reasons are many," he began. "Boston is the largest city in the English colonies, and if it fell to the French, the others would be badly weakened. Also, Massachusetts, together with Virginia, is the most prosperous of the colonies. As it is closer to New France than is Virginia, it is a much easier target for the French."

Renno smiled in approval, and glanced at Ja-gonh. "If you are in need," he told his son, "of a senior warrior to command a group of two times ten, I can commend my grandson to you. I think he is a fitting candidate for such a post."

"I thank my father for his suggestion," Ja-gonh replied gravely, "and I will keep it in mind when the next opening takes place."

Ghonkaba understood that he would be promoted soon, and was quietly pleased. The higher post was not very important, but the advancement was significant because it was a sign that the family had renewed faith in him. That, to him, was all-important.

Only one thing remained to make his happiness complete. He had unfinished business in Boston; specifically, he had to see Beth Strong again and to reach a decision with her on their future.

But he realized that it would be wrong to leave home so soon after he had arrived, so he was willing to postpone his departure for a full moon. Meanwhile, he would say nothing about his tentative understanding with her. That was not the Seneca way. When the question was resolved, and Beth had agreed to become his wife, he would have ample occasion to tell his parents and his grandfather of the decision.

A swift sloop-of-war, flying the navy's proud ensign from her masthead, sailed unheralded into Boston harbor, and the militiamen on duty at the fort saluted her with an eleven-gun greeting.

The sloop responded in kind, and when the master's gig was lowered, a colonel in the army's brilliant scarlet and gold uniform was rowed ashore.

When the junior officer on duty at the waterfront learned his business, he immediately sent for General Strong.

The general soon arrived and, hospitable as always, insisted that Colonel Townsend Whiting accompany him to his home. As Whiting explained his mission carefully, passing along William Pitt's message, formality between the pair disappeared.

"I'll arrange a meeting forthwith for you with the governor," General Strong said, "and I'll set up another with the leaders of the legislature and with some of our leading businessmen, such as the Hancocks. You can bet your boots they're all going to greet you with open arms, Colonel!"

Townsend Whiting laughed. His mission, it seemed, was going to be both simple and pleasant if the other colonies' leaders responded in a similar manner.

"We've waited a long time for the news that you've brought us," the general said. "How soon do you think Mr. Pitt's plan will begin to take effect?"

"That happens to be the last thing I asked him myself before I sailed," Colonel Whiting replied. "I'd estimate that at least one or two corps of trained troops should be available within twelve months, perhaps as soon as six months. It may be as long as two years before navy reinforcements of any consequence can be sent across the Atlantic, simply because it takes substantial time to build new ships, as you know, and to train the crews. But tangible evidence of Mr. Pitt's intentions should be forthcoming much sooner than you are now thinking, sir. When we set sail from Plymouth,

I saw two large merchant ships being loaded to the gunwales with ammunition, arms, and medical supplies."

"That," General Strong said expansively, "is the very best news that I've had since the war with the French started over a year ago. I think we will celebrate with a bottle of claret at supper tonight—a bottle that I've been saving for a special occasion."

He showed the colonel to the guest room, and then went in search of Beth to tell her to plan on having a special meal served for supper.

Beth shared her father's elation when he told her briefly of the good news. At last, England had become aware of the importance of the colonies, and real help would be forthcoming in a reasonable time. Furthermore, they need not wait indefinitely for some assistance, in that ships laden with supplies were already on the high seas.

After she instructed the cook about a festive evening meal, Beth went off to her room, and in honor of what was to be a very special occasion, she changed into her new gown of black lace, which set off her blond beauty perfectly. Although she seldom used cosmetics, she thought that she looked a trifle pale, so she put a rim of kohl around her eyes, reddened her lips and cheeks, and dusted rice powder liberally on her nose. Then, still excited about even the little that she had learned, she went into the drawing room to join her father and their guest.

Townsend Whiting was speaking when Beth entered. He glanced at her casually, then suddenly became so confused that he completely forgot what he had been saying.

Whatever it was could not have been very important,

he decided, instantly dismissing it from his mind. His whole being was filled with the radiance of this lovely creature who had stepped so unexpectedly into his life.

Beth, aware of the great impact she had created on the handsome colonel, was flattered. No, she was far more than flattered—whatever it was that he felt had communicated itself to her, and though she knew she was being most unladylike, she returned his gaze.

They looked at each other in a silence that crackled with suspense, and although their eyes met and held for no more than a moment, it seemed an eternity.

Townsend Whiting was not lacking in experience with women, but never had he encountered anyone like this blond colonial, never had he experienced such an amazing upheaval of emotions.

Beth shared his emotion. She felt dizzy, her mouth was dry, and when she tried to swallow, the sensation was actually painful. No man had ever created such an impression on her.

What bewildered her most was the total unexpectedness of this quite bizarre, unique experience. She had rejoiced when she had learned the news of Ghonkaba's achievements in battle, and had thought she was now betrothed to him. She had weighed carefully the problems entailed in a marriage to a Seneca warrior, and had decided that such a marriage would be worth whatever sacrifices she would have to make, and all the conveniences and comforts she would forgo.

Having already held a frank discussion with her father, she intended to speak with him further. Above all, she had been looking forward to Ghonkaba's return to Boston. She knew he was visiting his family, and she was counting the days until they were reunited.

Now, suddenly, Ghonkaba no longer mattered. Her

entire being was filled with this scarlet-uniformed officer, whose name she did not even know.

She heard her father's voice, as though he were speaking from a great distance. "Beth," he said, "I have the honor to present Colonel Townsend Whiting to you. Colonel, this is my daughter, Beth."

Her gaze still fixed on this stranger, Beth returned his smile as she dipped to the floor in a deep curtsy.

She had no idea of the effect that the radiance of her smile created, and Whiting was shaken to the core as he took her hand and bowed low to kiss it.

As their fingers touched, they reacted alike, both feeling as though struck by a severe jolt of lightning. All that they had experienced in the seconds that had preceded this moment faded from their minds, and yet lingered at the same time. Each was conscious only of the other's presence and nearness, of the fact that her small hand rested so naturally in his large, competent hand. The mysterious chemical flow that had started the instant Beth had entered the room soon was turning into a whirlpool that defied reason and left both of them weak.

Chapter XIV

The mutual infatuation of Beth and the British officer strengthened and grew deeper during the evening. They were conscious only of each other, and General Strong had to demonstrate patience whenever he tried to converse with them. His daughter and Colonel Whiting seemed scarcely conscious of his presence. After dinner, he soon retired, and they sat in the drawing room over innumerable cups of tea until long past the usual hour.

The following day, Townsend Whiting was received by the governor, and repeated his message from William Pitt. That evening, when Sam Adams dined at the Strong home, he immediately proposed that the colonel's news be given further circulation through his Committees of Correspondence. Adams wrote several paragraphs accordingly, the colonel approved them, and Beth went to work copying them for dissemination to the other colonies.

Seven of Massachusetts Bay's leading citizens were dinner guests of General Strong only a few evenings later, and at the conclusion of the meal, Townsend Whiting informally spoke to the gathering. He explained the plans that England was making for prosecution of the war, and at the conclusion of his remarks, he was roundly applauded.

Later, General Strong asked him, "Where are you going from here in your travels?"

"I thought I'd do the most convenient thing," Colonel Whiting answered, "and visit the other New England colonies before I head down to New York."

"If I were you," the general told him, "I'd give serious consideration to visiting our Maine District and the Vermont region of New Hampshire. Both stand perilously close to French Canada and are vulnerable to attacks by the Algonquian and the Huron, as well as by French troops. They are protected only by their local militia, and it will give the lads a tremendous boost in morale to hear from you that real help is to be forthcoming from England."

"By all means, I'll go to both," Whiting replied promptly.

"I have one additional suggestion, if you don't mind," General Strong said, "and this, I think, is vital. We're completely dependent on the Indian nations that make up the Iroquois League. With them, we can hold off any attacks from French Canada until help arrives from England. Without them, we're lost, even though Pitt pours troops and munitions and ships into the void. You would be very wise to pay a call on the Great Sachem of the Iroquois and inform him of Mr. Pitt's plans."

"If you think it's important," Whiting said, "I certainly will do it."

"I'll arrange a militia escort through the wilderness for you," the general said. "As a matter of fact, I think I should come with you, and we'll take Beth with us as an interpreter."

Townsend Whiting beamed at that idea.

"You'll find your visit a fascinating experience," General Strong said. "You'll meet Renno, you know."

The colonel was thunderstruck. "The famous white Indian? I am in luck! I didn't know that he was still alive. Among his other exploits, I have heard many stories of his appearance at the court of William and Mary."

General Strong immediately began to make plans for their journey, saying that they could leave for the land of the Seneca in two or three days.

The news struck Beth with the impact of a physical blow, for she knew she could delay no longer. She was relieved that she would be seeing Ghonkaba, even though she dreaded the prospect of telling him that another man had unexpectedly replaced him in her affections. At the same time, however, she realized that she must tell Townsend Whiting soon about the complications she faced.

After supper that evening, Kenneth Strong went off to recruit volunteers for the journey at the armory, where the local militia were engaging in a drill session.

Beth and the colonel were alone in the house, and as they sat together in the drawing room, she knew the time had come to speak.

"I find," she said hesitatingly, "that I must speak to you about something of great importance, but now that the moment is at hand, I'm tongue tied and confused, and I don't quite know how to put it to you."

Whiting smiled and, reaching over to her chair, put his hand over hers. "Perhaps," he said, "I can save you the trouble." He, too, was encountering difficulty, but he drew a deep breath and plunged on. "We have known each other for only a very short time, a matter of a few days," he said. "Yet I feel as though we have known each other always, and I have sensed that perhaps you feel as I do."

Beth caught her breath and agreed happily.

"I can't explain my feeling, or what has happened to either of us," he said. "I've never had an experience like this in all my life. I've had the acquaintance of many women, but I've never once reacted to anyone as I have to you. And I've been able to tell that you've been as bewildered as I by the whole experience."

"It's strange, very strange," Beth murmured, and instinctively rubbed her bare arms.

"I have no right to speak to you until I've obtained your father's permission," Townsend said, "but I find that I must. I am living in constant fear that you might rebuff me."

She laughed gently. "There's no chance of that," she said.

He brightened and peered at her intently. "You're sure?"

"Are you?" she replied, challenging him.

"Very sure," he said.

"So am I!" she responded.

"All that worries me is that we still know so little about one another."

"That concerned me, too, at least at first," Beth said, "but as I've thought about it, my concern has disappeared. There comes a time in one's life when it is necessary to depend on one's instinct and to act accordingly."

"I know what you mean," he said. "We've been defying logic and challenging reason. Yet I really don't believe we are undertaking anything unwise or improper."

"Nor do I," she replied, and they started to laugh together. Then, blinking tears from her eyes, Beth said, "I feel better now, much better. In fact, I have the courage to tell you what I could not bring myself to say earlier."

"You may tell me anything you wish, and speak your mind freely, now, and as long as we live," he assured her.

She nodded with appreciation. "I know."

He started to speak, then hesitated and waited for her to continue.

"Long before we met," Beth said, "I gradually became involved in a romance. I imagined myself in love with Ghonkaba, of the Seneca, the grandson of Renno. Before he went off to battle—he was involved in the campaign in which General Braddock was killed—we had almost reached an understanding."

Townsend, listening carefully, looked at her sympathetically.

"As one day has succeeded another recently," Beth said, "I've felt worse and worse about my relationship with him. Now that we're going to journey to the land of the Seneca, I'm relieved. I shall see him face to face, and I'll explain to him that, through no fault of my own—and certainly through no fault of yours—we've been drawn to each other so strongly that all other relationships have paled. I just hope that Ghonkaba will understand and that he won't be too greatly disappointed and distressed."

"You must know him well," Townsend observed. "How do you think he'll feel?"

Beth pondered the question at length, tugging at a small lace handkerchief. "I don't honestly know," she said finally. "I've asked myself that same question time after time, but have found no answer for it. I don't know you nearly as well, yet I can predict your reactions to various situations, possibly because we have somewhat similar backgrounds and come from the same civilization."

"That's true," he said thoughtfully.

"Ghonkaba's world bears no resemblance to your world," Beth said, "and very little in it is similar to what I've known. I just hope and pray that he will be able to accept the fact that I can't marry him. I would be living a lie, and you and I would be unbearably miserable."

He released his breath slowly.

"Ghonkaba is a savage, you see," Beth explained, sounding a trifle uncertain. "He's direct and forthright and primitive in his reactions." Then, suddenly, she laughed. "But he's good and decent, and so he will understand. He wouldn't want to stand in the path of my happiness any more than I'd want to spoil his!"

A strong hint of spring was in the air as the little

party, accompanied by its militia escort, set out for the land of the Seneca. The winds were less harsh, the snow melted gradually as the temperature rose each day, and at noon, the sun actually felt pleasantly warm.

Traveling was far easier at this time of the year than in dead of winter, and the party was in high spirits. On the first night of the journey, when Beth insisted on cooking the evening meal, Whiting took advantage of her temporary absence by formally requesting her father's permission to pay court to her.

"I've certainly seen this looming on the horizon," General Strong said. "I have kept my own counsel these past several days because I realize there's very little I can do about it, one way or another. My daughter is a grown woman, not a child, and she knows her own mind. You're an adult, too, and I presume you've had your share of experiences with women."

The colonel assented, but did not elaborate.

"I've watched you and Beth plunging into an emotional jungle, and have wondered how you intended to extricate yourselves," the general went on. "Ultimately, I realized, of course, that you are hardly intending to do any such thing. On the contrary, you are both in earnest."

"That's right, sir," the colonel replied. "As you know, my wages as a colonel are not adequate to enable me to support a wife in the style to which Beth is accustomed. However, I do have independent means that I inherited from my grandfathers, and—"

"I have been made adequately familiar with your situation," the general said, interrupting him, "and certainly I'm satisfied that my daughter would suffer no hardships as your wife. Your family stands a notch above us in the aristocracy, which is more important in

England than in this country, so I have no idea how your family will react to a bride from this side of the Atlantic."

"I assure you, General, my relatives won't give a damn about Beth's antecedents," Townsend said forcefully. "My father married a commoner, and so did my brother, who will inherit the earldom. It's people who matter in our family—not rank and titles and positions—and I know that they will accept Beth with open arms, all of them."

"I find that a great relief," General Strong said, and smiled. "You've relieved my mind considerably on many scores. What's more, it seems apparent from the rapport that you and Beth enjoy that you both have disregarded protocol and have discussed the matter."

"We have, sir, and for that I offer you my apologies," Townsend said.

The general chuckled and waved a hand. "Nonsense," he said. "We live in what is being called the Age of Enlightenment, so a great many of the old rules no longer apply. I don't blame either of you in the least, and I certainly have given neither you nor Beth any black marks in my private book because of it."

"Thank you, sir," the colonel said, feeling relieved.

General Strong's smile faded slowly. "That leaves just one serious problem that still stands in the way of your courtship," he said, "and it's as well, perhaps, that we're going to the land of the Seneca. A young warrior, Ghonkaba, is seriously interested in Beth, and I'm sure he entertains hopes of marrying her."

"So I understand, General. Beth has told me about him and has spoken quite frankly of the problem."

"The problem is more complicated than you know, and has ramifications that go far beyond my daughter's own personal feelings." The general shifted his weight on the boulder on which he was sitting, and became increasingly somber. "Ghonkaba is no ordinary Seneca warrior."

"I understand, sir, that he is the grandson of Renno—who is the Great Sachem of the entire Iroquois League."

"In addition, his father is Ja-gonh, the sachem of the Seneca, and he has an uncle who is the senior war chief of the Seneca. I don't know if Beth has described Ghonkaba to you, but I can tell you flatly that he's a firebrand. He was a rebel who got into hot water with his own people, and he rehabilitated himself by virtue of his heroic conduct against the French when Braddock made his futile attempt to capture Fort Duquesne. Now don't for one moment misunderstand me. I'm not suggesting that Beth maintain her relationship with Ghonkaba because of political forces that will assert themselves for better or worse. It's a woman's privilege to change her mind. She has chosen you, and I am prepared to stand behind her all the way."

"I'm grateful to you for that, General," Townsend Whiting said.

General Strong raised a hand. "Please," he said. "My daughter's happiness is my paramount concern. I do have other concerns and other interests, and foremost among them is the status of our all-important treaty with the nations of the Iroquois League."

"Let me get this straight, sir. Are you hinting that the state of the treaty with the Iroquois is dependent on Beth's relationship with this young warrior?"

"I'm making no hints, no insinuations," the general replied. "I am trying to look at a situation factually and unemotionally. Ghonkaba has a mercurial temperament, and from all accounts of him in battle, he's a ferocious fighting man. He comes from the first family of the Seneca, and they go back a long way. His great-grandfather was one of the primary founders of the Iroquois League and is still venerated by the Seneca as a near-god. Ghonkaba has pride in his nation, which in his case is justified, and I assure you, it's considerable. Now, if you will, put yourself in his boots, or rather, in his moccasins."

Colonel Whiting smiled in appreciation of the general's attempt to lighten the conversation with a dash of humor.

"Beth, the woman he loves and thinks he's going to marry, arrives in his town unexpectedly and he is delighted to see her. But his joy quickly sours when he learns that she has forsaken him for another, and that you're that man. You're slightly taller than he is, and I daresay, by most standards, you'd be considered better looking, a more handsome specimen.

"Don't ask me how he's going to react. I haven't the vaguest idea. All I can do is to hope that he doesn't influence his father, his uncle, and his grandfather in ways that could damage our alliance with the Iroquois, which we desperately need if we are to hold the French at bay until Pitt's reinforcements begin to arrive."

Townsend Whiting frowned. "It would be unethical and would place a terrible burden on Beth if she were to say nothing to Ghonkaba at present about the relationship that she and I have formed." He shook his head vehemently. "No, I—I couldn't permit that."

"I wouldn't want it, either," the general replied emphatically. "I'll speak to her before we reach the town of the Seneca, and I'll ask her to deal as diplomatically as she can with Ghonkaba. Beyond that, it's in her hands and in the Almighty's!"

The people of the Seneca had been told by the sentries' drums of the forthcoming visit of General Strong, his daughter, and their militia escort, so they created no stir in the town. But the Seneca were excited by the additional arrival of the tall, fair-haired English officer in the resplendent uniform.

Ghonkaba materialized almost as soon as the party had reached the fields beyond the gates, and he was on his best behavior as he was introduced to Colonel Whiting. Thanks to his training, he showed nothing of his pleasure at the unexpected appearance of Beth and her father. Not until they reached the town and he led her toward the house she had occupied previously, adjacent to the dwelling of El-i-chi and Deborah, did he reveal his curiosity.

"I was intending to visit you in Boston when the moon becomes new," he told her. "What brings you to this remote place?"

"The colonel," she explained, "brings messages of great importance from England, which he will explain more fully himself when he meets with the councils of the Seneca and the Iroquois."

It was apparent that she was aware of the messages that the English colonel was carrying. But because it was equally evident to him that she had no desire to break any confidences, Ghonkaba did not push the question.

When they reached the house she would occupy during her stay in the town of the Seneca, Beth maneuvered delicately, thanking Ghonkaba for escorting her as she stood in the open doorway, with one hand holding up the animal skins that would cover it when she let them drop again. She did not say in so many words that she preferred that he not enter with her, but was vastly relieved when he took the hint. She was relieved, too, that her approach was sufficiently subtle that he seemed to have no idea that she was avoiding him. She counted her blessings and was glad that the customs of the Seneca forbade any close contact in public between a man and a woman.

After Ghonkaba departed, Beth discovered that the ordeal had tired her unduly, and she needed time to compose herself. She vowed to speak with him at the first opportunity and to reveal her changed status to him. Otherwise, the tension would become unbearable.

Beth was alone no more than a few minutes when she heard her name called, and going to the door, she saw Deborah on the threshold.

Impulsively, she embraced and kissed her caller. "I'm so glad to see you!" she cried, meaning every word. She felt a kinship with Deborah, no doubt because the wife of El-i-chi was living as she herself would live if she were to marry Ghonkaba. Deborah was someone in whom she could confide, and from whom she could receive advice.

Holding her at arm's length, Deborah scrutinized her. "You look well!" she said. "You appear a trifle tired, but that's only to be expected after you've traveled all the way from Boston. I swear to goodness, child, you look prettier every time I see you, but you seem nervous to me, dreadfully nervous. Is something bothering you?"

Needing no further encouragement, Beth poured out

her story, explaining as best she could how she and Townsend Whiting had fallen in love at first sight.

Deborah listened, her eyes bright. "You needn't explain any further," she said. "I know exactly what you mean. Your reactions are very understandable, and entirely suitable."

Beth began to feel that some of the pressure weighing her down was now lessening.

Deborah continued to peer at her expectantly. "What of Ghonkaba?" she asked.

"He escorted me to this house," Beth said, "and we exchanged a very few words, all of them impersonal. I couldn't bring myself to break the news to him so suddenly. Perhaps I was a coward, but I told myself I needed time to gird for a confrontation with him."

"I see," Deborah murmured and fell silent. Beth, bewildered, was unable to understand the seeming withdrawal.

"You want to be honest with Ghonkaba," Deborah finally said after much thought, "and fair to him, as well. But you're afraid that your change of heart will severely hurt his feelings and make him miserable. Is that not correct?"

Beth indicated her agreement, one hand at her throat.

Deborah smiled faintly. "Ghonkaba," she said, "is a special member of a very special family. How they react to bad news is anybody's guess. I'll tell you a secret, if you don't mind my reviving ancient history. Many years ago, when I was younger than you are now, Renno rescued me after I was kidnapped by hostile Indians. They were Huron, I think, directed by a French officer, but it was so long ago that I can't rightly remember. In any event, he brought me here

317

and we fell in love. The times weren't what they are now, and I wasn't prepared then to spend the rest of my life in the land of the Seneca. I needed another marriage, a happy marriage of many years' standing, to prepare me for the years that I eventually would spend here with El-i-chi. Renno and I drifted apart when I returned to Fort Springfield, and I married Obadiah before he and Betsy found each other. I was very worried about him, very deeply concerned."

"I know precisely how you must have felt," Beth said compassionately.

"My sympathy was wasted," Deborah then said flatly. "I needed many years of living, and a far greater understanding of Renno, to realize that. He always accepted any situation for what it was worth, and didn't brood about it. His father, the great Ghonka, was the same way."

The knot of dread in the pit of Beth's stomach began to loosen.

"I've known Ja-gonh, our great-nephew, for the past quarter of a century," Deborah said, "and I've developed a great admiration for him. He bears a striking resemblance not only to Renno, but to Ghonka, though in that instance there is no blood relationship. Renno is a realist; he accepts what is. It's a wonderful trait, and it seems to have been passed from father to son and grandson."

"Are you telling me that Ghonkaba also is endowed with this trait?" Beth asked hopefully.

"There's such a great difference in our ages," Deborah said, "that I can't honestly say I know Ghonkaba that well. But it does appear that a certain tradition is followed in his family in each generation. So it stands to reason that he, too, is willing to accept a blow, and then to rebuild his life without creating a disturbance, and without great inner turmoil."

"I hope so," Beth said fervently.

"If there's one thing I've learned since I've lived here," Deborah told her, "it is not to judge how a Seneca warrior will react to any news, good or bad. He is a Seneca, which means he makes up his own mind, and no one can predict how he'll react or what he will do."

Townsend Whiting, in the presence of General Strong, held a private meeting with Renno and Jagonh. Also present were the senior male members of the family, including El-i-chi, Walter, and No-da-vo.

Renno was pleased with the colonel's report, and the other men seemed satisfied, too. No-da-vo looked less dour than usual, and actually managed to smile occasionally.

"This news," Renno remarked with evident gratification, "is the first sign in many years that this king of the English cares what happens to his people in the New World. The nations of the Iroquois long have waited for such word, and they will rejoice. This is a happy omen. He has been very neglectful, which year after year has surprised me, because I can remember well the cordial welcome that I received when I visited the Royal Court of the English and met King William and Queen Mary.

"I will send messengers today to the sachems of our brothers, and we will hold a council here as soon as they all assemble. In the meantime, I think it is right that you should give this news yourself to the warriors of the Seneca. They are the men who will fight and risk their lives for their own people and for their brothers, the English colonists. It will improve their spirits far more if they hear the news from you as the representative of the king of the English, rather than from me."

General Strong was delighted by the unprecedented offer, so Colonel Whiting promptly accepted, and the next day the warriors were gathered in a natural amphitheater, located near the lake, beyond the palisade of the town.

"Indians love flowery oratory, Townsend," Beth said before the gathering. "They expect it, and they're disappointed if they don't get it. So if you don't mind, I'll edit your words and will add to them if I think it's necessary when I translate for you."

"I'll do my best to follow your instructions," he replied with a pleased smile, "even though that type of speaking is hardly my style. But I give you carte blanche to do what you please with my words. Embellish in any way that you see fit!"

His smile faded. "When are you intending to speak with Ghonkaba about your personal situation?"

"Because I must be a coward, I've kept postponing it," she said. "But I can't delay any longer. His mother has invited me to dinner before your address, and I have prepared myself to speak to Ghonkaba after the meal, if it is at all possible."

Nervousness over her impending ordeal spoiled Beth's appetite for the simple, hearty meal that Ah-wen-ga had prepared, but she offered no excuses and her hostess seemed to understand. Occasionally their eyes met, and Beth was certain that Ah-wen-ga was looking at her with both sympathy and understanding.

It occurred to Beth belatedly that Deborah undoubtedly had said something to Ah-wen-ga about her predicament. Ghonkaba's mother was letting her know in the subtle fashion typical of a Seneca woman that she supported Beth, understanding that she would not reject Ghonkaba because of any failure within him.

After the meal, Renno donned his elaborate headdress and his buffalo cape, and the other males of his family fell in behind him as he started toward the natural amphitheater.

Ghonkaba brought up the rear, and Beth walked beside him. Turning to her, he said, "This is just the first of many processions like this in which you will participate in the years to come. You'll grow weary of marching behind Renno and Ja-gonh and No-da-vo."

Here, at last, was Beth's opportunity, and she knew she had to seize it. Doubling her fists and looking straight ahead, she spoke through clenched teeth as she said, "I think not, Ghonkaba. This will be the only Seneca procession in which I participate."

A curtain instantly descended, and Ghonkaba's face became wooden. Beth guessed that his reaction was a protective device.

He remained silent, Indian-fashion, and waited for her to continue. Whereas an Englishman might have asked what she meant, Ghonkaba assumed her remark was sufficiently provocative that she would explain it, and he waited.

Beth drew a deep breath; this was the most difficult moment of her life. "I have great respect for you, Ghonkaba," she said. "I admire your mind and your courage. I applaud your exploits in war, and I'm certain you'll be equally successful in time of peace. There is no doubt in my mind that the day will come when you will succeed your father, as he succeeded his father before him, as the sachem of your people. But I regret to say that I do not love you anymore."

He continued to walk slowly toward the amphitheater, his pace unvarying, nothing in his face revealing in any way that his world had just fallen apart.

Beth swallowed hard. "You are not to blame. I want to stress that. You have done and said nothing that has caused my feelings toward you to change. And strangely, I am not at fault either. Something totally unexpected happened to me, something that I did not anticipate in any way."

Ghonkaba nodded almost imperceptibly, his eyes still riveted on her.

She forced herself to continue. "Recently, very recently," she said, "a man came into my life. A man I'd never known or seen before, and of whose existence I had been unaware, just as he had been unaware of me. What happened is mysterious, and to us, at least, rather wonderful. We took one look at each other when we met, and we knew—both of us knew absolutely and finally, with no lingering doubts in our minds, whatsoever—that we were right for each other."

There! She had explained the gist of it and the ground had not swallowed her up.

Ghonkaba's eyes continued to be fastened on her.

"What happened to me is no reflection on you, Ghonkaba," she said. "I think you're a very fine, splendid person, and you will be a marvelous husband for some very fortunate woman. I'm sorry, in a way, that I won't be, and can't be, that woman. But what has happened to me is so stirring, so powerful, that I cannot resist it. It's as though I'm being forcibly tugged in a direction and have no control over my destiny any longer." She paused and tried to put her thoughts and feelings into concepts that he would understand. "It's as though the manitous had decreed long ago that this man and I were to meet and marry. Neither of us has had any choice in the matter. We've been swept along by a tide that's impossible to resist."

Ghonkaba still had not said a word.

The realization suddenly struck Beth that she had omitted one very important aspect of her confession. "If I sound evasive or mysterious," she said, "it's only accidental, because I've been concentrating so hard on how to put it to you. The identity of the man is no secret. He is Colonel Townsend Whiting, the officer whom my father brought here. He's going to address your warriors now." She saw Townsend standing at the base of the amphitheater, speaking in a low tone to her father, and her eyes glowed as she caught sight of him.

Renno moved slowly to the base of the amphitheater, followed by his son and son-in-law, brother and brother-in-law. The warriors who had already gathered immediately rose to their feet in a silent gesture of respect for the Great Sachem.

Ghonkaba halted when they came to the section where the young senior warriors were gathered.

Beth's heart went out to him, and impulsively, scarcely aware of what she was doing, she placed a hand on his arm. "I'm sorry, my dear," she said softly, "truly sorry."

He turned and joined his fellow warriors.

Only after Ghonkaba had left her did Beth realize that he had not spoken a single word.

But she had no opportunity to dwell on the painful scene, or to relive it in her mind. As soon as she reached the base of the amphitheater she was, once again, plunged into the present.

Ja-gonh, acting in his capacity as sachem of the Seneca, presented Colonel Whiting to the men of his nation. He lived up to the traditions of his people, and in his long, flowery address, he praised the young officer extravagantly, even though he actually knew almost nothing of his military record or his abilities.

Then, Townsend Whiting rose to his feet, and when he started to speak, Beth instantly began her task of translating his words, phrase by phrase.

Mindful of what Beth had told him, he did his best to make his address unusually ornate.

Beth proceeded to add embellishments of her own, and was so caught up in the game that the scene in which she had just been a principal player soon faded from the forefront of her mind.

Occasionally, as Colonel Whiting spoke and Beth translated, the warriors rose to their feet, raised their tomahawks high over their heads, and emitted the blood-chilling Seneca war cry, a sign of approval.

Ghonkaba rose when the others stood, but he neither brandished his tomahawk nor raised his voice. Perhaps he remained silent because he already knew what the colonel was telling his fellow Seneca.

After the colonel finished speaking, Ja-gonh again addressed the warriors and exhorted them to do their best to achieve the victory that was so vital to the future of the nation. Then he dismissed them.

Ghonkaba drifted back to the town with scores of other warriors as the shadows grew long. His mind still did not seem to function adequately, and he continued to remain silent.

He went direct to the lodge of the unmarried senior braves, where he kept most of his belongings. From a worn, oversized pouch of rawhide that Ba-lin-ta and Walter had given him many years earlier, he extracted a long knife with a steel blade. Manufactured in the English Midlands, it was reputedly the sharpest weapon that a man could use. Grasping it by its bone handle, he tested the knife with his thumb.

It did not satisfy him, so he went out-of-doors again, and walked to the rear of the lodge, where a large boulder had been used as a whetstone by generations of Seneca.

Seating himself on the ground, Ghonkaba used short, sharp strokes as he methodically sharpened the double-edged blade, honing it until its cutting edge was like that of a razor.

As he worked, his eyes were on the building where Townsend Whiting would be, within the next few hours, sound asleep, little suspecting the full depth of the bitter enmity that his conquest of Beth was to cost him.

Suddenly, Ghonkaba's vision blurred momentarily, and he realized something had floated before his eyes. His whetting of the knife forgotten, he reached up and, to his astonishment, discovered that his hand had closed over a gray feather.

In perplexity, he realized that what he was holding was a hawk's feather. Nearly four inches long, it was sufficiently sturdy that it appeared to be from a bird's outer coat.

Jumping to his feet, he looked at the sky and, seeing nothing, carefully scanned the entire heavens. He could find no trace of a hawk, and his mystification grew. The feather was very real, and the hawk that had dropped it must have been flying very low, and directly overhead. How could it have disappeared so completely, he asked himself, in the short time the feather would have taken to float down to him? Yet undeniably a hawk, flying overhead, had shed it. He gripped it tightly between his thumb and forefinger, turning it over repeatedly as he stared at it, incredulous.

If the feather had been cast aside by any bird other than a hawk, Ghonkaba would have easily dismissed the matter as a coincidence. But he could not ignore one significant fact: hawks were messengers of the manitous—the omnipotent, unseen spirits of the Seneca—and, in particular, they watched over the destinies of his own family. Hawks had intervened to save the lives of Ghonka, Renno, and Ja-gonh. No man in the family ever dared to ignore them or to thwart their will.

Ghonkaba knew beyond any shadow of doubt that the appearance of the hawk feather could not be accidental. It had a deep meaning, intended for his guidance. The manitous were sending him instructions, and he was to do their bidding. Taught to fear no man, he likewise had infinite respect for the manitous, and under no circumstances would he dare to disobey any message from them.

But the question was: what was the message that the spirits were sending? He pondered at length, and finally became acutely conscious of the knife he still held.

Now beads of cold sweat ran from his forehead into his eyes and chilled his entire body. He knew what was expected of him, what orders he was being given.

The manitous strictly forbade him to raise his hand

in anger or vengeance against Townsend Whiting, who so unexpectedly had won the heart and person of Beth. Ghonkaba was to accept the situation with as good grace as he could muster, and somehow find the strength to shape his own life accordingly.

Slowly sheathing his knife, he realized that he would not be using it for its recently intended purpose, for the hawk had been sent to convey the will of the manitous that he allow the passage of time to clarify his outlook.

He was a man, a responsible Seneca warrior, son of Ja-gonh, grandson of Renno, great-grandson of Ghonka. He was being required by the manitous to live up to the promise of his heritage.

Slowly, his feet feeling like lead, he left the whetstone. He looked at the feather once more, and a firm resolution formed within him. However long as was needed, he would rely on the manitous' guidance to show what was right.

In his day, he had caused problems enough for the Seneca. Now that day was ended, the nation came first, and his course would be the one that would honor and benefit his own people.

**FROM THE PRODUCER OF WAGONS WEST
AND THE KENT FAMILY CHRONICLES—
A SWEEPING SAGA OF WAR AND HEROISM
AT THE BIRTH OF A NATION.**

THE WHITE INDIAN SERIES

Filled with the glory and adventure of the colonization of America, here is the thrilling saga of the new frontier's boldest hero and his family. Renno, born to white parents but raised by Seneca Indians, becomes a leader in both worlds. THE WHITE INDIAN SERIES chronicles the adventures of Renno, his son Ja-gonh, and his grandson Ghonkaba, from the colonies to Canada, from the South to the turbulent West. Through their struggles to tame a savage continent and their encounters with the powerful men and passionate women in the early battles for America, we witness the events that shaped our future and forged our great heritage.

☐	24650	White Indian #1	$3.95
☐	25020	The Renegade #2	$3.95
☐	24751	War Chief #3	$3.95
☐	24476	The Sachem#4	$3.95
☐	25154	Renno #5	$3.95
☐	25039	Tomahawk #6	$3.95
☐	25589	War Cry #7	$3.95
☐	25202	Ambush #8	$3.95
☐	23986	Seneca #9	$3.95
☐	24492	Cherokee #10	$3.95
☐	24950	Choctaw #11	$3.95

Prices and availability subject to change without notice.

SPECIAL MONEY SAVING OFFER

Now you can have an up-to-date listing of Bantam's hundreds of titles plus take advantage of our unique and exciting bonus book offer. A special offer which gives you the opportunity to purchase a Bantam book for only 50¢. Here's how!

By ordering any five books at the regular price per order, you can also choose any other single book listed (up to a $4.95 value) for just 50¢. Some restrictions do apply, but for further details why not send for Bantam's listing of titles today!

Just send us your name and address plus 50¢ to defray the postage and handling costs.
